Two Little Boys

Two Little Boys

Duncan Sarkies

JOHN MURRAY

First published in Great Britain in 2009 by John Murray (Publishers)
An Hachette UK Company

First published in New Zealand in 2008 by Penguin Group (NZ)

1

© Duncan Sarkies 2008

The right of Duncan Sarkies to be identified as the Author of the Work has been asserted by him in accordance with the Copyright, Designs and Patents Act 1988.

Lyrics from 'Loyal' by Dave Dobbyn reproduced with permission from Mushroom Music Publishing
Lyrics from 'Two Little Boys' originally written by Edward Madden and Theodore Morse, 1902
Designed by Anna Egan-Reid

All rights reserved. Apart from any use permitted under UK copyright law no part of this publication may be reproduced, stored in a retrieval system, or transmitted, in any form or by any means without the prior written permission of the publisher, nor be otherwise circulated in any form of binding or cover other than that in which it is published and without a similar condition being imposed on the subsequent purchaser.

All characters in this publication are fictitious and any resemblance to real persons, living or dead, is purely coincidental.

A CIP catalogue record for this title is available from the British Library

ISBN 978-1-84854-090-3

Printed and bound in Germany by GGP Media GmbH, Pößneck

John Murray policy is to use papers that are natural, renewable and recyclable products and made from wood grown in sustainable forests. The logging and manufacturing processes are expected to conform to the environmental regulations of the country of origin.

John Murray (Publishers)
338 Euston Road
London NW1 3BH

www.johnmurray.co.uk

CONTENTS

for Stanley,

for the penguins and the sea lions and the dolphins,

for my friends and family.

CATLINS MAP

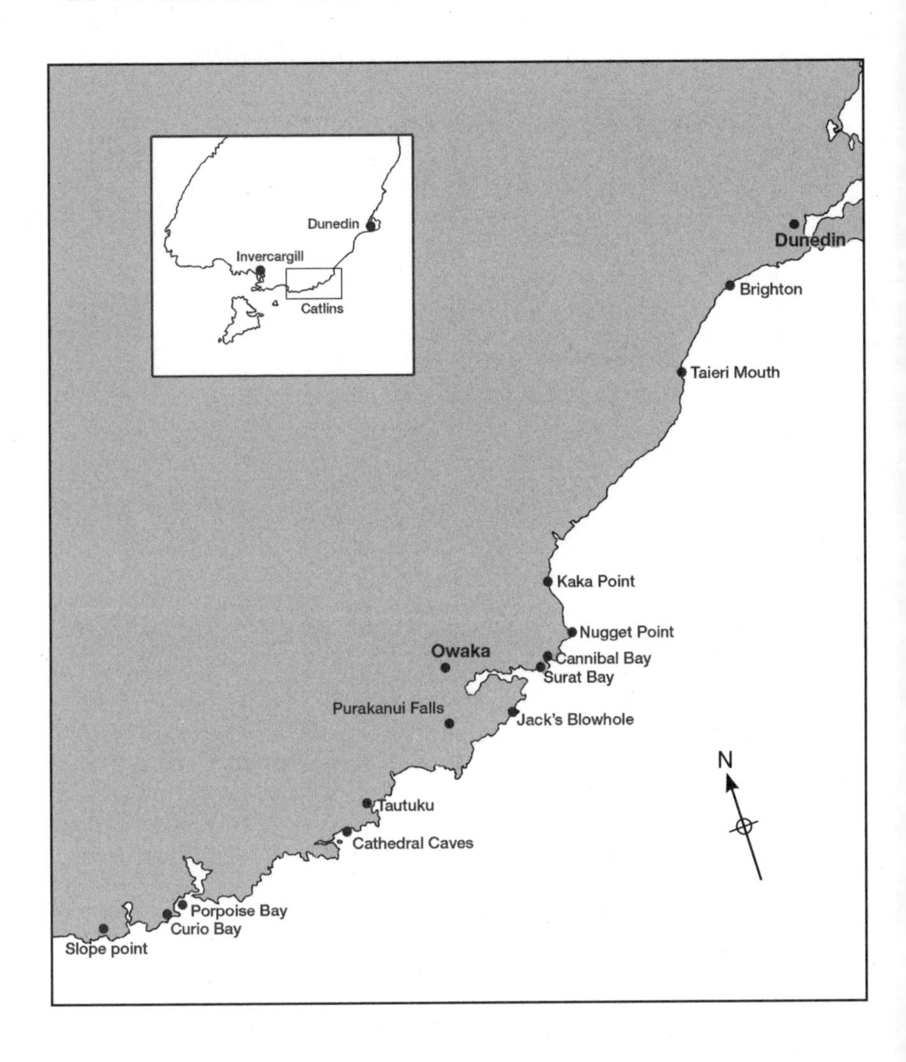
Dunedin
Invercargill
Catlins
Dunedin
Brighton
Taieri Mouth
Kaka Point
Nugget Point
Owaka
Cannibal Bay
Surat Bay
Purakanui Falls
Jack's Blowhole
N
Tautuku
Cathedral Caves
Porpoise Bay
Curio Bay
Slope point

Did you think I would leave you crying
When there's room on my horse for two
Climb up here Jack and don't be crying
I can go just as fast with two

When we grow up we'll both be soldiers
And our horses will not be toys
And I wonder if we'll remember
When we were two little boys

– as sung by Rolf Harris

I WASN'T DRUNK

NIGE

I wasn't drunk. I hadn't had anything to drink for over an hour. I was a bit stoned, I spose. But it was fuckin two o'clock in the morning, you know? Who's awake at two o'clock and not out of it? No one, that's who, so if anything I was less out of it than most people who were awake at the time. Still, Gav's cone blew me away a bit more than expected, but I was sure I was okay to drive.

And it wasn't a joyride either. I was just tryin to make it to the petrol station. From there – you know – the world's my oyster, but the gauge was a good centimetre below E for Empty, which I took to be a bit of a bad sign.

Now, the petrol station is down South Dunedin way, and I figured the fastest way there is straight down Rattray, and just do one last bit backwards up the one-way. Given it was a Thursday I figured there wouldn't be that many people about, so it felt like a pretty safe bet at the time.

The plan was to kill the engine and ride with my foot on the clutch all the way down Rattray, and then clutch-start the old girl once I hit the flat.

It wasn't a joyride. It was just a case of me bein practical. Makin what little I had left last the distance.

It was no joyride.

Anyway, I guess where I kind of went wrong was in underestimating the *steepness* of Rattray and how much speed you can build up on the slope in a short distance. Ridin the clutch got me up to a good 90k, with no juice bein drained from the tank. Now that's pretty quick, unless you're on a motorway, where 90 is pretty slow. So I was coasting all the way down and I really thought my luck was with me – the lights at the bottom of Rattray were green, which meant I didn't have to run a red, so all was well.

Well, I can tell you one thing. All would not be well in a few seconds, cos as I slipped around to the start of the one-way I saw this cat. I thought it was a black cat at the time but it turns out it was a ginge, but it looked black in the night, and maybe my brain thinkin it was a black cat is what kicked off my run of bad luck. Anyway, I swerved to miss the cat . . . and the next thing I knew it I was headed in the wrong direction, so I swung the steering wheel a hard right and pulled out the clutch to get her started but I had my foot on the accelerator pedal and . . . I kinda sped up even more and did a full sideways swerve one-eighty at the same time and . . .

I don't know how to describe it really.

Have you ever driven over something big, you know, like a full rubbish bag? Or a giant judder bar or . . .

I can't really think of something that it was like, but here I am sittin in the car, and I'm scared to get out and look. I've got this feeling some bad shit has just gone down my fan.

So I get out of the car and look at what I just run over . . .

It isn't a rubbish bag or a giant judder bar . . .

It's a backpacker.

'Ooooooooooohhhhhhhhhh,' I'm sayin to myself.

'Oooooooohhhhhhhhhh . . .' I'm sayin. The backpacker's still got his backpack on and everything. His face is on the ground and his backpack is in the air, but there's no movement or anything. And I look around to see if anyone saw it, and the only witness is the ginger moggy.

'Oooooohhhhhh,' I go, and the cat comes up to me and tries to rub its arse against my leg, and I yell, 'Fuck off' at it, cos I'm in a state of shock, eh.

'Okay, Nige,' I think to myself. 'Okaaay . . .' I'm not actually sayin the words out loud, I'm thinkin them, like ESP. I'm tryin to stay calm is what I'm doin, and I'm also picturing lots of bad things that might happen, you know, like that movie where the guy goes to prison and becomes an accountant? So I'm tryin to stay calm, and also I'm thinkin about the backpacker, and how he must be feeling too.

And that makes me think, what if it's not a he?

What if it's a girl?

And so I turn the body over and I'm bloody relieved when I see whiskers on his face. Don't ask me why, but if I had to run over someone I'd rather it would be a guy than a woman, just like I'd rather kill an old person than a baby. So I'm relieved when it's like a twenty-year-old man. It's kinda ideal in some ways. But then I look at his eyes and I feel bad all over again.

Like, I start to feel real sick, like – I want to have a big retch right there, so I stick my fingers down my throat and nothing comes out, so I figure I should just, you know, stick to the job at hand, and maybe not think about myself, but more about the backpacker.

'Mate,' I say to him, 'what's your name?'

'Yuckin,' he says, or something like that.

'Eh?'

'Yuckin.'

'Yuckin?'

'No. Yaaagen.'

'Yoooogen?' I say, slowing down the vowels, but I'm not good on foreign pronounciation.

'Yaaagen with J. Jaaagen. Ah . . .'

He reaches for his pocket but his arm's pretty fucked. He pulls out a wallet and then he drops it and I pull out his driver's licence and his name is Jeurgen, with a J, like he said, but you say the J like a Y, so instead of saying Jeurgen you say Yeurgen. He's from Norway, like those vikings who wear the funny hats with the horns.

'You're gunna be okay, Jeurgen,' I say to him.

Then he dies, the very next second.

How do I know?

A noise comes out of his throat and his pants and a big pool of muck comes out of his rear end, not just . . . like . . . number twos, but also some blood and . . . I mean, like . . . and it's *flooding*, you know, like . . . a big flood – like they had in New Orleans after that earthquake.

'Oh fuck . . . fuck,' is all I can say.

It's funny how when something really bad happens, the only word you can think of is *fuck*. It must be that all the adrenalin blocks all the other words from gettin to your brain.

I slap the backpacker in the face, but he is definitely dead. There is no way he is *not* dead.

Well, actually, maybe he's not dead. Maybe I'm jumping the gun a bit.

No. He's definitely dead.

I can kind of tell he's dead not just by looking at him, but from this feeling I get. All I can say is I just *know*. It's a bit of a . . . ohhh . . . you know where your body knows something and your mind has to catch up? I just *know*, in the same way I know the sky is blue and the sun is yellow. I just *know* Jeurgen is dead, and the fact that his guts are all over the road around him doubly shows to me what I already *know* in my heart of hearts, which is that Jeurgen is *dead*.

I don't know what to do cos I'm in a fully blown state of shock.

So I run across to the other side of the road, to get a wider view and that. And from a wider view I see that no one is around. Not one person, anywhere. It's one of the advantages of it all happening at two o'clock in the morning instead of six o'clock in the morning (which is just four hours later).

So I run back to the backpacker, and I take off his backpack. Don't ask me why. I'm on a lot of adrenalin. And then all I can think is 'Fuck, fuck' and then 'What will I do now?'

Now obviously the police station is an option, especially since it's so handy location-wise – just around the corner, in fact. And I really do give it some thought . . . like . . . I run it all through my brain and I realise that to the police I might appear a bit *guilty*. And I get a flashback to when I once went to a court case for reckless driving when I took out a lamp-post back when I was a fifteen. And I was fully shitting myself then, so I . . .

I . . . I just don't think I can deal with all of this now . . . I mean it goes without saying that this is worse. This is much worse. This is so worse it's badder than bad, you know. This is pretty fucked. It doesn't matter whether you're a glass-full person or a glass-empty person – the situation at hand is pretty bad and the only one that's goin to go down is yours truly, in other words *me*.

I could strangle that fuckin cat. You know how they say don't cross the path of a black cat? Yeah, well add ginger to the mix, that's what I say.

Anyway, I make a snap decision to explore other options than the police, and that's when it hits me . . .

Or I should say flashes at me.

You see, the only sign of life is twenty metres down the road, a big amber flashing light at the bottom of Dowling Street. A big glowing amber flashing . . . flashing at me . . . with a whole lot of orange cones all around it . . . flashing away . . . calling out to me . . .

Like a sign.

Well, it is a sign, actually – a road works sign, but I can see now that it is another type of sign too. The sign is calling me, sayin, 'Niiiige, Niiiige,' you know, and I look down at Jeurgen and I say to him, 'Sorry, mate, I gotta do this.'

And I drag him by the feet to the road works.

Bodies are heavy, you know? I'm struggling with the weight and his head is bobbing up and down on the tarseal, and I feel sorry for him so I change sides and try to drag him by the head, which means I have to do a full one-eighty to get back into the right direction. I get the best grip on his arms, but it's a lot harder, and I realise it would be easier after all draggin him by the feet, so I go back to his feet and I pull with all my might and *we* (it feels like Jeurgen is with me in spirit, so that's why I use the word *we*) make it to the hole, where I get one last chance to have a good think about how things stand . . .

You know how they say time slows down when you have an accident and that? Well, I can tell you from experience that time doesn't slow down. It's your thoughts that speed up. Like, if you normally think about one thing every ten minutes, well now I'm on about ten things every *minute*, and I'm not exaggerating!

I think about Mum and Dad up in Oamaru and I know I could never tell them cos they'd hit the fuckin roof, and I think about their neighbours, Mr and Mrs Staples. I don't know why I think of them – just mind association, I guess. I think about Monica, and then I think of Gav and what his reaction might be, and I have to say with Gav it's hard to tell cos he's so easygoing.

And then I think of Deano. Ohhhhh shit. Deano, who's been with me through thick and thin before I turned into that guy Judas from the Bible, except I didn't kiss Deano – I just took off, and even though he bashed in my car with the toasted sandwich maker it doesn't make up for how I hurt his feelings . . .

And then I think about the last time I was covered in blood – blood that's not my own, that is.

And that sends my mind hurtling back to when me and Deano were kids, out at my folks' crib down at the Catlins . . .

ME AND DEANO AND THE POSSUM

NIGE

Deano was ten and I was nine. We were already best mates by then, even though we'd only had less than a year of knowing each other.

Deano was like another member of the family. He stayed with us heaps. He told me he liked my folks' cooking more than his folks', and he started comin around every second day for tea. I never stayed at his place cos his Dad once threw him at a wall – he made a hole in the wall and everything – so Deano reckoned me and his Dad might not get on.

It all happened at my parents' crib, down Kaka Point way, in the Catlins. The Catlins is like the drive you do from Dunedin to Invercargill if you go down the coast. It's a beautiful part of the country. Our family used to go down to the crib every weekend, and Deano always came with us.

The whole possum thing was Deano's idea all along. It was pretty late. I was sleeping in the top bunk and Deano woke me up, shining my dad's Big Jim in my eyes. Deano loved that torch. When it shone in your eyes it was like lookin at the sun – except even brighter.

Deano said, 'You ever killed an animal, Nige?' and I said, 'I've killed loads of slaters,' and Deano was like, 'Slaters aren't animals. Get dressed.'

Next thing we're huntin around for weapons and that. Dad's shed was locked up and there was loadsa stuff we coulda used there, but we couldn't get into the shed, so I grabbed my old cricket bat. And Deano took Mum's Staysharp knife from the kitchen.

We snuck out into the woods behind the crib. It was real dark and freaky. We were, like, in our PJs but with jackets and shoes and socks on. My heart was beating real fast and loud – like, I could hear it in my ears. I had to yell to Deano to slow down cos he had the torch and I couldn't see where I was goin.

After walkin through the woods for, like, ten minutes we heard this rustling, and Deano stopped dead still, and I copied him . . .

He shone the Big Jim up a tree and we saw, like, these eyes staring back at us.

Big fuckin glowing eyes . . .

'Holy shit!' I said and I started giggling, and I also started pissing in my pants.

'Hit it with something!' Deano said.

The possum's eyes got stuck staring at the Big Jim light, so I hunted around the ground and found pine cones and a few acorns, too. I threw lots and lots of cones up in the air and they went everywhere. A lot of them hit Deano but it musta put out the torch for a second, and in that time I half saw the possum make a run further up the tree.

I shone the Big Jim up at the branches while Deano started shakin the tree, real hard, as hard as he could. He almost looked like he was humping that tree, shaking it back and forth with all of his manhood. He was never that big but he was pretty strong for his size, but even he couldn't get the possum down.

So we went lookin for another one. I was like, 'Deano, let's go home,' but he was like, 'I'm not goin home empty-handed.'

Next thing I remember we were moving through some bush. I was shining the torch at my feet and we were both walkin real quiet to listen for a rustle.

And suddenly I heard Deano yell, 'Fuck!' and I nearly shat my pants, and Deano yelled, 'Nige, come fuckin here!' and I went over and Deano grabbed the torch off me and shone it down at a possum caught in a gin-trap.

Deano was real excited cos it was still alive. It was staring up at us, tryin to move but it was stuck. The jaws of the gin-trap were right in its hind leg, high up, and it was stuck bigtime and screamin blue murder.

Deano put the torch underneath his chin and did this real evil face at me, like you'd see in a horror movie. Then he got me to hold the torch while he picked up my cricket bat and pounded the crap out of the possum. Like, he really went for it, and I kinda don't blame him cos after the first hit the possum went fuckin psycho – I've never heard anything so loud except maybe a fire engine if you had your ear real close to the siren or something. It was *that* loud.

Deano was yellin, 'Keep the torch pointed at it, Nige!' and when I pointed the torch back it was mostly dead, but its mouth was open and its teeth were sharp as.

Fuck, I was shaking. I couldn't look at it but I knew it was still alive cos it was still screaming but then Deano whacked it in the face and then there was no more screaming.

'Far out,' I said. I wanted to say *fuck*, but I didn't say *fuck* as much when I was a kid as what I do now.

Deano took the Staysharp knife out from the thing that makes it sharp and he handed it to me and said, 'Stab it,' so I took a big breath and I looked down at the possum, and it was still moving a tiny bit. I wanted to retch but I knew it was one of the things I had to do to be a man. So I stabbed the possum once in the guts. Then Deano took the knife off me and said, 'I want a go,' and he stabbed it twenty times. I know cos he counted every single one of them out loud. I thought Deano would stop at 10, you know, but he stabbed it again and said '11', and then I joined in the counting and both of us were counting, '18 . . . 19 . . . 20,' and I shone my torch down at my feet and blood was everywhere.

'I think that'll do,' Deano said, and we both had a good look at its guts and stuff. 'Hold still,' Deano said, and he dipped his fingers in the blood and wiped them on my cheeks. I knew that I had to do the same for him. He didn't even have to ask.

'Shine the torch at me.' Deano said, and I did. 'What do I look like?'

'Pretty scary.'

'Really?'

'Yeah. Shine it at me,. I wanna know what I look like.'

He shone the Big Jim at me and I got blinded by the light while Deano said, 'You look cool, like a wild animal,' and I went quiet cos I didn't know what to say.

Then Deano put his hand over his mouth and made a high-pitched Red Indian sound, you know the one: *Ooo/ooo/ooo/ooo/ooo/ooo/ooo*, with your hand goin up and down over your mouth. He did it in a real high voice, and then he cut the possum's head off.

'Deano, I wanna go home.'

'We could put the head on a stick and carry it home.'

'I'm going home,' I said, and I headed off, but Deano grabbed a stick and put the possum's head on it and ran after me and caught up.

'Wanna hold it?' he said.

'No,' I said. He kept holding it, walkin behind me, and I ignored him and just shone the torch in front of me all the way back to the crib.

MAN FOR A CRISIS

DEANO

It's about three in the morning when there's this loud knock on the bedroom window. I know it's Nige straight away. I get up and open the curtains and sure enough, a big crop of curly hair and there he is, just as I predicted, all jumpy, like he's had a good think about his actions and he's come back to grovel his way back into my good books.

I give him the finger. I mouth 'Fuck off' to him, but I suspect he doesn't hear it so I say it out loud a second time: 'Fuck off, Nige.'

He's practically beggin on the other side of the window. 'Deano, pleeeease.'

I put on a pair of tartan boxers and a T-shirt that says 'Fuck off Tweety' and a picture of Sylvester with a mouthful of fleshy yellow bird. I go to the front door and open it, but I stand right in the middle of the door-frame, wide stance, so he can't come in cos I'm blockin him.

'Haven't you got a life?' I say to him.

'Deano, I'm in trouble –'

'Did ya finally get her pregnant? It might not be yours, you know. Monica's a slutbag. Could be anyone's. Could even be mine.'

And he says, 'It's not that. I . . . ohh fuck, I need your help. I've fuckin –'

I shut the door on him and go to the kitchen. Nige comes to the kitchen window and knocks from the outside. He goes, 'Deeeano, pleeease!' I decide to really piss him off by making myself a cup of tea. He keeps pounding the window, lookin real desperate, like one of those refugees tryin to get a ride on a boat. Serves him right.

I hold a tea-bag up to the window in front of him.

'Would you like one?'

'I'M IN TROUBLE, DEANO!'

I really draw out making my cup of tea for as long as possible. I let the tea seep into the water in my cup. Makin a good cup of tea takes time. Most people dunk their tea-bag in and as soon as they see the water go brown they think 'That's it' and they pull it out, but you're actually sposed to wait a bit so the flavour can really get into the boiling water.

I ignore Nige, even though I can feel him watchin my every move from the other side of the window. I squeeze everything out of the tea-bag slowly and he's like, 'COME ON!' and I take a sip and I say, 'Actually, it's a bit peaty,' and I pour it out and start again.

'So what's the prob?' I ask, real casual.

'I don't know where to start –'

'How bout you start with sorry?' I go, and he blurts out like a baby: 'I'VE KILLED SOMEONE! I'VE KILLED SOMEONE!' and I have to open the door and tell him to 'Shhhh' cos of the neighbours upstairs. I point to my brain and I say to him, 'Use that, ya knob-end!'

I look at him and he does have a bit of a wild look about him. You know, the kind of look you see an antelope get just before it's attacked by a cheetah.

'I need your help,' he goes.

'That's a pity,' I say, pulling the tea-bag out of my cup, 'cos I washed my hands of you after the events of last Tuesday.'

'Fine!' he says, and storms off to his car.

I go back to my cup of tea, and as much as I really am enjoyin the cup of tea, I just can't stop thinkin about Nige.

There's another knock so I open it and Nige speaks so fast it's like he can't get the words out quick enough. 'Please don't tell anyone what I just told you. I shouldn't've told you. I'm sorry, man, I fucked up, I fucked up.'

And my heartstrings just kinda go like *that*. I mean, he's a pathetic sight, but for fuck's sake, it's *Nige*, you know? He's like a little brother to me . . . even more than that – he's . . . he's like a girlfriend, except that I'm not attracted to him or anything. I say to him, 'It's gunna be all right, Nige. Take me to the scene of the crime.'

On the drive there I manage to chain-smoke my way through three whole cigarettes. I guess I'm tryin to build up some strength for what's gunna come next. I have cigarettes for breakfast and it helps kick my brain into action, and I'm gunna need my brain more than ever at a time like this.

Next thing we're in the middle of town. Nige parks the Mazda up Moray Place, next to First Church, and he says to me, 'I'll never forget this, Deano.' We walk down to Dowling Street and there's a road works hole in the ground and Nige says, 'Look in there.'

And I look in there and I see . . .

'Holy shit, Nige!'

'I know. I'm a fuckwit. I'm a fuckwit –'

'Nige, you're not a fuckwit but I need you to calm the fuck down and take some deep breaths.'

And he's like, 'Yeah, course.'

'I'm gunna go down the hole. I need you to keep an eye out.'

I go down there and I light a flame for a better view of the body and Nige yells, 'Are you sure that's a good idea?'

'What?'

'What if it's gas?'

And I'm like, 'Fuckin A, what was I thinking?'

Nige hiffs me the flashing orange light and I shine it down below. I stare at the backpacker's face and one of his eyes is staring at me.

'Jesus,' I say, and then I close his eyes, which feels like such a weird thing to do. Then I kinda flick his forehead just to see if he suddenly comes alive, but he's pretty dead, you know?

I'm in a bit of shock, cos I've never seen a dead person before. I've seen lots of dead animals, but not, like, a person. Looking at a dead person makes you feel real . . . *alive*, you know? It's a weird feeling but Nige is in such a state I have to stay calm for both of us. My shoe has a hole in it and I can feel some liquid in my feet so I shine the torch down there, and I see . . .

'Blood!'

'Eh?'

'Oh shit –'

'Yeah, I know –'

'No, I . . .'

I'm standing in it, like, the bottom of my jeans has a blood line, so I take them off so they won't incriminate me.

Nige says, 'What are you doing?'

'Stop talking to me. You'll draw attention.'

'Have you got a plan?'

'No. Not yet. I'm *thinking*.'

What I'm thinkin is 'Holy fuck!' but I know I won't be doin anyone any favours by losing my rag at a time like this.

Nige says, 'I need to have a piss. Do you mind if I go?' and I fuckin let him have it.

'Do not draw attention to yourself!'

'Shhhh! People are coming! Shhh!'

I crouch down in the hole. I hear some people go past. Nige says, 'Evening, ladies,' and then a chick's voice goes, 'Hello, handsome,' and Nige yells after them, 'Have a good night!'

Then it's all quiet again, and I look up and Nige is staring back at me.

I say to him, 'What are you talking to strangers for?'

'I was acting normal. If I don't act normal people will get suspicious.'

Never mind that he's talkin to a fuckin hole in the ground.

I get an idea. I start digging, to cover over the body. I'm thinkin the longer it takes people to find the body, the harder it'll be to figure out the time of death and all that. And the better chance Nige and I will have of gettin away with this. I say that to him and he says, 'It's me that'll go to prison, not you.'

'I wouldn't let that happen to you, Nige. You have a bright future. We can't let a little mishap get in the way.'

'Yeah, but I did it.'

'Mate, when you do something I've done it too. If you win a million bucks so do I. If you kill someone then me too. For better or worse, Nige. For better or worse . . .'

Nige looks at me as if he's just spotted a pimple on my nose. Something in his look sends shudders down my spine.

And then he yells, 'Fuck, the cops!' and, and he's goin 'Run!' and he runs away, leaving me stuck in here. It's hard to get a footing but I fumble about and get out fuckin quick. I don't even look to see where the cops might be, I just run an Olympic sprint up Burlington Street, through the church, and out to where the car is parked.

Nige is already in the car. I hop in and we take off. Nige drives down the one-way system and I suddenly yell 'FUCK!'

'What is it?'

'My pants! My fuckin pants!'

We both look down at my bare legs and my undies and he says, 'Did you have any ID in them?'

I search my jacket pockets. 'Only my keys, my driver's licence and my video membership card.'

Suddenly up ahead on the one-way we see a police car. Nige pulls over and turns the lights off. I say, 'What are you doin? Just act normal. Take off again!' He pulls out again but he's forgotten to turn the lights back on. I flick 'em back on just before we pass the police car.

They're breath-testing people but they don't stop us cos they're busy with someone else. I look out the back window. I say, 'Don't ask me how, but I think we got away with it.' I look down at my bare legs and I think to myself, 'My pants. My fuckin pants,' and I must've been thinking out loud cos Nige says, 'Don't worry about it. It's a pair of pants, not a murder weapon. There's no way you'll be incriminated,' but somehow that doesn't ease my mind.

I say to him, 'You do realise this could be our last night drinking together?' and Nige says, 'Yeah. Do you think we should have a final piss-up? Is there anywhere open?'

'There's the 24-hour on Regent.'

As we head down Great King Street I stare down at my bare legs. Nige must see me lookin at my legs, and he says, 'I know. We'll nip to my new flat. I've got some acid-wash jeans I can loan you. And I've got a bottle of Seagrams and some pot.'

'Now's not a good time to smoke pot, Nige –'

'Okay, well, we'll just get the Seagrams and then we can head to the 24-hour and stock up on some more bevvies and get hammered and it'll be like an alibi, even.'

'I dunno if that's a good plan or a dumb plan but I sure wouldn't mind getting pissed.'

So we head to his new pad.

HOW I ACCIDENTALLY BUMPED INTO THE ANSWERPHONE WITH MY ELBOW

NIGE

I park up outside Gav's pad and turn the ignition off and there's nothing but silence. You know that saying 'Silence is louder than words?' Well, this really proves it, cos for the first time in my life I can hear how *noisy* silence is.

It starts freakin me out, and it must be freakin Deano out, cos he's talkin a bit weird.

'Nige, I'm really touched that when the shit hit the fan, you thought of *me*. You *chose* me.'

And I'm like, 'Oh, totally, I mean . . . who else is there?' and then I kind of think to myself that I should be careful about what I say, so I just shut my mouth.

Deano goes, 'There's your mum and dad . . .'

'Oh yeah, but . . . you know me better than Mum and Dad . . .'

'There's Monica –'

'Oh yeah, but Monza isn't . . . I mean, she's studying for

her exams and she doesn't understand me anyway.'

'. . . and there's Gav.'

I knew it was coming. He wants me to say something bad about Gav, but there isn't anything bad about Gav. Gav is a security guard who comes in and out of the bank I work at. I've only known him for three months but you'd think we'd known each other for over a century. He's a big Maori from Northland, and I haven't really been good mates with a Maori before. It's weird that he came down to live in Dunners, but that's the kind of guy he is. He makes interesting choices. Like, he's been to Spain and South America and everything. Gav's just an all-round good guy, and deep down I wonder if Deano knows it and won't admit it.

Still, I know I have to keep Deano happy, so I say, 'Yeah, you know, when the whole thing happened I thought of you straight away, like, I just got this mental picture of you. I thought . . . I wish Deano was here.'

'And now I am here.'

'Yeah, you are. Thanks, man.'

I'm the only one Deano ever shows emotion to. He doesn't mind havin a blub in front of me, but I'm not allowed to tell anyone about it. And things have got the better of him now – he's all emotional and he has to wipe his eyes on his sleeve.

You see, it's been a bit of a saga.

Me and Deano went flatting when he was seventeen and I was sixteen. We shared the same bedroom in the same flat for almost ten years. We had two double beds side by side and not much floor in between.

We were pretty tight, you know? We've been best mates for fifteen years. I mean, we've done everything together. We went on holidays to the Catlins, we scored the same women, we even went on our first and only overseas trip together: to

Surfers Paradise. We were like a pair of likely lads, like those guys from *The Dukes of Hazzard.*

We even both got our jobs within, like, a week of each other. I work at the bank and Deano works as a part-time bus driver. He used to be full time but he's had a couple of incidents at work, like leaving a porno under the back seat of the bus when there were schoolchildren on board. All the kids started calling him a wanker, like all yellin it together, and then Deano started drinkin on the job, too. He got so fucked up one time he had a big argument on the bus with the tough kid of the high school. Deano told him to 'step outside' and have a fight outside the bus, with all the other kids watching. The kid wouldn't fight him but Deano got in real trouble at work. Then there was the time he slashed the tyres of his own bus. I'm amazed he hasn't been fired but Deano reckons it's pretty hard to fire people these days.

Anyway, me and Deano were on the verge of our fifteenth anniversary when I shifted out, and I've been crashing at Gav's pad while I get my head together. I've even got my own room, which is a bonus. I knew me shifting out would be hard on Deano, but I also knew there was a whole world out there waiting for me, like that place Shepherds Bush in London.

I mean, I thought we would still hang out, ya know, cos Gav's is only about fifteen minutes' walk away, but Deano didn't see it that way. With him it's all or nothing. He's that sort of guy.

When I left, Deano didn't take it too good. He went real psycho with the toasted sandwich maker he'd got me for my twenty-fifth birthday. It was a good toasted sandwich maker. Deano knew I loved a good toasted sandwich and when he gave me it he also gave me three wrapped tins: spaghetti, creamed corn and baked beans. I felt guilty accepting it, cos by then I knew I was shifting in with Gav, but I hadn't had the guts to tell him.

I tried to shift out when he was at work. I'd shifted all my stuff into the car and was taking the last load when Deano came home in his bus driver's uniform. He started making a toasted sandwich for each of us, without even asking me if I was hungry. He hadn't twigged that I was ready to go and he hadn't had a look around – he'd just gone straight for the toasted sandwich maker like a man on a mission. He came through to see if I wanted baked beans or creamed corn and that's when he saw me packing up my last box.

He went completely apeshit. I had to run straight out to the car cos Deano ripped the toasted sandwich maker from the wall and was goin to hit me with it. He was screamin so loud the whole of the road heard it. I started the car just in time, but not before he'd bashed the back indicators in. He was so mad he was holding the toasted sandwich maker by the hot bit, and he branded himself on the hand.

So here I am sitting in the Mazda with him just one week later, and Deano's crying has got the better of him. He wipes himself with an oily rag and he gets a bit of a black mark on his nose.

'I've missed you,' he goes.

'I've only been gone a week.'

'I couldn't get out of bed. You know what that's like, when you can't get out of bed?'

'Remember that time I couldn't get out of bed?' I say, trying to lighten things. 'We thought I had meningitis but it turns out it was food poisoning from that dodgy chicken we found at the back of the fridge. I never thought I'd get out of bed then.'

'Yeah but this was different. This was like . . . what's the point, you know?'

'Yeah,' I go, but I don't really know what to say.

I open the door to head in to Gav's but Deano doesn't want to come in. He says he's happy in the car.

I say to him, 'I have a feeling those acid-wash jeans have got a bit of sick on them, but I could loan you some other jeans. What sort of jeans do you want?' He asks for my faded Levi's with the holes in the knees that I cut myself, and I say to him, 'No problemo.'

As I approach the door I get mental flashes of Jeurgen the backpacker. I can see his eyes staring at me, kind of lifelike, and the thought of it puts me on the verge of a freakout, so I change the subject in my mind by thinking about the last time I had sex with Monica, and that brings a smile to my face. I love lots of different positions, and we've invented a few new ones, me and Monza, and given them names like the Vacuum Cleaner and the Rhino. Her one was the Vacuum Cleaner and mine was the Rhino, and whenever I think of doing the Rhino with anyone, let alone Monica, it makes me, you know, go a bit hard. Usually I'd find that frustrating, having a hard-on and not being able to do anything with it, but this time it actually relaxes me.

I grab the spare key from under the outside ashtray and head inside. I hear a noise from behind me and it's Deano in his underwear. He looks real funny, not that now is the time for laughs and believe me, no one is laughing, which goes to show how full on we're feeling. Deano says, 'It's important you don't wake Gav.'

'Right on. You might as well come in now.'

'I don't want to.'

'Gav doesn't bite.'

'It's not Gav, it's just . . . you can't ask me to get over what you did *instantly*.'

So I say to him, 'The past is the past; let's think about the now,' before I think that the now is pretty fucked too.

'Come on, man,' I say to him. It must have been the way I said it, cos he nods and goes, 'Okay.' I push the door open and go to turn on the light but Deano says, 'No lights,' and I think to myself, 'Good thinking.'

I go to my room and grab the Seagrams and spot the jeans Deano wanted. I go back to the kitchen where Deano has the fridge open. I whisper, 'Deano, are you sure you want these ones? The fly doesn't do up.'

'I don't care.'

He wouldn't care either. That's classic Deano all the way. He's always flopping it out at odd moments. He used to love putting on the top half of his bus driver's uniform and nothing on underneath. He'd just walk about the house, to gross me out and that. I've seen his dick lots of times. We're not gay or anything – he just likes to show it to me. Whenever he gets a rash or an STD he'll say, 'Nige, come and take a look at this,' and I'll tell him what he's got cos my mum trained as a nurse, so she was quite good at first aid. Deano would even whip out a hard-on from time to time. He'd go, 'Nige, check it out' when he was in bed, and he'd have his hard-on under the sheets but tightly wrapped like a mummy so you could make out everything. And then he'd make it go up and down all by itself and say, 'Look, Mum, no hands,' and I'd say, 'Classic.' So it's no surprise to me that Deano doesn't mind a pair of jeans with a fly that won't zip up, cos that is exactly the sort of guy he is.

'So what are we gunna do?' I say to him.

'I thought of a plan, but I don't know if it's dumb or not.'

'Okay, I'm all ears,' I say.

I lean back and I accidentally hit the answerphone with my elbow . . .

MY REACTION TO WHAT I HEARD ON THE ANSWERPHONE

DEANO

Nige has accidentally hit his elbow on the answerphone, makin it do a big beep. I say, 'Shhhhh!' cos I think we shouldn't wake Gav, but Nige is a bit retarded and he's like, 'I dunno how to work this thing,' and the first message comes on, and I recognise the voice straight away . . .

It's Nige.

'Oooooohhhhhhhhhhh fuccckkkk! Gav, wake up, maannn! Gaaavvvv!'

Nige finds the stop button and manages to turn it off and just stands there, lookin at me like nothing's happened.

He says, 'There we go. So aah . . . what were you . . . what were you sayin?'

'Was that you, Nige?'

'Eh?'

'On the answerphone. Was that you?'

'Um. Well . . . yeaahhh . . .'

I stare at the answerphone but Nige moves in front of it so I can't see it.

I say, 'Is that message from tonight?'

'Ummmmmm . . . oooohhhh, yeah, actually, I was, aaah . . . you know, I was calling from the petrol station. I wanted to know if Gav wanted some ciggies.'

'Is that right?'

'. . . Yeah.'

Have you heard of micro-explainings? I saw it on TV. These crims were pulling massive micro-explainings on their faces and in slow motion they looked guilty as. So I'm lookin into Nige's eyes for micro-explainings, you know, and his eyeballs are workin overtime. He's scratching his hair and chewing his lip. Nige's micro-explainings are really going for it.

Nige says, 'So what were you sayin about a plan?'

I don't say anything. I just move over to the answerphone machine but Nige blocks me. He says, 'Maybe we should get out of here.'

'I'm in no rush, actually.'

'Yeah, but we don't wanna wake Gav.'

I just stare at him. I point up to the ceiling and say, 'Dead bird,' and he goes, 'What?' and I say, 'Look out! There's a dead bird!'

He looks up at the ceiling and goes, 'Wh-what?'

I shove him off balance, push the button on the answerphone and Nige's voice comes back on.

'Ooooooooohhhhhhhhh,' it's goin. 'Ohhhhhhhhhhh.' Nige tries to get in to push the stop button but I crowd my body around it, like a prop lying on the ball in a ruck. He tries to get his hands through but I slap them away. So he starts pullin at my hair, like a girl.

On the answerphone his voice is goin, 'Gav, pick up the

phone, man, I'm in trouble! I'm in trouble! I'm in fuckin trouble!'

The phone beeps and a voice says, 'You have two more messages.'

I push the button and his voice has gone all high-pitched on the answerphone. He sounds like a dog that's just been shot in the nuts. 'Ohhhhhhhhh, mannnnn . . . Ohhhh fuuuuuuuck . . . Help, Gav, I'm in trouble, maaaaannnn . . . I've ki . . . I've ki . . . Ohhhh fuckinnnnnn . . . fuckinnnn . . .'

I don't know whether to laugh or cry, so I choose laughing. I'm laughing at how pathetic he is. Nige has gone to the oven and he sits down on the floor in front of it. Probly he wants to stick his head inside and cook his brain into action, the dipshit turncoat fuck.

'What's up?' a new voice says, and it's Gav, standing there in some boxers and a tight singlet so you can see his bitch tits.

On the answerphone Nige is goin, 'Ohhhhhhhh, fuckin pick up the fuckin phone, maaaan . . . pick up the fuckinnnnn phone, maaaaan . . . ohhhh fuckin . . .'

I suddenly think of how suspicious we're looking, and how suspicious we must be to Gav. I push the stop button on the answerphone. And I'm thinkin it would be real smart here to put my emotions on hold and pretend like nothing's just happened.

'Um, eh?' I say to Gav.

Nige goes, 'Aaah . . .'

Gav does a big loud yawn and says it again. 'What's going on?'

'Yeah, I could ask the same question, actually,' I say, staring at Nige the turncoat little Judas little betray-your-best-friend fuck. I'm so angry at Nige I don't care how suspicious we look. I go right up to Nige's face and shove my finger straight in front of his eyes. I say, 'DON'T YOU EVER ASK ME FOR A FAVOUR AGAIN!' and I storm out of there.

Except I still haven't got any pants on so I head down the hallway and I go into what looks like Nige's room to grab some pants. I can't see anything so I turn on the light. I find some jeans on the floor, with old undies still inside them, and I throw the undies against the wall and yell, 'Aaaah!'

And there, right next to his fuckin bed, above his Stephen King collection, is a photo of Nige and Gav in front of the old crib in Kaka Point, where me and Nige used to go every holidays. Even after Nige's parents sold it, me and Nige kept going every second weekend, since the new owners are hardly ever there. That place is sacred to us. And here's a photo of Nige and Gav in front of our special place.

I look at Gav in the photo.

Fat prick. Big fuckin smile, which is all part of his act.

Nige and Gav are standing real close together so they will fit in the photo, cos it looks like Nige has taken the photo with the camera in his outstretched hand. They're holding up beers to the camera and smiling, like a couple of homos in love.

I track back a little and realise they must have gone on that little trip when me and Nige were still living together. I remember one weekend Nige was away on a banking conference, and I couldn't really figure out why they'd send Nige – the stupidest person working at the bank – to a banking conference. It never made sense to me, but it really makes sense now.

I feel a rush of crying coming on, so I get out of there as fast as I can. I don't even put on the pants. I wait until I'm outside and I put on the pants there, and they're fuckin tight. I can't get the arse part of them up over my arse. I go to the car but Nige has the keys so I punch the fuckin bonnet and my hand is fuckin sore now so I go, 'AAAAAAHH!' and I run along the street, trying to pull my pants up, shaking my fist and yelling, 'AAAAAAAHH!' and crying.

Behind me I can hear Nige yell, 'Deano!' and he's runnin after me so I run faster, so he won't catch up. We end up on fuckin Stewart Street, which is one of the steepest streets in Dunedin. Dunedin's got the steepest street in the world, Baldwin Street, but, like, Stewart Street is almost as steep but much longer – it must be about the tenth steepest street in Dunedin or something. It's fuckin steep and I run up, thinkin there's no way Nige will keep up with me, cos I know Nige hates running uphill. But he keeps running after me . . .

STRONG ENOUGH TO LIFT AN ELEPHANT (MEMORIES AT THE EIGHTEENTH HOLE)

NIGE

I wish I was better at lying, you know? I'm real shit at lies, and that's why I'm runnin up this fuckin hill after Deano, who's really pissed off. And you know, life is full of lies – white lies they call them – and sometimes you have to do a white lie to make someone happy, but I've never been good at white-lying.

Sometimes I think I should tell the truth all the time, but whenever I open my mouth to say the truth I get this brain-fade condition and my mouth comes out with a lie, and it's always pretty lame and it gets me into a lot of trouble.

I think one of the reasons I'm not good at lying is cos I'm a bit stupid. Deano knows me well, and he always tells me I'm stupid. And you know, whenever I look at something I've done, I always think, 'You fuckin stupid idiot' and stuff like that. I am stupid. I'm cool with it, kind of.

At least I know I'm not brainy. Some people think they're

brainy when they aren't brainy, and they're actually dumber than me, cos at least I know I'm dumb.

Gav doesn't think I'm dumb, but I think Gav's just bein nice, cos it must be obvious.

Deano says to me that even though I'm a bit thick, I have the potential to be a polytech student or something, which is a few steps down from being a brainiac, but still. I mean, I guess what he's sayin is that there are stupider people out there than me. I reckon Deano thinks I can't be too thick cos I read books and that. Like, he doesn't know many people that read books. The only thing he ever tries to read is those *Penthouse Forum* letters, and even then he reckons he skips the story after a few paragraphs and goes straight to the pictures. He knows the girls in those pictures real well cos it's been a good three months since we last got a new girlie mag.

Anyway, my mind isn't on girls or sex or reading at the moment. What's on my mind is the backpacker, and that without Deano I'm screwed cos I'm no good under pressure.

'Deeeeeano!' I yell. 'Deeeeeano, wait up!'

He comes down the hill to me. He says, 'Keep quiet you dumb fuck. You wake the neighbours with my name you might as well be sendin a note to the police sayin suspect number one, Dean Ormsby.'

I say, 'Oh yeah. Good point.'

Then he turns around to run away again and I go, 'Wait . . . I need you, man . . . I need you.'

He just stares at me with this face that looks like a smile, but it's not a happy smile, it's more like an unhappy or angry smile. I know that sounds like it doesn't make sense but next time you get angry have a look at yourself in the mirror and you might just be doin an angry smile like Deano is doin, and then you'll know what I mean.

He says, 'Let's go somewhere quiet. The eighteenth hole, eh . . .'

'Yeah, I get it,' I say, and I head up with him.

He's bein smart cos he knows we have to clear the air, but that we have to do it in a place where people won't hear us, and he's chosen the eighteenth hole of Belleknowes golf course cos it's a place where we've had a lot of real big talks in the past.

DEANO

The eighteenth hole at Belleknowes contains a lot of memories for me. Like two Christmases ago, when Nige and me poured petrol all over a Christmas tree and planted it in the green and lit it. I said to Nige at the time, 'Nige, you can't buy memories like that,' and he agreed with me.

Then there was that time after I came on to Monica. That was a real test of our friendship.

I think it was a case of Nige forgetting the things that brought us together. Like sharing, for example. And girls.

And sharing girls in this case.

When we were kids I taught Nige a lot of things when it came to girls. I taught him how to talk to a girl, how to kiss a girl, how to get down her pants, and what to do when you get down her pants.

I'm a big believer that you can copy any body part using a piece of fruit. Once I took Nige to the supermarket and asked him to choose one, and he chose a nectarine. I picked out a ripe one. We put a slit in it and took some flesh out, and I demonstrated for him – I told him about the clitoris and I taught him how to dart your tongue around and all that.

And he learned it. I asked a girlfriend of his a fuckload

of questions about their sex life and she said it was great. I smiled and said, 'I taught him everything he knows.'

I asked Megan Hutcheson to the formal for him. We all headed to my house beforehand and I made him do a yardy and he was sick all over her dress, which was fuckin funny. He was a bit pissy with me on that one, even though if it wasn't for me he wouldn't have gone to the formal with Megan Hutcheson. He gets a bit mad at me, cos I tend to give and then take away. He gets all hung up on all the girlfriends I've taken away from him when he should be thinkin about how I got him most of those girlfriends in the first place.

I got him girlfriends in all kinds of ways. I'd do the small talk at a nightclub and we'd take a girl home, but instead of having sex with me she'd have sex with him. I always gave them privacy by sleeping in the lounge, but I often did that thing where you listen with a glass against the wall, and I can tell you right now, it works. You can hear quite a lot.

I could hear a lot even when Nige was tryin to be quiet. I once told him he didn't have to be quiet on my account, and as time went on he started being less quiet when he was scoring.

We once had a deal with an early girlfriend of mine. I said to him, 'I'll have her for one month, and then you can have her for a month.' That was hard cos she was into me. She had great tits – an early developer – and beautiful eyes. Beautiful eyes really give me a permanent hard-on. Anyway, a month ticked over and I thought, 'A deal is a deal,' and I dumped her.

That wasn't easy for me or for her, and of course I didn't tell her I was dumping her cos me and Nige wanted her to fuck *him*. I played it real cool: said I wasn't into all-out misogyny and she corrected me and said monogamy and I said, 'Same thing,' and she said, 'No. There's quite a big difference.'

She was kind of into me still, so I started being mean to her in public and encouraging Nige to 'pick up the pieces'.

Sure enough, I told her she smelled in front of a whole lot of people and I was Public Arsehole number one, and who stepped in to fill the hole? You guessed it. He didn't stick to a month, though. He went out with her for six months. In the end *she* broke it off with *him*. I was real mad at him but I didn't complain. He broke the deal but he needed it for his confidence, so I thought, charity begins at home, and what I did was charity. But he never thanked me. Not once. Nige can be real ungrateful.

Anyway, fast forward to about a six months ago and Nige started going out with Monica. She's one of those university students. She's like, well, a bit too flabby to be a supermodel but she's got a good body shape for a porn star – not the headline act, more the one they bring in last to join in the final group sex scene. Nice body, terrible face. You know the type.

But was I attracted to her? Was I fuckin what.

I waited a fair amount of time, like about three months, and then I said to Nige, 'What do you think of this one?' and he was kinda like, 'I dunno,' and I said, 'Well, I'm ready to step in,' and he just nodded, said nothing.

Well, six more weeks passed and I woulda thought he woulda helped me out by then. But did he? He left the bathroom door unlocked for me and I walked in on them in the shower and I saw her tits – well, one tit – but apart from that he was *no use*. So I said to him, 'Mind if I elbow in now? You've had this dance for a while.'

He said to me, 'I don't . . . I mean . . . I don't want you to . . . I like her, you know? Like, you know, love.'

'You don't love her,' I said to him, and he said, 'I think I do,' and I said, 'You don't know what love is, Nige.'

Anyway, he kept going out with her so I started embarrassing him – showing Monica baby photos of him, including one of him as a three-year-old and he's crapped himself. She found it funny but she was still into him.

One night when I knew Nige was out at karate practice I hopped into his bed naked and waited for Monica to come home.

Did she get a shock when she saw me! I'd draped the sheets around myself so you could make out a bit of shape and she said, 'What are you doing?' and I was like, 'I thought we could . . . you know . . .' Get this – she just stood there, real still, staring at my *member*, bobbin away under the sheets. I said to her, 'I love you, Monica,' cos I thought she might like to hear that. She went to leave and I said, 'Come on, Monica, who's gunna get hurt?' and she said, 'Nige, you dick,' and I could feel I was losing her attention so I whipped the sheets right off, leaving the tent pole standing proud without the tent, and she just screamed and ran. Some people are pretty strange, eh? You'd think I'd just shown her a dead baby.

It's not quite how I expected it to turn out, but I knew instantly that it would be one of those things that later on I'd have a good laugh at, even though it wasn't funny at the time. I've had lots of those times. In fact, thinking about it was already making me crack up. I couldn't wait to tell Nige.

When I did tell him he really surprised me. He flipped out bigtime. I said to him, 'What's up, Nige? You look like a ghost or something,' and he yelled, 'Get the fuck away from me!' Can you believe it?

He ran away from me and he headed out to the Belleknowes golf course and sat at the eighteenth hole – right where we are now. I went and joined him. I said to him, 'You know what you are? You're a fuckin hypocrite.' That surprised him cos usually

I don't use big words, but I knew exactly what I was saying, and so did he. 'A what?' he said and I was like, 'You heard me. I won't repeat myself. You're a fuckin hypocrite,' and he went, 'I'm getting a new flat,' and I'm like, 'Fine, fuckhead.'

Shit – as soon as I said it he was out of there, so I picked up a golf flag like a javelin. I threw it fuckin hard and yelled out, 'FUUUUUUUUUUUUUUCK!'

And I fuckin ran to him and I said, 'Hold your horses, Nige. I've done a lot for you. I got you girlfriends when no one wanted to fuck you, so what about a little bit of payback? Or if not that, then how about a bit of appreciation? Huh?'

We had a big talk and it took him a while to see my point, but we really bonded later that night. I realised then that no one or nothing could come between us. Our bond is like superglue. You know that ad where they superglue two pieces of metal and use it to winch an elephant? Well, that's us. Our friendship is strong enough to lift an elephant.

I still feel that, even though he shifted to Gav's. Nige is just going through a bad patch of treating me like shit and taking me for granted.

When I think about the way he treats me, I start to feel a lot of anger inside. Like, I'm *always* there for him on a rainy day but what about the other way around? I've had a lot of rainy days since he's gone, and when do I finally hear from him? When the shit hits the fan in *his* life. Selfish.

I say to Nige, 'I can't believe you took Gav to the Catlins.'

'I only took him there for a day.'

'It's *our* place!'

'I just wanted to show him Kaka Point. What's so bad about that?'

I just stare at him with tears in my eyes, so he can really see the pain he's causing.

He goes, 'We're sposed to be going this weekend. I was gunna show him round the Cathedral Caves,' and I just yell, 'AAAAAAAAAAAAH!' to the air, and that really scares him and shuts him up.

I chuck a ciggy in my mouth to get calm again, but it's a bit windy and the fuckin childlock on the lighter is being a real bastard, so I can't light the fucker. I leave it in my mouth anyway, and it kinda calms me down a little.

'You know that song "Loyal" by Dave Dobbyn?' I say.

'Yeah.'

'The lyrics go: *I can't remember last time you thanked me . . .*'

'Oh yeah.'

I've made my point, but Nige doesn't say thank you, so I start singing to make him take a good look at himself. '*Keeping my distance unintentionally. But if it were different, but you know it ain't. Let's get on with it . . .*'

I get to the chorus and Nige starts singing too: '*Call me loyal, I'll call you loyal too . . .*'

He keeps singing for a bit but I go quiet and he kinda tails off in the middle of the chorus, and there is one of those silences where all you can hear is the wind in the trees.

'What happened, Nige? What the fuck happened to loyalty?'

'I dunno,' he goes.

And I'm like, 'Nige, I know this is a pretty freaky time for you, but if you want me to help you there's gunna have to be a few changes.'

'. . . Like what?'

'No more running to Gav. Who knows you better, me or Gav?' and he goes real quiet cos he knows the answer so well he doesn't need to say it.

'You're in big shit, Nige.'

'I know.'

'You're in big shit, but I'm gunna help you, Nige. But I don't want you to see Gav any more.'

'Gav didn't do anything wrong,' Nige says, and I say, 'Nige – read my lips. He's *using* you.'

'No he's not.'

I just stand up and say, 'Okay, you've just dug your own grave, then,' and he says, 'Stop. Okay. I'll stop hangin out with Gav.'

But I'm not satisfied. I say to him, 'I need you to *hate* Gav,' and Nige says, 'That's a bit rough,' and I say, 'If you want my help then look in my eyes and say *I hate Gav*.'

He won't say it so I walk away and he says, 'Wait,' and I turn around and look at him and he says, 'I hate Gav,' real quiet.

So I sit down again.

I say to Nige, 'I'm gunna use letters as a way of ordering the things we've gotta do. A – we have to get rid of that body. We can't leave it in the road works, especially with my pants in there. B – we've gotta dump it somewhere it won't be found. And C – we've gotta deal with Gav.'

'What do you mean "deal with Gav"?' he goes.

'What's Gav doin now?' I ask. 'We just made the biggest fuckin ruckus. You think that might make him suspicious?'

'Spose so.'

'And the answerphone –'

'Fuck, I knew I shoulda taken the tape out. I knew I'd forgotten to do something but I was in such a rush to find you –'

'Sloppy, Nige. It's all too sloppy. You've gotta start usin your brain.'

'My brain's playin tricks on me. I can't trust it any more.'

'Then we'll use my brain. We have to befriend Gav again,

and win his confidence. Do you think you can do that?'

'What?'

'Pretend to be friends with Gav.'

'Oh yeah, Gav's great.'

'Yeah, well, that mindset of yours is gunna help us now. We have to go back and pretend everything is normal and we have to come up for a reason that you got so upset on the answerphone that has nothing to do with Jeurgen.'

'Yeurgen. You don't say the J out loud. It's Yeurgen.'

Poor Nige. He looks fragile, like a leaf that's fallen out of a tree in a hurricane.

I stand up and hold out my hand to help him back onto his feet. And I give him a hug. Not a *gay* hug. Just like a man-hug where you keep your heads well away from each other but the rest of your body is doin the hug, except for the pelvic area, which you arch back out of touching distance so you don't cause each other any embarrassment.

He says, 'Thanks, man. Do you think we might get away with this?' and I say to him, 'It's gunna be fine,' even though I have a weird feeling everything will turn to shit.

GETTING DRUNK IN DAD'S STATIONWAGON

DEANO

We've returned to the scene of the crime to clean up the mess we've made. It's only a couple of hours before it gets light so we haven't got much time left and my heart is beating fast like I'm one of those horses that's just been injected with steroids so that it'll win a race.

Even though I have never dealt with anything as big as this, I somehow feel calm. Like, I feel like I know exactly what to do.

I think it's a bit like being at war. I watch the news and all the reports of the troops in Iraq, and I wish I was over there with them, dealing with resurgency and that. Life and death is so much more real when you're in a war zone. Once you've killed someone – Nige knows this, I guess (I don't, cos I haven't killed anyone yet) once you've killed someone you realise that you're part of a big food chain. And that if insects eat flowers, and spiders eat insects, and rats eat spiders, and dogs eat rats, and people eat dogs – well, Asian people do – well, what eats people? Well, vultures eat us after we kill each other and the whole food chain starts again with dogs eating vultures leading all the way back to people again. And so on and so on.

So I have already grown hard to the idea of manhandling a dead body before we get to the road works.

I say to Nige, 'Are you cool with this? Cos I am.'

He's like, 'Maybe we should go to the police,' and I tell him to use his brain. I say, 'Go to the police and you go to prison, no matter what. If you don't go to the police, if you try and get away with it, then you might not go to prison.'

'Yeah, but if we don't get away with it I'll have to go for longer –'

'Yeah, like maybe ten years. What's ten years? Ten years is about as long as it takes for an elephant to grow a new set of tusks. That's nothing.'

'Eh?' Nige goes.

'Nige, do you want to have a limp cock about this or do you want to walk around like a man?'

Nige gets this determined look in his eyes and he says, 'Right,' and jumps into the hole of the road works.

Now we're both down there together and it's quite a big hole. Getting Jeurgen out of there is gunna be a tough haul. Like, have you ever shifted a mattress in your house and it's not that heavy but bloody difficult cos there's no handles? Well, me and Nige lifting the body is a bit like trying to take a mattress out of your house and then up some steps. Not easy.

Jeurgen's insides are coming out all over the shop. We have to lift the body real high to get it out of the hole in the ground. We get it to our chest height but we have to somehow lift it above our heads. Nige looks like he's struggling but I think he just doesn't wanna get dirty, cos he can be a real pretty boy. I try and think of how weightlifters do it, you know, with the clean jerk and snatch, and I say to Nige, 'On the count of three: one, two, three,' and we both lift, but Nige is holding the legs and they get wrapped around his head, pulling him down, and I end up going down too. The body doubles over itself a bit and I end up on top of Nige, with the body sandwiched in between us.

Nige looks like he's gunna spew and I say to him, 'Hold it together, lieutenant,' and I salute him and he just looks at me strange.

'Let's do it again,' I say, and Nige goes, 'Yeah.' This time we manage to lift him up to a ledge bit. I scramble up and pull the body out onto the road. 'Don't forget my pants,' I say to him, and he comes out of the hole with my pants, and also Jeurgen's backpack. It's a pretty big backpack. One of those old-school ones with the big metal bars on the back.

We've only got about an hour and a half before it starts to get light so we need to act quick. Nige elbows me cos he's spotted a street-sweeper truck that looks like it's coming our way.

'Come on, mate,' I say, and we quickly drag the body over to the car. I open the boot and there's a blanket and we try our best to wrap the body in that, but time is of the essence so we only get the body half wrapped.

I have a feeling there's blood on us so I grab some newspapers out of the boot and put them all over the front seats of the car. I say to Nige, 'Sit on these,' and we sit on the newspapers inside the car. I wipe my hands on newspaper and then put newspaper on the steering wheel so that no blood will get on it. Then Nige says, 'Duck down!' cos the street-sweeper is coming past . . .

Those street-sweepers are amazing machines. It's funny how if you've had an all-nighter you're usually real wasted and this street-sweeper comes past and you just look at it and feel like a legend for staying up so late. This time we don't see much. We just hear the noises real loud, like a big vacuum cleaner but also with those beeps that a truck makes when it's reversing. Nige and I duck down below the windows. I look at him and he's staring back at me.

As I look at him I get a mental flashback to when we were kids, drinking his old man's tequila in the stationwagon out at the Catlins on that golden Easter holiday, back when everything was good and our friendship was blossoming like gorse on the New Zealand countryside . . .

NIGE

Deano whispers to me as the street-sweeper goes past, 'Remember that time we got drunk in your dad's stationwagon?'

'Ohhhh yeahhhh,' I say, and it makes me think back to us at the Catlins, when he was thirteen and I was twelve.

Deano had raided my parents' liquor cabinet of tequila and we'd snuck out to get hammered once everyone had gone to bed, but it was pissing down with rain so we snuck into the car and started drinkin there. My parents came outside for a bit of a smoke and the two of us ducked down in the stationwagon, just like we are ducked down now. I thought they'd see us for sure, cos I'd left my door a bit open and the light was still on. Deano leaned over and shut the door proply so the light would go off. I was sure we were gunna get busted.

But we didn't. My parents didn't seem that interested in the car, but they stayed outside for ages, just talking.

I kept sneakin looks at them through the windscreen. It

was funny watchin them when they thought no one could see them – they were different, like. I know this might sound corny, but you could see the love.

And I remember Deano started doin that thing where you open and close your eyes as fast as you can. I sculled some tequila and started doin it too. 'Hey, Deano, look how fast I can do it,' I said.

He went, 'I can do it faster,' and we started havin this race for who could open and close our eyes the quickest.

'I'm winning!' says Deano.

'I am!' I said, not that any of us could see who was winning.

'Are you drunk yet?' Deano asked me.

I just giggled, you know. 'No, but I'm a bit happy.'

'Me too,' Deano said, pouring the tequila worm into his hand while still opening and closing his eyes real fast. 'I'm really happy.'

And now here we are almost fifteen years later, and Deano is opening and closing his eyes at me, smiling.

It makes me feel a bit creepy, you know?

He gives me the shits sometimes.

The street-sweeper has gone past and we peek up and breathe a big sigh of relief that they didn't notice any blood on the footpath. In fact, with any luck they cleaned some of it off for us. It's hard to say cos it's still dark.

'We have to go to Mum's,' Deano says.

HOW THE BMX ENDED UP IN THE BACK SEAT OF THE CAR

NIGE

So we drive to Deano's mum's to get some rope and some rubbish bags. We park up real quiet. I turn the ignition off a good block before we get there so we won't make any noise parking.

We sneak out to the front gate and I start to open it and it makes a loud scraping noise so Deano tells me to go over the fence, which I do, and then he goes over too. For some reason he takes a running jump and hurdles it. I don't know why. I think it's a dumb move but there's no problems – Deano used to be good at the highjump, and even though he didn't do the Fosbury Flop, he made it over with centimetres to spare.

So far, so good.

'Mum doesn't sleep too well,' Deano says. 'She goes to the toilet every half hour, so we gotta be quiet.'

We sneak around the side of the house to get to the basement. Unfortunately I don't see the electric fence. Deano's mum's neighbours have some sheep so there's an electric fence and I accidentally brush against it and I get thrown. 'Aaahh!' I yell, and Deano goes, 'Shhh!' and I say to him, 'I just got electrocuted!' and he goes, 'Shhhhh.'

We sneak inside the basement and it's as dark as pitch black. Then there's a flush of a toilet upstairs.

'She's got a bladder like the Niagara Falls,' Deano says.

He finds a torch and we make it to a back part of the basement, but we can't find any rope. Deano bangs his head on something and there's another scrape and then there's a voice from upstairs going, 'Who is it?'

'Fuck,' Deano whispers. A light flicks on outside. 'C'mon,' Deano says, and we run out but his mum's already made it outside so we hide under the apple tree.

'Who is it?' Deano's mum says. She's come out the back in her nightie.

Deano and I just freeze under the apple tree and she comes straight to us. She says, 'Dean, what are you doing under the apple tree?'

Deano gets up and brushes some leaves off and says, 'Hi, Mum, um, Nige and I came to get my old BMX bike for this, um, this kid that lives in our building. We didn't want to wake you, with it being so early and that.'

'Hello, Nigel,' she goes.

'Hi,' I say, feeling a bit weird.

Deano's mum likes me a lot. Deano hates how much she likes me, cos he's real good to his mother, doin all sorts of stuff, like looking after the apple tree and unblocking the toilet and stuff like that, but she really likes me, even though I never help out. She always invites me around for dinner with Deano and her but I never go. She still thinks I'm the bee's knees and Deano can't stand that.

'The bike's by the washing machine,' Deano's mum says, and Deano goes back into the basement and says, 'There it is,' and takes out a BMX bike. 'Oh, and Mum, do we still have all that rope?'

'What for?' she goes, and Deano looks at me, hoping I'll have an idea.

'I dunno,' I say, and Deano goes, 'It's a surprise. You'll have to wait till Christmas to find out.' His mum just nods in a kind of slow way that makes it look like she's not very happy.

'Mum, what is it?' Deano says, and she says, 'It's Patty.'

Patty is a cat. Deano's mum is always having trouble with cats, cos she lives next to a real busy road, so they keep on getting mashed by oncoming cars and that.

Next thing, Deano and I are sitting in her lounge upstairs, with a BMX bike, a pile of rope and some yellow rubbish bags. Deano whispers to me, 'Nige!' and I see my shirt has some blood on it, so I take it off, and now I'm in my singlet, which I spose looks a bit strange but Deano's mum doesn't say anything. That's cos all her attention is on Patty, the cat. She's a little grey moggy. Looking at the cat makes me think of the ginger one that caused my whole life to change, and I find it hard to feel sorry for Patty. But she is in a bad way.

She's got a big lump in her throat, and her breathing is making a sound like one of those people that smoked too much and they have a hole in their neck. Deano strokes the cat's neck and it's like it's got a golf ball in it. Real freaky.

'You'll have to have her put down, Mum,' Deano says, and his Mum looks real upset.

She says, 'I don't know if I can do that,' and Deano says, 'It's the human thing to do, Mum.'

Deano's Mum just pats her cat on top of the head, and the

cat isn't purring or anything. It sounds kinda half dead, and in a lot of pain.

Deano says, 'Give it here,' and he holds on to the cat and rocks it back and forth a bit, singing 'Rock-a-bye baby, on the treetop'. It's weird seeing Deano like this. He's quite different around his Mum. Sometimes he reminds me of a woman, but then at other times he's like the biggest meathead you'll ever meet.

Deano winks at me and he suddenly stands up and says, 'Mum, we gotta fly. I'll love you and leave you.'

She gives him a hug and a big sloppy kiss, and then she gives me a hug and a big sloppy kiss.

At the car I open the boot to put in the BMX but Jeurgen's body isn't leavin much room to cram in anything else. Deano goes, 'Don't put it in there, it'll get DNA,' so I put it in the back seat with the yellow bags and the rope.

BURYING JEURGEN DOWN AT TAIERI MOUTH

DEANO

It's six-thirty in the morning as we arrive in Taieri Mouth. We drive through a sunrise that is real spectacular. Taieri Mouth has a nice little beach area. Me and Nige once did a 'Big Dig' here. That's like a contest where they bury treasure for little kids, like lollies and stuff. Me and Nige dug up lots of prizes one time. We were so good the organisers told us to stop digging, and to let the smaller kids win some prizes. I was pissed off so I broke a bottle and buried the glass right in the middle of the 'Big Dig'.

As we drive over the bridge I'm thinkin it's important that me and Nige find a good, well-hidden spot. Obviously we should dump Jeurgen in the river, and given that Taieri Mouth is the mouth of a river, I'm running through my mind whether that means the water is coming in or out, which makes a big difference, cos if it is goin out that means it is heading out to sea and Jeurgen will never be seen again. If it's comin in, then . . .

I mean, you have to be good at maths to work out all the possibilities. I just know that time is of the essence cos at this rate Nige is gunna be late for work today, and that might appear highly suspicious.

We drive along the river mouth looking for a good spot. A good spot for dumping a body is a bit different from a good spot for doin a bit of fishing or gettin your feet wet. For a start, public access is a no-no. If you find a spot with public access, chances are the public will accessorise it, and they'd find Jeurgen tomorrow.

That's when I get this idea that we could pull over by a farm and walk the body to the river, away from any people. So me and Nige go down this dusty road and over a cattle stop, and we pull over.

Nige doesn't want to get out of the car cos he's all scared and that, but I say, 'Now is the time to overcome your fears, Nige.'

I think about it further and I'm starting to think that, as bad as it sounds, this experience is gunna be good for Nige, you know – like soldiers in the army coming back after having seen their mates blown to bits and when they come home they're no longer freaked out by big cities and that's cos they've seen worse, and nothing fazes them.

I'd be good in a war. I was born in the wrong decade. I never got the chance to go to Gallipoli. If I had got that chance I would definitely have got a purple heart or something. I often have the same dream, where I'm in one of those MASH tents, and the doctor is sawing off my leg. And in my dream when they saw my leg off I don't cry or anything. I just grit my teeth through all the extreme pain. I woulda been great in a war.

So I'm thinkin maybe this experience could be good for

Nige in the same way a war would be good for me. You know what they say – if it doesn't kill you it makes you stronger. No pain, no gain. Nige is in a lot of pain right now cos he's fallen in a whole lot of brambles cos of a hidden hole in the ground and he reckons he's twisted his ankle but that's just his way of gettin me to do more of the work and I'm not falling for it this time. He can fuckin do his share. I even make him carry Jeurgen's top half while I take the feet. Me and Nige come to a fence, so we lift Jeurgen over the fence and dump him, but when he hits the ground Jeurgen's body rolls roly-poly style down a bank. Me and Nige climb through the fence and chase his body to the side of the river.

Trouble is, the river isn't very deep in this bit.

I pull open a rubbish bag and I say, 'First we fill half of this bag with rocks.'

Nige looks around at all the rocks. 'Do you want me to get some rocks, then?' and I say, 'No, Nige. I was hoping the rocks would somehow make it into the rubbish bag all by themselves.'

Nige goes off to get some rocks and I get a good idea that it might be better to put Jeurgen in the bag first, and then fill the rest with rocks second. That way we'll know how many rocks to put in.

I get Nige to hold the rubbish bag while I try and put Jeurgen in it.

'Do you think we should take his clothes off?' Nige asks, and I'm like, 'What the fuck for?' and he says, 'There might be air in his clothes that makes him float.'

In a weird sort of way he might have a point so we take off Jeurgen's clothes. 'I don't want to take off his undies,' Nige says, and I say, 'We don't need to. I don't think there'll be much air in his undies.'

'Now what do we do with the clothes?'

I say, 'Let's put the clothes in the rubbish bag,' and Nige goes, 'But what about the air?'

'I reckon if we put enough rocks in it doesn't matter how much air is in his clothes.'

Jeurgen and his clothes and his backpack and the rocks are too big for one rubbish bag, so I get another rubbish bag and pull it over Jeurgen's head and tie it on.

Nige spots a tree trunk that hangs over a deep part of the river and I say, 'Perfect.' It's not easy dragging the rubbish bag with Jeurgen to the tree – it's about four hundred metres away. I know distances pretty good cos I used to be good at the hurdles back in the day.

We make it to the tree and climb across the wide trunk. It gets wet in the middle and there's a danger we'll fall into the river, so Nige plays it safe by sitting on his arse and shuffling forward like some kind of monkey with diarrhoea tryin to wipe its arse on the whole length of the tree. It's bloody slow going.

Finally we're ready to go, sitting on a branch hanging over the middle of the river with Jeurgen in between us. I say to Nige, 'You cool about this?'

'What? I mean . . . I can't think of a better plan,' and then I say to him, 'Perhaps you should say a few words,' and he's like, 'Why?'

I say to him, 'Nige – the guy is *dead*. He's not gunna get a funeral with his body,' and Nige goes, 'So?'

'Well, think of his parents. Don't you think they'd sleep better if they knew at least someone gave him a bit of a send-off, you know, with a few words?'

'I don't know what to say . . .'

'Fuck, I'll do it. Let us pray.'

Nige looks at me funny. 'You don't believe in God.'

'Yes I do.'

'No you don't.'

And I'm like, 'It doesn't even matter if I believe in God, cos Jeurgen might. We must think of Jeurgen's needs.'

'I get it. Cool,' Nige goes, and he shuts his eyes and prays.

I say, 'We are here to celebrate this life cut short at the knees by a horrible accident. Jeurgen. Even though I never met you I'm sure you're a good guy. I hope you enjoyed your time in New Zealand. The mountains and rivers are very beautiful here, and I bet you enjoyed the fiords. Anyway, death means many different things to many people. It may be a completely black world like living in a cave without a torch. Or you might be turning into a ghost, or you might be in heaven, in hell, or somewhere in between. You may even be turned into nothing. Ashes to ashes, dust to dust. RIP Jeurgen. RIP.'

'RIP Jeurgen,' Nige says. 'I'm sorry.'

Then we drop the bag in the water.

NIGE

It doesn't sink. Instead it floats in the river. The current takes hold of it and pulls it out towards the sea.

'How many rocks did we put in there?' I ask, and Deano says, 'I thought we'd put in enough.' We watch the bright yellow rubbish bag wind its way down the river and I feel a bit sick watchin it head off like one of those yachts in the America's Cup.

Deano scoots off the tree and tries to keep up with Jeurgen. I get this real bad feeling in my stomach. It's a bit like the feeling you get when you break your mother's favourite Toby Jug. My mum used to have a Toby Jug on the mantelpiece and

I broke it one time with a tennis racquet. It was an accident. I was just practising my backhand in the lounge. I knew Mum would be pissed off with me so my stomach did a big freakout, just like now.

Like . . . maybe Jeurgen is tryin to tell me something, by not sinking and that. Maybe he's sayin, 'I'm angry at you, Nige,' or something like that. I kinda panic and I chase Deano, who's chasing after Jeurgen's rubbish bag. The rubbish bag makes it about another hundred metres and then gets caught in a dead tree that has fallen into the river.

Deano tries to pull a branch off the tree so that he can pull Jeurgen back in, but the branch is a bit big. He keeps tryin anyway, cos when Deano has got his mind on doing something he won't give up. So he's really yanking and twisting it, and goin, 'Fuck,' and finally he yanks the stick free.

Deano fishes the stick in the river and tries to push Jeurgen down, but the yellow bag just won't go down and Deano says 'Fuck' quite a few times. So he pulls it back to land. He tells me to pull it out but I can't reach it and he says, 'Just get in there, Nige,' and I'm like, 'I don't wanna get wet,' and Deano just looks at me and I can tell he's a bit pissed off so I wade into the river.

I grab hold of the yellow bag and I pull it in, using all of my strength. Deano helps me – it's not easy cos Jeurgen and the bag are full of water, but we drag it back in. Deano is panting like he's just had a big sex session with himself, and I feel a bit out of air too.

'Why won't it sink?' he says, and I say, 'Maybe it's not meant to be,' and Deano says, 'Fuck that hippy shit,' and starts dragging the yellow bag back.

I help him and it takes us ages to get the bag back to where we first dropped it in.

'What are we gunna do?' I say, and Deano looks around and spots this big drainpipe on the beach. He says, 'We'll put it there in the meantime,' and I say, 'Isn't that a bit dumb?' and he says, 'Have you got a better idea, Nige? Cos I'm all ears.'

I can't think of any ideas. In fact, I'm freaking out bigtime, but Deano has no sympathy. He drags Jeurgen to the drainpipe by himself, cos I have no energy to help him. 'I'm fuckin dead,' I say to Deano and he says, 'Keep calm, Nige. Where there's a will, there's a way.' He drags Jeurgen's yellow bag into this drainpipe.

Deano says, 'We'll come back tonight after we've made a better plan,' and then we head back to the car.

Suddenly Deano has a bit of a meltdown. 'Ohhhh fuck,' he says. 'Fuck, fuck, fuck.' I have no idea what's got into him until he says, 'Our fuckin footprints! We have to clean our footprints!' I look out at the beach and it's full of our footprints – hundreds of them – and like, you can even make out our shoe treads in the sand.

Deano goes right to the water's edge and starts pickin up sand and throwing it over his footprints, and so I copy him, except I find I'm making new footprints, so Deano says to me to get on my knees and do it, so we are both on our knees now, coverin over our footprints with our hands. We're doin this for about ten minutes and there's still a fuckload of footprints to go. Like, more than a thousand or something. And Deano goes, 'Fuck it. We just gotta get back and hope for the best,' and he runs back to the car, kicking sand over any footprints that are on his way. So I copy him by doing the same, but when I get back to the car and look back at the sand, all I see is quite a lot of footprints.

I HAVEN'T SLEPT FOR TWENTY-FOUR HOURS AND NOW I'VE GOTTA GO TO WORK

NIGE

We've headed back to Dunners to figure out our next move. Deano takes the wheel cos I'm totally freaked out. My heart is beatin real loud. Like, so loud I can hear it, even though Deano is drivin full tit. I guess I must have a real loud heart.

On the drive home I keep thinking about Jeurgen, and what it must feel like to be dead and stuff.

I mean, I hadn't thought a lot about death until now. And now I'm thinkin about death all the time and that freaks me out, so I think of other things, like sex in a three-way with two lesbians – which I've never had, but I have had sex with a lesbian and it was a bit like having sex with your hand. Hard to explain but the lesbian didn't even pretend she was into it. She never touched my cock – I think she was pretending my cock was a vagina and she started fingering my poo hole and I wasn't into it and the whole experience was a bit of a turn-off.

That's what I'm thinkin about as we drive along the road from Taieri Mouth to Brighton. As we pass a river I get a picture of Jeurgen in the yellow bag again, so I try and think about the first time I saw Monica naked, but then in my brain as I scan up her naked body and I come to her face I see that her face has whiskers on it and it is actually Jeurgen's face, and seeing Jeurgen's face on Monica's naked body makes me think about death again, like I've come full circle.

This is what it must be like when they say you have a hard time getting over a death.

My heart is beating louder than ever. 'Can you hear that?' I say, and Deano goes, 'What?'

'My heart is beating real loud. Can you hear it?' and Deano's like, 'Yeah, I think I can,' and he gets up over a rise and now we're into a long straight flat bit as we head past Brighton Beach.

Deano says, 'I spose your heart is gunna freak out along with the rest of ya.'

'Can you really hear it?' I ask him.

'Yeah,' he says. 'You have a loud heartbeat. I hear it all the time – especially when we're in bed and you're asleep.'

'I need to make it shut up. That could be our downfall,' I say.

'Don't worry about it,' says Deano. 'You gotta act normal if we're gunna get away with this.'

'Okay. Normal,' I say, but I can hear my heart chugging away. 'Shut up, heart,' I say to it.

'What do you reckon our chances are of not getting caught?' I say.

'Don't worry about a thing,' he says. 'Everything's gunna be *sweet.*'

But I can tell even Deano is a bit freaked cos he suddenly

puts his foot on the brake and then drives at the speed limit all the rest of the way home.

When we make it back into town Deano seems pretty amped. He drives me to Gav's and says, 'Go and get dressed.'

'I am dressed.'

'In your work clothes.'

I feel a need to point out the obvious to Deano. 'Deano, in case you missed it, tonight I *killed* someone. Now if that's not grounds for sick leave I don't know what is.'

'That's the point,' Deano says. 'If you'd just killed someone the last thing you'd do is just go to work like everything's normal . . .'

He leaves this big silence and I just know he's just had a really good idea, you know, from his tone, and I know that he's just told it to me, but he's makin me read in between the lines, and I don't get it yet, but I know that if I trust him, everything'll be fine.

'Don't fuck around,' Deano says. 'You need to be on time.'

I head inside to Gav's. I put on my bank uniform while Deano waits in the car. Gav is getting changed too. He's getting fatter so his security uniform shirt is getting a bit tight and he can't do up all of the buttons any more.

'Bro,' Gav says, 'are you really going in to work today?'

'Yeah, why wouldn't I?'

'Well, on account of pulling an all-nighter. What was going on last night?'

'Eh?'

'With you and Deano.'

'Yeah, um, that got a bit full on.'

'Are you okay?'

'Fuck yeah,' I say to Gav.

You know that song 'You Can't Hide Your Lyin Eyes' by

the Eagles? That's how I feel, cos Gav's lookin me in the eyes and I feel like my eyes are havin a freakout so I just kinda walk away from him.

I head back into the kitchen and go over to the answerphone.

Gav passes through the hallway and heads to the bog for a bong. He's got a cannabis plant next to his dunny. He likes to take a crap and have a bong at the same time. He says marijuana has made him really appreciate all of his bodily functions.

I try to pull the answerphone tape out but I can't find the right button to get into the machine. I rip the tape out but I pull it out while it's going so there's a bit of tape hanging out.

I take the tape and I put it in the foot-pedal bin. Then I think, what if Gav opens the bin? So I open it again and fish around pulling out the tape and it's covered with leftovers that have got a bit of mould and stuff.

My hand's still in there when Gav comes back in and I get a fright and my foot comes off the pedal of the rubbish bin and the lid slams down on my hand. I pull my hand out and try and think of a way to change the subject.

I say, 'Yeah, me and Deano ended up on a real bender last night.'

'So you made up, then?'

'Yeah, totally.'

'Cos you guys were pretty intense.'

'Yeah, I had a bit . . . a bit of a freakout about . . . um . . .'

'If you don't wanna tell me that's fine, Nige, but I can see you and Deano are . . .'

'Are what?'

'Nothing. It's cool. Did you stay the night at Deano's?'

'Nah. I . . . I didn't really sleep.'

Gav does a big loud laugh that scares me a bit.

'Fuck. Who was she?' Gav goes, winking at me.

'Aahhhhh . . .' Gav thinks I slept with someone, and with my track record I can see why he thinks it, cos I've been a real stud lately. I say the first thing that comes back into my head. 'Monica,' I say.

Now I'm in my room, looking for my bank uniform, which is somewhere on the floor underneath all my other stuff.

Gav calls out, 'I thought you and Monica were history.'

'Yeah, but . . . she could only resist me for so long.'

'Fuck, that's great news, Nige. You must be stoked.'

'Uhhh . . . yeah.'

I'm having a bit of trouble with my tie so I get Gav to do it up for me.

'Mind if I score a lift to work?' he says, and I'm like, 'Um . . .'

DEANO

Gav's in the back seat, next to the BMX bike. 'Cool bike,' Gav goes. I see a whole lot of bloody newspaper also in the back seat. I get in a panic about it, so I turn on the car stereo as a distraction. It's Bachman Turner Overdrive, singing 'You Aint Seen Nothing Yet'. I've got the Bachman Turner Overdrive CD, but I can't really get into it. I don't like how they stutter in the song. Like, why can't they just sing it normally?

Gav likes the stutter though – he leans forward in the car and yells out, 'Choooice! I love this song!' and I really crank up the volume until the speakers are rattling, and Gav is singing the whole chorus real loud, with all of the stuttering and everything. Fuck he sounds like such a fuckin retard. Gav's totally distracted so I quickly grab the bloody newspaper and shove it in under my arse.

They might have been a one-hit wonder, but Bachman Turner Overdrive have just saved our bacon.

As we arrive, Nige is bein real friendly to Gav, just like in our plan.

Nige says, 'Fuuuck, maaan, you know that fish we caught the other day that we threw back? I reckon it was a baby.'

'Oh yeah, that's why you throw it back,' Gav says. 'You know that fish are gunna become extinct in our lifetimes?'

'Really?' Nige says.

'Yep. All animals are becoming extinct.'

'What about rats?' I say, in quite a friendly way, even though it sends daggers into my heart.

'Not scavengers, they're fine, but . . . like . . . you shouldn't eat tinned fish, bro.'

'Ohhhhh,' Nige says, all serious.

'I love a tuna sandwich,' I say. 'So do you, don't you, Nige? One of your favourites.'

'Yeah, but . . . wooohhhh . . .'

We arrive at the bank and I drop Nige off. I say to him, 'Nige,' and he goes, 'Yeah?' and I say, 'Just stay cool today. Focus on the customer and put all the other stuff out of your mind.'

'Okay.'

Then fuckin Gav pipes up. 'A good hangover food,' he says, 'is chicken livers.'

'Where can I get them?' Nige asks, and I say to Nige, 'Just don't do anything that's not normal, okay?'

'Sure thing,' Nige says, and I wait until Gav's not looking and I shoot Nige a wink, and he winks back but Gav sees Nige's wink unfortunately, but I don't really think he suspects anything, the dumb ugly fuck.

And now here the two of us are in Nige's car. I say to Gav, 'You wanna hop in the front?' and he says 'Nah, I'm just a block away. No point.'

What a prick. He expects me to drive him around like a chauffeur, like I'm the scum of the earth and he's a multi-millionaire. Who does he think he is? I keep an eye on him through the rear-vision mirror to make sure he doesn't look inside the car too much. He's just lookin out the window, not saying anything to me, like he's better than me. Just cos he's a world traveller. I'd like to have a look at his passport just to see if he has been where he says he's been. I mean, what's the big deal anyway? You're still the same person. Just cos you go to Spain and you throw a few tomatoes at a few bulls it doesn't mean you know more than I do right here in Dunners. Just cos he speaks in big sentences – not that they're that big. I reckon he doesn't know the meaning of some of the words he says. The other day he said *extrapolate* and I got Nige to look it up in a dictionary and Nige couldn't find it. My guess is the word doesn't exist and Gav is just showing off cos he's so desperate for someone to like him.

'Who's Jeurgen?' he says to me.

'Eh?'

'He a mate of yours?'

I look around behind me and Gav has a small piece of plastic in his hand. He's staring at Jeurgen's fuckin driver's licence.

'Yeah, I found that on the . . . on the bus the other day,' I go.

Gav is staring at the photo on the card real close. I wanna grab it off him but I know that might look a tad suspicious so I just keep driving like nothing's a drama.

'Fuck, he looks like an albino. You reckon he's an albino?' Gav goes.

I've pulled up at a red light and Gav shows me Jeurgen's photo and Jeurgen does look pretty white.

'Fuck, maybe,' I say, tryin to act normal.

'I've always wanted to know if albinos have white pubes,' Gav goes.

I take the driver's licence off him.

'I don't reckon we should go lookin through other people's stuff,' I say.

'Yeah, fair call,' Gav goes.

'This is the one,' he says as we approach the security building. He gets out of the car. 'Thanks, bro. Ka kite.'

That fucks me off. For one thing, I speak English, and for all I know he's just said 'You're a real fuck-knuckle' to me in the Maori tongue. I wouldn't put it past him.

Secondly, I am so *not* his *bro*. Bro is short for brother and if I'm related to him then I'll go and slit my wrists right now.

'No worries, mate,' I say to him, but I say it nice, so he won't suspect I hate his guts.

Gav gives me a wave but I pretend I'm concentrating on drivin by craning my neck back in the other direction to look for oncomin traffic. I pull a Uey and head back to the house.

I get stuck at a traffic light and watch Gav in the rear-view mirror. He's talking to a parking warden. Can you believe it? Like, who makes friends with a parking warden?

I don't know if Gav can be trusted.

ADVICE FROM GOD, AND WHAT I DID WITH MY HARD-ON

DEANO

In the shower I talk to God. I don't know if it's actually God. It's just the way the sunlight hits the water vapour makes for a real 'God' feel. I say to God, 'Any ideas of how we can get out of this one?' and God shrugs his shoulders. You can't see him shrug his shoulders, cos vapour doesn't have shoulders, but I can *feel* God shrugging his shoulders.

I say to God, 'Is this really happening, God?' and God says, 'Sure is,' and I say, 'Is it like a test?' and God says, 'Nah, it's just bad luck,' and I say to God, 'Or good luck, depending on how you look at it. There's a good chance that this whole experience will bring me and Nige closer together.' God doesn't comment on that one.

I use conditioner in my hair but not shampoo, cos you're sposed to let the natural oils in your hair clean itself. Like, your body knows a lot that you don't. Like, when a woman has a baby, her whole vagina gets larger and larger, and don't ask her how she did that – it just happened cos her body knew more than her brain. I only know this stuff cos one of my favourite porn stars got pregnant and she wrote about it all in gory detail in her blog.

Anyway, where was I? Oh yeah. My hair cleans itself, much like a pregnant woman havin a baby for the first time. But I put conditioner in cos I'm going bald and I figure that might keep the wolves at bay, if you get my thrust.

God tells me I should have lunch with Nige today, just so we can get our story straight and to make sure he doesn't say anything stupid to anyone. I'll make him a toasted sammy and keep it warm by wrapping it in tinfoil. I might also whip to the bakery and get him a custard square as a treat for after he's finished his sammy. I'm picturing the look on his face when he sees I've got him a custard square. Nige loves custard squares. He loves all custard. He even had sex with custard once, but he got burns on his dick cos he poured it on too hot.

I feel a real need to get in touch with Nige and check he's doin okay so I phone him, even though I'm naked and I haven't even dried myself. If some chick wanted to have a perve through the kitchen window she'd cop an eyeful right now, and she might like what she sees.

The thought of it gets me goin so I hold on to myself loosely with my right hand while I phone Nige with the other. When Nige comes on the line I say to him 'So you wanna have lunch?'

'Yeah sure,' Nige says. 'As long as you think it isn't . . . you know . . . suspicious.'

'There's nothing suspicious about having lunch with your best mate of fifteen years.' I say, peering down at my penis.

'Hey Nige,' I say, 'are you acting normal?'

'Yeah. I thought it would be hard,' he says, 'but it turns out acting normal is pretty easy, cos if you think about it, we act normal every day, so we get lots of practice.'

'Good boy, Nige. You have master criminal potential. Hey, I reckon you, me and Gav should go down to the Catlins together. This weekend.'

Nige suddenly freaks. 'Ohhh . . . what if they tape the phone calls?' he says.

I'm lookin around on top of the telly for that porno we got out the other week. All I can find is Sandra Bullock in that movie *Miss Congeniality 2*, so that'll have to do.

'Nige, don't worry about it. I've gotta go and wash the dishes. See you at twelve.'

'Okay, mate.'

I hang up and try to rewind the vid to a good scene with lots of beauty queens but a good car chase comes on and I'm pretty excited anyway so I work myself over while watching the car chase and I catch my reflection in the TV, which puts me off so I close my eyes and do a mental picture of all of the girls I've ever slept with, but bloody Nige keeps popping into my brain – must be all the worry, and I'm about to finish myself off with a picture of Nige in my brain and there's no way I'm gunna let that happen so I quickly think of Miss November from the *Penthouse* under my bed, and that completes the job.

I look behind the TV on the wall where there's a photo of me and Nige at Surfers Paradise. He's holding a koala and I've got a couple of fingers sticking up behind his head.

Nige looks real happy in the picture. He's holding the koala real tight, like it was his own child. We had a lot of fun in Surfers Paradise. We went to Dreamworld and Movie World and Sea World and loads of stripclubs. We went to this place where a barman threw drinks around in the air like in that

Tom Cruise movie *Cocktail*. I love that movie, and so does Nige.

Poor Nige.

As I wipe myself on the sheepskin rug I look at the photo of me and Nige and the koala, and I vow to myself to find a way out of this for Nige.

THINKING ABOUT MONICA ON THE TOILET

NIGE

I'm serving a customer when I see a backpacker in my queue. He's got his backpack on and everything. It really freaks me out.

I have to do a withdrawal for the guy but I catch myself kinda just staring at him and thinking about Jeurgen.

Geraldine, the redhead who works next to me, can see that I've gone into a bit of a mental spin while I'm serving the backpacker. Like, I'm really having trouble counting his money. She has to finish off the transaction for me.

She says, 'Are you okay?' and I'm like, 'Yeah. Just . . . yeah, nah, I'm good. Box of birds.' She goes back to her counter.

Geraldine has no idea that I've recently become a murderer. For the next part of the day she talks to me a lot – you know, about things that don't matter, like, how to work the computer and stuff when I get stuck, but I don't want her help cos I've got so much goin on that it makes things that used to seem big, seem small.

Like the bank. When I had my first day here I thought it was like . . . really intense, you know, but now it's not intense. It's just a place where people get money, and what's money anyway? I mean . . . what I'm going through right now is so much bigger than money.

If I was a genius I'd be able to put it into words but I'm not so I won't. All I can say is, when you've killed someone, the first twenty-four hours is a bit like being on a rocket going to space. You've left planet Earth and there's no going back. Although I spose astronauts do come back, but . . . I mean . . . well, I guess their situation is different. I'd love to go to space, though. That'll never happen now.

See the way my brain is working? Going round and round with one thought and then another thought and then another one after that. I've had more thoughts in the last twenty-four hours than what I've had in my life so far. That's how intense I am.

Geraldine says to me, 'You look like shit, Nige. You must've heard the news.'

I look at her and suddenly feel, like, this intense sense of panic.

'What?' I go.

'About Monica.'

'Eh?'

'Your ex? Monica?'

'What about Monica?' I go.

Geraldine looks at me all weird.

'She had a bump.'

'Eh?'

'You know. A bun in the oven –'

'Speak in English, Geraldine!'

'Either she's suddenly got fat or she's having a baby, Nige.

I was wondering if it's yours.'

I go even whiter and I shut my eyes and open them again.

I say, 'Are you bullshitting me?'

'No, Nige. You go see for yourself. She's dropped and everything. Must be in her last trimester. Mustn't be yours, otherwise she woulda told you, eh?'

This guy comes up to the counter with a huge bag of change. I just freeze, like one of those wax statues at Madame Thingy's place in London. I can't deal with the customer in front of me.

I say to Geraldine, 'Can you cover me for a bit?' and I head to the only place I can be alone . . .

The toilet.

I shut the door of my cubicle and I look into the toilet bowl and picture all of my sperm swimming around like goldfish and that makes me think, if I go to prison how am I going to be a father to Monica's baby? That is, if it's mine. Fuck, I wonder if it's mine . . .

Imagine if I was a dad. I picture playing with a big Tonka toy with a little boy, only in my picture I'm not really a grown-up, I'm more like I was when I was at school, and I don't want the other kid to play with my Tonka truck, even though the other boy is my son.

It's just like a mental picture. It's not really happening, which explains why it's not very realistic.

I have to really sit down and have a think about this for a good long while, and so I'm not suspicious I decide to take a long shit, you know, as an alibi for not serving customers. And I'm picturing if I did have a son – I spose I could have a daughter, but given I'm a guy it's more likely I'll have a son – I'm picturing my son visiting me in prison, and handing over a loaf of bread, and I open up the loaf of bread and inside is a knife, for escaping out of prison, and I'm proud of him for bein so caring, but I'm a bit ashamed cos I'm not doin much of a job of being a dad in prison.

As I wipe my arse I realise I need to stay calm.

I've made some pretty bad smells in the toilet and my stomach is gurgling cos of all the trauma I've been going through. As I pass motion number two I think about my life so far and my life in the future and I think about Monica.

She was the only girlfriend I've had who ever made me feel good about myself. She gave me confidence, and even though she was brainier than me, she never made me feel stupid. Like, she was real patient. When I didn't get something she'd explain it again and again, without getting angry or anything. I wonder if I should drop around and say sorry for bein such a dick, and see if maybe we can get together again. It's funny with her – the sex was real good when we got things up and running, like *real good*, but it wasn't just the sex – it's what she would say afterwards that would make me . . . you know, *think*. She told me I was like a little frightened rabbit, and I really thought I was more of a rhinoceros, but right now, as I think about everything that's happening to me and how full on it is, I'm starting think that maybe she was right. Maybe I am a bit of a frightened rabbit.

THE TOOTH AROUND NIGEL'S NECK

DEANO

It's a nice day so me and Nige eat outside at the Octagon. I watch his eyes as he unwraps the tinfoil and sees inside a ham, cheese and pineapple toasted sandwich. Then he looks in the brown paper bag I gave him and he sees a great big custard square.

'I don't like custard any more,' Nige says to me, and I say, 'Bullshit,' and he says, 'It's bad for you. Ask Gav. Gav says they make it out of pigs' feet.'

Fuckin Gav. What does he know about custard squares?

Nige can see I'm more than a bit fucked off so he says, 'I'll eat it anyway,' and he takes a bite from his custard square – skipping the sammy and just concentrating on pudding. Even though he pretends not to like it, I reckon he's secretly enjoying that custard square.

'Hey, Gav saw this,' I say, and I hand over Jeurgen's driver's licence.

'Ohhhhh,' Nige goes, and he stares at Jeurgen's face.

'Yeah,' I say, 'so I'm figuring we should keep Gav well away from newspapers. I reckon this is gunna make the news. Not front page, but it'll definitely get on the news, I reckon. Plus there's the small matter of shifting Jeurgen from Taieri Mouth. We need to bury him somewhere better.'

Nige yells, 'I CAN'T HANDLE THIS, OKAY?' so loud that a busker on the street stops playing mid-song and looks over.

I say to Nige, 'You're experiencing psychological damage,' and he says back straight away, 'You just broke your big-word rule,' and I go, 'Fuck, I did,' and then I think to myself, 'I must make Nige eat his sandwich – he needs some strength right now,' so I say, 'Eat your sandwich,' and he opens it up and pulls out the pineapple and I say, 'Since when did you stop liking pineapple?' and Nige says, 'I don't feel like eatin anything from a tin.'

I tell you, Gav is turning him into a hippy. Not good.

Nige is struggling to eat his toasted sandwich. Usually Nige eats food really fast, like he can't get it into his body quick enough. He loves it when I cook Wiener schnitzel and he practically swallows it whole. He loves breadcrumbs on meat. I put breadcrumbs around a steak once and Nige loved it. So to see Nige struggling to eat a toasted sammy and refusing pineapple, which is one of his favourites – well, I know that everything must be affecting him pretty bad.

All of a sudden I feel like I was put on this earth for a purpose, and that purpose is to protect Nige.

I've always looked out for Nige. Right from his first day of school, when he was the new kid and he turned up at school and on his teeth were, like, the most ridiculous braces you ever saw. They were old-style braces, which didn't just sit in your mouth, but there was a whole contraption thing attached to your face to keep them in place. He looked like a robot and a real retard.

I talked to him for the first time that lunchtime. At school I was a real loner. That's how I wanted it. Kids stayed away from me cos they knew I had a short fuse. I was playing cricket with myself against a brick wall that had some wickets painted on it. Nige was lookin for a spot with no people, I reckon, cos he was scared of bein picked on. I bowled really fast at the wall and I hit the stumps and yelled, 'Howzaaaaaatttt!' real loud, and I could tell Nige was impressed.

I bowled a few more balls and took a few more wickets but I also got smashed for a six. Even though the wall was an imaginary player, I was really pissed off with it and I came down the pitch and spat on the wall, then I bowled it out the very next ball.

Nige just quietly ate sandwiches the whole time and pretended to be lookin at the ground, but I could tell he was impressed.

'You look like a robot,' I said to him, and he said nothing. 'What's your name?' I said, and he went, 'Nigel,' and I laughed cos I thought it was quite a girly name. Little did I know that that name would become itched into my future history forever.

I asked him if I could have one of his sandwiches, but he'd already eaten them, and I said, 'What about that?' There was this thing wrapped in greaseproof paper, so I knew it was some kind of sweet treat. He opened it up and it was a Belgian biscuit. He broke it in half and gave me the small half, which was a bit selfish, but that's Nige – he hasn't changed one little bit.

I remember we had this one teacher, Mr Forsyth, who was a real prick. Mr Forsyth made a joke about Nige's braces in front of the class. He called him the bionic man. 'We can rebuild you,' the teacher said, and the class laughed.

I found it pretty funny too. I hadn't decided at that stage whether I was gunna like Nige or not. But he got called all sorts. He always sat on his own and ate his lunch and I think he cried a bit. I kind of kept an eye on him from a distance cos I didn't want to be seen with him at that stage.

Then I heard about it in maths – Jason Farquhar had punched Nige in the face and he'd gone home early. I didn't find it funny any more. I went and found Jason after school. I dropped my bag and just went for him. He was much bigger than me, but I climbed into him with everything I had, while everyone yelled, 'Fight! Fight! Fight!' He gave me a bloody nose but then I punched him in the face and there was blood coming out his mouth and I climbed on top of him and rubbed his face in the ground and said to everyone, 'YOU CAN LEAVE NIGE ALONE! HIS NAME ISN'T BRACEFACE OR ROBOT OR LEE MAJORS, HIS NAME IS NIGE, AND IF I HEAR ONE FUCKIN WORD ABOUT HIM I'LL FUCKIN KILL YA, I DON'T CARE IF I GO TO PRISON, YA HEAR?'

Jason was crying and I yelled in his ear as loud as I could, 'YA HEAR?' and he nodded. He was spitting blood out of his mouth.

I turned up at Nige's place – even though I'd just met him I knew where he lived cos it was on my way home. His mum answered the door and I said, 'Is Nige in, please, Miss?' with manners and everything. I went in to see Nige and I could tell he'd been crying cos his eyes were all red and he was trying really hard not to cry by doing this funny face, and my heartstrings just snapped lookin at him. I saw where his braces had been broken and I felt a second wave of anger build up inside me.

I held out two fists and said to him, 'Pick one.' Nige picked the left one and I opened it and showed him Jason Farquhar's front tooth.

I said to him, 'Jason Farquhar won't bother you again. No one will.'

'Woooohhh,' he said.

'It's his adult tooth, too, so his looks are fucked for life.'

'Did he cry?' Nige asked, and I was happy to report, 'Like a baby.' That made Nige smile.

'Shall I keep the tooth for the tooth fairy?' he said, and I said, 'Fuck that shit. I'll make it into a necklace for ya. Have you got a power drill?' Nige shrugged his shoulders.

Nige used to wear the tooth necklace all the time, but he stopped wearing it about a year ago. He said he'd lost it but I found it in the rubbish bin, and I don't reckon it got there by accident.

I've got it in the top drawer of my tallboy.

I always felt good when he wore that necklace, like . . . the bond of friendship was secure. And I realise that since I'm helping him so much, then maybe Nige should start thinking what he can do to make *me* happy. I want to see Jason Farquhar's tooth bouncing around Nige's Adam's apple again.

GAV'S THEORY ABOUT SEX

NIGE

Getting rid of Jeurgen's driver's licence turns out to be a bit of a drama. At the bank we do a lot of cutting credit cards with scissors, and the idea is that the credit card is invalid. So I cut Jeurgen's driver's licence and throw it in the bin. I realise that that in itself is not enough so I chuck it in the shredder, but the shredder makes a real bad sound. I think you're only sposed to put paper in it. I take the plug out and I fish it out with my fingers and Jeurgen is half shredded, half not.

On his photo he's smiling, like he's having the happiest day in the world. He must have been happy coming to New Zealand and I hope he liked the scenery – what he got to see of it anyway. I make a mental note to myself to learn more about Norway, as a way of staying true to Jeurgen, you know. Even though I never met him I feel like I would have really liked him. It's like we're connected. It's like that with me and Gav – right from the first day we hung out and smoked pot and he showed me the inside of a video recorder and told me all the ways that the inside of a video recorder was like the inside of your body. I don't remember what he said but I do remember I got real blown away by every word he said. And then later on I told him all about the Catlins and he got so excited by the way I talked about the Catlins he told me I should work in tourism. Ever since that day it felt like me and Gav were old friends.

It sucks that Deano doesn't like Gav cos they're so alike, apart from Gav being easygoing and Deano always throwing tanties, and apart from Deano being quite mean and nasty a lot of the time whereas Gav is kind and thoughtful. And also I guess another difference between them is that Gav is Maori and Deano is a hundred per cent white, and also Gav has travelled a lot, which makes him wiser, while Deano thinks the world revolves around Dunedin and the only decent overseas destination is Surfers Paradise. Deano loves Surfers Paradise. I like it too, but I reckon Deano should 'broaden his horizons', as Gav would say. Gav's really been encouraging me to broaden my horizons. That's why I've been thinkin about Shepherds Bush so much. It's like this place in London, but everyone there is either a Kiwi or an Australian or a South African. It's like being overseas but at home at the same time. One day I'm gunna go there all by myself.

I'm so relieved when Gav finally gets to the bank. He does some security here. He comes in every day at about three o'clock, you know, taking money in and out and all that. It's a real responsibility, he reckons. He reckons it has given him a new understanding of, like, how *cheap* money is. Like, it's just stuff printed on bits of paper.

Did you know it costs less than fifty cents to make a one-hundred-dollar note? And Gav reckons if you gave that note to starving children in Africa they'd just laugh at you, cos in Africa they use different money, so our one-hundred-dollar note is worth less than a handful of sand over there.

Gav reckons people think about money too much. He reckons that if money is what makes the world go round, then the world is gunna stop going round one day, and when that happens there'll be an ice age and we'll all be dead.

Anyway, I know that Gav is a good person to talk to about Monica. So as soon as Gav's van comes in I put up the 'Next Teller' sign and I say to Geraldine, 'Can you cover for me?' and she says, 'No,' but I go anyway and I know she will cover for me cos she's got a secret crush on me.

I head straight outside to where Gav is standing. His security mates are loading and unloading and he's just keeping an eye on things.

I say to him, 'I been thinking, Gav –' and Gav says, 'Don't strain it too hard, bro,' and I say, 'What?' and he says, 'Your brain.'

He's just joking. Gav knows that thinking isn't bad for your brain.

Deano told me it was. Deano said that we can only have so many thoughts in our life, so every time you have a thought a part of you is dying. He reckons if we think less and do more without thinking we'll live longer and have more smiles.

Gav thinks that thinking is a bit like if you got a pimple, and you pick at it, and lots of pus comes out, and by thinking more you help more pus come out, and that there is like a never-ending supply of pimple pus.

'I was thinking about children,' I say.

Gav goes, 'Yeah?'

'And then I was thinking about sex.'

'Woo, I don't think I like where this is going –'

'No, hear me out. I was thinking that when you have sex it leads to children, which doesn't make any sense, cos the two couldn't be further apart. So I'm thinking about sex and children, in like, the same thought and I start realising that the two are connected, and that one leads to the other, which leads to the other, which leads to the other.'

And Gav says, 'It's a trick.'

He's kinda lost me.

He says, 'Think about it, Nige. Why do we like sex?'

'Is it cos it makes ya horny?'

'No.'

'So we can have better orgasms?'

Two of Gav's workmates comes back with some money. They put it in the van and me and Gav go quiet. Gav raises his eyebrows at them and they give him a bit of a nod, like a way of saying hello without using words. Then they go back into the bank, and Gav keeps on his thought.

'Slow down and think about it, Nige. Why do we like sex?'

Now I'm starting to feel dumb. I just go, 'I dunno. It feels good?'

Gav slaps his hands and goes, 'Yes! And why does it feel good?'

Fuck, I still don't get what he's talking about.

Gav says, 'If you think about it, Nige, sex is ridiculous. Two people get naked and they push each other's buttons and wham-bam thank you ma'am, and a transaction is made –'

'Yeah, a transaction –'

'Just like at the bank, Nige. Deposits and withdrawals.'

'Yeah, yeah,' I go.

'And what does it all lead to?' he says.

That's when I get it.

'Babies,' I say.

And Gav goes, 'So let me ask you again. Why do we like sex?'

And I say, 'Babies.'

'It's a trick,' he says. 'We've been tricked into liking sex in order to have babies so the whole world can procreate and regenerate and repopulate! Survival of the species, bro.'

And I'm like, 'Wooooohhhh, that's true.' Even though I didn't pick up on what some of the words meant, I knew exactly what he was saying. He's a real life teacher, Gav is.

I've been tricked into having a baby with Monica. But not *by* Monica. I've been tricked by the survival of the species. I've been tricked by . . . I dunno . . . some other . . . force.

I really wanna tell Gav my news about Monica but I'm a bit worried that if I tell Deano one secret and Gav a different secret I'll end up tellin both of them the opposite secrets and then they'll both know how fucked I am.

So I keep it to myself.

Gav's mates have got back and the queue is getting up and Geraldine is lookin a bit fucked off. It's a pity Gav has to go right now. I wish he could hang out with me while I serve the customers. Ah well.

'You sure you're okay, bro?' he says.

'Oh yeah, I'm . . . a box of birds, Gav.'

Gav says, 'Hey, I got the day off tomorrow.'

'Awesome.'

'Yeah. And the van's got a warrant, too. So it's all on.'

'Eh?'

'The Catlins.'

'Ohh. Yeah . . . um,' I go.

Gav hops in the front of the van and gives me a real thumbs up.

I give him the thumbs up back, and then I wave goodbye to him as the security van heads off down George Street and out of sight.

PUTTING DOWN THE CAT

DEANO

I give Nige a call at the bank cos I have to take Mum to the vet's, and I'm worried about how he'll cope once banking hours are finished, so I reckon he should come with me and Mum, for company and that. Nige says he's going to the pub with Gav, which puts me on edge straight away. I say to him, 'You're not gunna tell him anything, are you, Nige?' and Nige says, 'Course not,' and I say, 'Well, even if you feel the urge, *don't*. If you tell Gav you might as well kiss your chances of getting away with this goodbye.'

'Okay,' he goes. They're heading to the Robbie, so I figure I'll go there after we've put down the cat.

At Mum's, I put Patty in a box. Patty puts up a real fight. It's like she knows what's gunna happen, so she tries real hard not to go in the box. She's got a real burst of energy and all four of her legs are kicking at the box and it's bloody hard to get her in. After a bit of a struggle I manage it but you can hear all this scratching inside the box, and a paw sticks out where the air holes are. She's got her claws out and is trying to get out of there. That's the kind of fighting spirit I think Nige needs to find.

Next we rock on up to the Mornington Veterinarian's Clinic and take the cat out in the waiting room. Mum strokes it and I try making eyes at a forty-year-old woman with a labrador. I make friends with the dog but the owner's not really into me. She just keeps reading, ignoring all the attention I'm giving her dog. 'Are you a mother?' I ask her and she says, 'What?'

I say to her, 'Oh, I just thought you might be a mother and just that that's not a problem for me.'

'Pardon?' she says.

'That's my mum over there,' and I point to my mum with Patty lying half dead in her arms. 'Our cat's got cancer,' I say, and the woman with the labrador says, 'I'm very sorry,' and I say, 'Yep – it's hard.'

I look down at my pants and my cock is doing what I call the 'let me out' throb. The forty-year-old keeps reading her *Woman's Weekly*.

'Nice dog. Boy or a girl?'

'Girl.'

'Nice bitch,' I say.

She ignores me so I go back to Mum, give her a big hug so the mother with the labrador can see us out of the corner of her eye. Then we're called in.

I hold Mum while they inject Patty. Patty starts doing these heinous long meows – ones that tug at your heartstrings, and Mum is crying, and I say, 'Be strong, Mum. Be strong.'

As the needle goes into the cat I look into Patty's eyes and she looks back at me. We spend a while looking at each other while she drifts off to another place. I know that my face is going to be the last thing she sees so I kind of do a bit of a smile so that Patty might die feeling a bit happier. Patty closes her eyes and her purring gets louder for a bit, so I know she's in peace, cos cats don't purr when they're freaking out. The purring goes for another minute and then no more purring. Just the sound of Mum crying.

'Mum, give her a pat while she's still warm,' I say, and Mum and me pat the cat. Mum says to the vet, 'Is she dead now?' and the vet says, 'Probably.'

The vet looks at his watch and Mum gets out a hanky and wipes her nose, which is dripping watery snot everywhere. I hold her, but I leave a bit of a gap so none of Mum's snot will fall on my neck.

Afterwards we have the body of the cat in the back seat, wrapped in newspaper.

Mum says, 'I'm a murderer.' She sounds like Nige, the way she's going on.

I say, 'You're not a murderer, Mum. Patty's in peace now.'

'Will you bury her for me? I can't face it.'

'I can't do it straight away.'

She says, 'Plant a nice tree for her,' and hands me twenty dollars. 'You can pick up a nice seedling from the garden centre.'

'Okay, Mum,' I say.

QUACK LIKE A GOOSE

DEANO

I spend Mum's twenty bucks on a round of drinks for me and Nige and Gav. I spit in Gav's beer before I take it over to him, but then I forget which beer I've spat into, so I randomly choose a beer for Gav and one for Nige, and when they take a drink I realise that Nige is drinking the beer I spat into. Oops.

I've been running over some real big decisions in my head, like, what are we gunna do with Jeurgen. So I say to Nige, 'Can I have a word? Alone?' and Nige just looks at me strange.

Gav says, 'I'll go and enrol us in the pub quiz. What's our team name?'

Nige looks at me and says, 'Can't we talk about it later?'

'How about the Shaggin Wagon, after my van?' Gav says.

'How bout the Wild Pig-fuckers?' I say to Gav, looking him right in the eye, but I say it like a joke. Ever since I found out Gav once went pig-hunting I've been having a field day on it.

Gav goes off to get us drinks. I'm a bit worried about that, cos who knows what Gav might slip in my drink. I reckon he's got a dodgy side. I reckon he hides that part of himself from Nige. Like, he seems like one of those guys that get on with everyone, right? I don't trust those guys. It's not natural to get on with everyone. I only get on with about three people: Nige, my mum and maybe Les from work, who works out all of the bus schedules. People that get along with everyone can't be trusted, if you ask me.

I say to Nige, 'How are you coping?' and Nige says, 'I'm trying not to think about it,' and I say, 'You have to think about it, Nige.'

'I know! Can't we talk about something else?'

'Jesus, Nige! We need a plan!'

'Can't you think of it?'

'Jesus, what am I? An A-plus student?'

'Can't we just deal with this tomorrow?'

'For fuck's sake, Nige, I mean –' I'm about to launch into a big rant but Gav comes back to the table. Gav says, 'We are the Minge Munchers,' and he's smiling.

The Minge Munchers? Fuck, talk about a dumb name.

It turns out Gav is pretty good at a pub quiz, but for some reason he always wants to hold the pencil cos he reckons he thinks better when holding a pencil. So I say to him, 'Is that pen-cil or pen-is?' and I whack Nige in the ribs to make him laugh, but Nige is concentrating on a question. It's the geography session and Nige is right into it, even though he couldn't find his way to the sea at a beach.

So Gav is saying, 'I'm not sure if the answer is Lithuania or Latvia – I get them mixed up,' and Nige is like, 'I think it might be Latvia,' and I'm lookin at Nige thinkin, what does he know about fuckin Latvia? He can't find his way from the couch to the TV sometimes, so I wouldn't rely on Nige to take us to the fifty-dollar winners' bar tab prize with Latvia.

I get bored watching them fill out their questions like little suck-the-teacher's-cock schoolboys, so I take Gav's pencil in between a round and draw a big cock on the page with hairy balls, just like mine. Then Nige takes the pencil off me and gives it to Gav, cos it's time for the next round, which is 'Who Am I?' For fuck's sake.

'Whose round is it?' I say, just as the questions are being read out loud. Nige goes, 'Shh, Deano,' so I say, 'What was that? Do you want a beer, Nige, or some top shelf?' and Nige goes, 'I'm tryin to hear the question,' and I say to him, 'I wonder if there'll be any backpackers here tonight? I wonder if there'll be any questions about Norway?' And Nige goes quiet. 'A round of sambucas on me,' I say, and I head off to get some sambucas.

At the bar I scull back a beer and buy a round of sambucas. I've decided to let Nige have a night off thinkin about it. I think a good unwind will give him strength for the hell that is to come.

I move past a table of blondes and brainiacs. They must be a family cos there's no way these girls would go out with these geeks – I mean, one of them admittedly has muscles but they can't disguise a face like a rottweiller's arsehole.

I say to one of the girls, 'Do you want to see my hard-on collection?'

She says to me, 'What?' and I suddenly think she might not be used to colourful language, so I just say, 'Nothing.'

Then she goes, 'No, what did you say to me?'

I say, 'It doesn't matter,' and she says, 'No. What did you say to me?' Now the whole table is listening, and the next table too.

'I said, do you want to see my hard-on collection?' and a

tall blonde chick says, 'How many have you got?' and I say, 'Hundreds. I make a new one every night.' and they laugh, and I'm thinkin I should get Nige over here.

I look over at Nige and Gav and they're doing a big laugh together, which makes me feel pretty shit. Then the tall blonde says, 'Fuck off,' and they all laugh at me. I could throw the fuckin sambuca in her face but I 'keep cool till after school' and head back to Nige and the big fat fuck.

When the quiz is finished our team has come third last and they're both a bit gutted and I'm secretly pleased. Gav comes back to the bar with some whiskys. 'It ain't Jim Beam,' he says as he slides one over to me, waiting for me to say thank you or something, like he's a fuckin war hero or something.

'So, Gav,' I say, 'Lookin forward to getting down to the Catlins?'

'Bro, I wanna see a penguin at dawn,' he says, and I say, 'A penguin at dawn is all very well, but it doesn't beat seeing a hot chick naked,' and he says nothing.

I say, 'Do you guys mind if I tag along? That place has a lot of memories for me and Nige,' and I wink at Nige and Nige nods slowly, like he is trying to understand my master plan. Gav goes, 'Fuck, of course you should come. The more the merrier –'

'Actually, I reckon three of us is enough,' I say.

Gav goes, 'The Catlins won't know what hit them.'

'The penguins will all take a big shit when they see you coming,' I say, and I punch Gav in the arm so that he thinks I'm joking, but it's actually a real punch in the arm cos I wouldn't mind inflicting a bit of violence on the cunt. Nothing would give me more pleasure.

I'm in a dark mood tonight.

As the three of us walk home I suggest we detour past the road works cos they are kind of on our way. Nige goes, 'Oh, naaa . . .' and I'm like, 'Why don't you wanna go that way, Nige?' and Nige doesn't say anything. He walks off ahead and up the hill, walking a bit faster.

I'm glad I freaked him out a bit. It's a good reminder to him that all this cosying up to Gav is for a reason, and that he shouldn't get too jokey with him. Not at a time like this.

I say, 'Hey Nige, let's go back to our place,' and Gav goes to me, '*Your* place, you mean,' and Nige goes, 'Oh yeah, I guess it isn't my place any more. It's your place,' and I say to Nige, 'It'll always be your place, Nige,' and Nige doesn't say anything back.

When we get to my place I have to do a quick tidy before they come in, cos when Nige left I demoed the living room and broke quite a lot of stuff. It's a real sty, and I can't clear the mess completely, so I just shove a lot of broken shit behind the couch and plug the TV in. I yell, 'Come in,' and Gav's eyes roll when he clocks the mess.

'Been partying, Deano?'

'Yep, I've been hitting the piss hard and . . . You know, what's stuff anyway? Stuff is made to be broken.' Nige looks around in a bit of shock too so I yell, 'Sit down. Can I get yous some beers?' and they sit down on the couch while I flick open three bevvies with my cigarette lighter.

Now we're all sitting on the couch. I've found the porno tapes we got out about a month ago and 'forgot' to return. Gav's is rolling a joint as we all watch a threesome. It's a bit like that show *Survivor* but after they do stuff like climb across a rope ladder and throw a coconut at a target then they just all get down to it and fuck each others' brains out.

Gav passes his joint to me but I refuse it, so Gav passes it to Nige. I look at Nige and shake my head so Nige passes it back to Gav.

'Fuck, am I the only one smoking?' Gav says.

Then he nods his head and smokes the whole joint all by himself.

And now Gav won't stop talking – he's like a fuckin breakfast radio DJ. 'The thing I found hard when I had a threesome,' he says, 'was that other set of eyes staring at me.'

'Did it put you off?' Nige goes, as if he's receiving the Ten Commandments from God himself.

'Fuck yeah,' he says. 'It's like at the urinal when you got some fella next to you lookin down at your cock. Hard to piss in those circumstances.'

'Fuck, that's true!' Nige yells.

'Not a problem for me,' I say, but no one builds on it.

Nige says, 'Speaking of, I've gotta take a fuckin slash,' and he heads off.

Now me and Gav sit at opposite ends of the couch, watching the porno. No one says anything. I'm not fooled by his *easy-going* bullshit – I know he doesn't like me, and that's fine cos the feeling is mutual.

'So how long have you known Nige?' I say to him finally, as a black guy unzips a big cock from his pants and strokes it while two chicks do a full 69.

'Not sure, ah –' and he counts on his fingers. 'Three months?'

I just smile cos he has just fallen into my trap.

'Fifteen years,' I say to him, and he has no comeback to that one.

I get up and leave him to ponder that, and I find Nige in the bedroom, sitting on my mattress.

'Sorry, I shouldn't be in here,' he says to me, and I say, 'You're always welcome in this room, Nige.'

Nige says, 'It looks different without my stuff.'

It sure does.

It's like the room has been divided in half. His whole side of the room is empty. There's scunge on the carpet underneath where his bed used to be – lots of it cos he never bothered to vacuum, did he, and I've just let the dust sit there as a reminder of him. Did you know that humans shed skin more often than a snake – like, one tenth of our skin comes off every day? So basically that empty floor is covered in Nige's old skin, and I can't bring myself to vacuum it.

Nige says, 'Remember that time we scored those two chicks that night after we learned a synchronised robot-dance routine to 'Is There Something I Should Know?' by Duran Duran and we wowed them on the dance floor?'

'I remember that, Nige. You were wearing your Surfers Paradise shirt and it really glowed in the UV.'

'Yeah, and then we came back here and you guys went for it in the bathroom and me and . . . what was her name?'

'Susan or something?'

'Yeah, we went for it in the bedroom.'

'I wanted you to be comfortable.'

'Yeah . . . well . . . I always thought that maybe we shoulda had our own rooms.'

'Economics.'

'Yeah, but . . . I mean, we coulda shifted into a bigger flat.'

'Economics, Nige. You don't understand economics.'

'I work at a bank.'

'Not the bank I bank at. There's no way I would let you administer my account.'

Nige looks around at the peeling racing-car wallpaper on his side of the room.

'Do you miss it here, Nige?' I ask.

'I don't know.'

His 'I don't know' makes me want to cry.

'You should stay the night, Nige.'

Nige looks at me. 'I live with Gav now.'

'Are you gay?' I ask him. 'Is Gav a homo?'

'Fuck off.'

'Well, stay the night here then.'

'Don't want to.'

'You owe me, Nige . . .'

He looks at me and goes quiet.

'Hey, shall we have a playfight?' I ask him, and Nige says, 'Not in the mood.' So I throw a pillow at him and he goes, 'Fuck off,' and so I give him a horse bite and he says, 'Fuck off,' but giggles at the same time, and then I launch at him bigtime – I wrestle him to his bed and we're both wrestling on the floor and I've pinned his face to the wall. Gav comes in and yells out WWF style – 'Annnd in the bluuue corner wee have Deeee-noooo and in the red we have the Niiige Maaannn' – and then he jumps on top of us, and he's fuckin big, you know. Nige is getting squashed and I'm like thinkin, 'Jeesus . . .'

Gav gets off and fuckin goes and lies on my bed. My fuckin bed!

I mean, what a weird cunt.

I leave the room. I flick off the porno. 'Hey Gav,' I yell to him. 'Time to go, buddy.'

'I'm fucked,' he yells out. 'Can I crash here, bro?'

'Not on my bed,' I yell, and Nige goes, 'I'll make up the couch for ya.'

Which is fuckin ironic, considering all those years I stayed at his house he never *once* made up a fuckin bed for me. Not once. And to be honest I'm bloody stunned as I watch Nige get fuckin *sheets* and *pillows* and shit and makes Gav up a bed.

'C'mon, Gav,' he yells, and Gav comes through off his face and practically falls on the couch. 'Don't break it, ya fat fuck,' I say, and Nige says, 'Deano!' and I say, 'Fuck, it was a joke,' and head off to bed.

When Nige comes in I'm lyin on the floor, which is carpet laid directly onto concrete – not so good. He says, 'What are you doing down there?' and I say, 'I thought you could take the bed, mate,' and he goes, 'That's not very . . . fair,' and I say, 'Don't look a gift horse in the mouth, Nige. Take the bed. I fluffed up the pillow for you,' and he goes, 'Thanks,' and he takes off his shoes and some clothes and gets in my bed.

I feel like a man-hug but there's no way to do it in this situation without being a bit gay so I just lie on my back and stare up at the ceiling. 'Hey Nige,' I say.

'Yeah?'

'I was thinkin about how nice it was of you to make that bed up for Gav on the couch.'

'Yeah, well . . . you know . . . I was just being helpful.'

I look up to where he's sleeping and he's facing my way and that kinda feels nice, like, that close feeling you get when you're with your best mate and all else is quiet in the world.

I say, 'I was thinking about when we were kids.'

'Oh yeah?'

'When I used to crash at your place and you never ever made a bed up for me. Weird, eh?'

'Yeah, fuck,' he goes. 'Kids are weird, eh?'

'Yeah,' I say, and watch him as he rolls over to face the wall.

I just lie and stare up at the blackness of the ceiling above me. There's some cracks in it. I follow the lines of the cracks with my eyes, close my eyes and I can see a ceiling without cracks – Nige's place, back when I was twelve and he was eleven, and we were both happy as fuckin Larry.

Eleven-year-old Nige says to me, 'Deano,' and twelve-year-old me says, 'Yeah?'

'You're my best friend,' he says. 'And you're my second-best friend. And my third-best friend. In fact, if I was to make a top ten list of best friends you'd be one, two, three, four, five, six, seven, nine and ten.'

'You missed eight ya dopy shit.'

'Did I?' he goes. 'Did I really? Fuck, I'm a goose.'

I giggle, and he giggles too.

'Such a goose,' I say.

He goes, 'Quack quack.'

And I say, 'Geese don't quack. They honk, like *hooonk hoooonk*,' and he giggles even more.

'Do it again!' he says, and I go, '*Hoooonk hooooonk*,' and he's laughing and laughing.

Twenty-six-year-old me stares up at the cracks and goes, '*Honnnnnk honnnnnnk honnnnnnnk*,' to the ceiling, but Nige is already asleep.

NEWSPAPER FREAKOUT

DEANO

I wake up a good half-hour before the sun comes up. I lie in the darkness and watch Nige sleeping. He's way comatosed and that makes me feel good, cos he needs his sleep at a time like this. He won't get much sleep in prison, that's for sure.

Not that we're in that deep yet. If I can figure a way out of this mess for him, I will. In fact, I have decided to let my subzero think about it for me. You might not have heard of the subzero. It's like when you wanna think about something you can't solve, like in maths or science. You can think about it without thinking about it by letting your subzero have a think while you go about your daily business. So I figure that's what I should do. So far my subzero has come up with nothing except for the idea that we should definitely take Gav to the Catlins, cos once he clocks that Nige is a murderer his whole nice guy act is gunna come to an end and he'll betray us, just like Nige betrayed me a week ago.

I get up and take a shower, cos I'm figuring God must have some ideas on this one. Between me, God and my subzero, we should be able to come up with a solution. Fuck knows Nige won't be much use.

There's a lot of vapour this morning and God says to me, 'You're almost out of conditioner,' and I say to him, 'If I go bald shall I get a hair transplant?' and God says I should find out if there's any testosterone pills on the market, and that ought to make me as hairy as a goat.

It's weird though, cos I'm losing hair on my head and gaining it on my balls. I ask God, 'Why are you shifting all my hair down to my balls?' and God says nothing.

'So, any ideas, God?' I ask, and God tells me to fetch the newspaper.

I head out in nothing but my towel into the cold air and up the neighbour's stairs where they get theirs home-delivered, and I get the royal shock of my life when I see a picture of Jeurgen on the front with a big headline saying 'MISSING'.

Fuck!

Suddenly I'm not cold. I'm sitting outside in nothing but my towel, and I'm not cold any more. The fuckin newspaper has a photo of Jeurgen on it and he's standing in front of a mountain. The police won't give away any details except to say they hold 'grave concerns for the safety of Jeurgen Larssen (23)'.

And I'm thinkin, 'Ohh fuck a duck. This isn't fuckin going to plan . . .'

I smoke a cigarette to jolt my brain into action. I really need my brain right now. I often dreamed at school that I would be brainy one day. You know, I'd look over at all the bright kids in class and I'd think, 'Well, you're only doing well in the tests cos you're trying – fuckin try-hards.' But then I went through a spell where I thought maybe they were just brighter than me. I'm still in that spell. It makes sense now. Maybe the reason I wasn't trying was cos they are brighter than me. Instead, I just surround myself with the only person I can find who is stupider than me, and that's Nige. Even though he reads books I know he's stupid as. It's a bit like how Sylvester Stallone cruises around in glasses. Nige reads books to look brainy, but it doesn't work cos he's as thick as two planks. Come to think of it, he's thicker than two planks – he's as thick as about four planks, which is twice as thick as two planks, according to the law of maths.

Anyway, my brain does kick in after a couple of drags. This newspaper article doesn't change a thing. In fact, it confirms that the plan we had was spot on. We gotta get Gav to the Catlins quicksmart, and we can't let him near a fuckin newspaper. That might be a bit of a challenge, cos Gav likes to bang on a bit about the news. I reckon he's just pretending, though. I reckon if you asked Gav what was goin on in the news he'd have to make up a big lie, and most people would fall for it, but not me.

It's time for actions to speak louder than words, so I head inside the flat and clap my hands together and I say to Gav, 'Wakey wakey! The Catlins await! Wakey wakey!' Gav opens his eyes and looks at me with half-asleep eyes. He says nothing and I just stare at him – the kind of stare that John Wayne would give a Red Indian. Then I smile, cos I have to use my head over my heart, and it is more important than ever that the big fat fuck likes me.

'I reckon we should get moving,' I say to Gav. 'There's a lot of nature out there waiting for us. You want some toast and a cup of tea?'

Gav nods and sits up, bleary-eyed. 'Kia ora, bro,' he says. 'That'd be cool.'

NIGE

This morning I dreamed it was all a dream but then I found out that I was dreamin when I woke up, and I found out that none of it has been a dream.

It's all *real as.*

Deano showed me the front page of the newspaper and I straight away felt this bulge in the bottom of my stomach and I had to take a dump to relieve the load. I sat on the toilet lookin at the photo of Jeurgen and he was standing in front of Mt Cook – he looked like he was really enjoying New Zealand.

I can understand that. It's such a beautiful country. Like, cos I'm from here, when I see a mountain I just kind of go, 'Oh yeah,' like it's no big deal, but for Jeurgen coming from a country that like is probly a bit shitty in the scenery department, well . . .

I mean, he must have been blown away when he saw Mt Cook and Tekapo and all of those places. That's where he'd just been, before he made it down to Dunners. He was hitching and he musta been looking for a place to crash when I flattened him accidentally. Just goes to show you can be at the wrong time at the wrong place, and that describes Jeurgen and me to a tee. Anyway, the police sound like they're lookin for whoever gave him a lift, which means they're barking up the wrong tree in the meantime, so that's something, I guess.

But you know, with DNA and science and that, I just don't know who's gunna come knocking at my door. Deano's all amped cos he reckons Gav might get suspicious of us, with all of our acting strange and that. I haven't been tryin to act strange, I've been tryin to be real normal, but being normal isn't as easy when you've killed a man. I didn't know that before but I know it now. I'm learning heaps at the moment, which I spose is a bit of a silver lining.

Anyway, Deano's all 'We have to go now' – no fuckin around and we can't let Gav see a newspaper. He has to be watched 24/7. I tell Deano before I go that I have to see Monica and he flips his lid bigtime.

He's like, 'Fuck off with that shit,' and I say, 'Deano, what if I love her?' and he says, 'Do you?' and I go, 'I haven't figured that out, but I was always gunna try and get back together with her. I just wanted to wait until she was done with her exams.'

Deano goes, 'You're not seeing Monica right now. You'll fuck everything up.'

I'm not backing down on this one. No way. For some reason my body is saying, 'Go and see Monica, go and see Monica,' over and over again, like one of those hypnotists. I've been thinking about her face and what a nice face it is. One of those faces that the first time you look at it you don't get what a nice face it is, but then you fall in love with her and you think she's got the best face in the world.

I tried to write her a poem in my head the other night when I was in bed, but I didn't have a pen and I couldn't be bothered getting up so I thought I'd keep it in my mind, but most of it bloody left me, just like Monica left me six months ago after Deano tried makin his move on her.

Anyway, Deano doesn't know that she might be carrying my baby. I mean, I know it's cool she hasn't contacted me, which means I'm off the hook in some ways, but maybe I would be a good dad, you know, cos when I'm around kids, even though they annoy the fuck out of me, I'm still nice to them.

The point is, I was a kid once, which means I know what kids are thinking. In some ways I'm still a kid, so if I was a dad maybe I'd be like a second kid, you know, like, the bigger kid, and Monica would be like a mother for both of us, except then I'd go and do a job and get some money and stuff.

Deano can see I won't back down on this one, so I'm going to see her before we go to the Catlins, not after, cos who knows if there will be an after?

There's no toilet paper and all I have is the newspaper with the article about Jeurgen so I look at his face and say, 'Sorry, mate. I don't mean any disrespect,' and I wipe my arse with the newspaper and flush it down the bog, although I have a floatie so I have to flush a second time and push it all down with the toilet brush.

REUNION WITH MONICA

NIGE

I've pulled up the Mazda outside Monica's. Gav and Deano are behind me in Gav's van. Deano reckons he is keeping an eye on Gav while I try and talk Monica into . . . shit, I don't really know what I'm gunna talk her into.

I get like a real quick urge to turn up with a flower, and cos Monica lives close to Woodhaugh Gardens I sprint off into the bushes and come across a rose bush, and I try and pull it out but it's hard to pull out a rose bush without getting prickled so I kick it out at the roots, but the whole plant is a bit much to give her, so I just pull the flowerheads off and take them in my hand, and I cup them in my hands as if I was carrying a small sick bird.

I have to take a piss cos of all the nervousness, so I put them down again and take a piss, but a little spray falls on the roses I just picked, so I pick up the ones that were furtherest away from my 'friendly fire' and I take them and head to Monica's and knock on the door, real loud.

DEANO

I'm stuck in the van with Gav and his BO so I wind down the window and say to him, 'Your van smells a bit, Gav,' and Gav goes, 'Does it?' and he has a big sniff and says 'Smells like cat piss,' and I say, 'I think it's BO,' and he says, 'I just had a shower,' and I say, 'What about stale BO?' and he says, 'I don't reckon. I'll open the doors and windows, though,' and he opens up all the doors and windows while we wait for Nige.

Then Gav grabs a little black notebook from under his seat and starts writing some note or something. 'What are you doing?' I ask, and Gav quickly shoves the notebook in his pocket and says, 'Nothing. Hey, do you know Monica?'

I'm not going to tell him that Monica has seen my tent pole standing proud without any tent. So I say, 'Yeah, I kinda know her,' and he says, 'Nige is real into her, eh?' and I say, 'She's too bright for him,' and Gav says, 'I think Nige has untapped potential.'

I say, 'Oh yeah, well, good luck untapping it.'

Then Gav starts banging on about Nige's potential. Fuck, I really wish I was deaf right now. If I could stick on a big pair of headphones and not listen to any more of Gav's boring thoughts I would, but there's no headphones in sight. Who does he think he is?

Also, I'm distracted. Nige has gone inside and for all I know he might be having a right old blab about the situation at hand. Nige has always been a bit lousy on secrets, unless they are secrets that would drop him personally in the shit, which makes me feel okay at the moment, except for all I know he might be giving clues, saying things like, 'I'm going away and I won't be back a while,' or, 'I've changed,' or shit like that.

NIGE

'I've changed,' I say to her, and Monica says, 'Too little, too late, Nige,' and I say, 'How do you know too little? I've been through heaps lately.'

'So have I,' she says, feeling her bump.

'I heard about it, Monz. I . . . can I stick my ear on it?' and she says, 'It's not yours,' and I say, 'Can I stick my ear on it anyway to see if it kicks me in the head? Please, Monz? It would mean something to me,' and she lets me stick my head against her tummy.

'I can't feel anything . . .'

'Did you feel that?'

'Wooo . . . yeah, I did. Wooo . . .'

She pushes my head away from it and I look up at her and I'm crying. God, she's beautiful. I could stare at her face for a whole day.

'It's not yours, Nige,' she says.

'Are you sure, Monz? I mean, remember how I had that run of bad luck with the condoms –'

'Nige. It's not yours.'

She makes me a cup of tea. As she brings it to the coffee table I can see she's been crying a bit too.

'I know you liked me, Monz.'

'I'm not denying that.'

'So what about it?'

'Nige, we're too different. You have a different life. I'm studying to be a lawyer. You're . . . you're stuck, Nige. I can't be with someone who's stuck.'

'What if I unstick myself?'

'Nige, I shouldn't've let you in. I don't think you should come round here.'

I can feel tears running down my cheek, so I wipe my face

with my sleeve. I want to yell out to her: 'I'VE KILLED A MAN, I'VE KILLED A MAN' but I realise it's not in my best interests, so I keep the secret of Jeurgen to myself. I'm a mess.

When Monica shows me to the door I say to her, 'I love you,' and she says, 'Don't say that, Nige,' and I say, 'But it's true,' and she says, 'You need to see a shrink, Nige. Are you still living with Deano?'

'Nah, I got out. Me and Deano aren't best mates any more, Monica. I don't even hang out with him. I've really changed.'

'Well, next time you see Deano, why don't you ask him where my Kate Bush CD is, where my Beatles *Abbey Road* CD is, where my Billy Bragg is, where all my fucking Bowie CDs are?'

'Eh?'

'He stole my B section, Nige. He stole the entire B section out of my CD collection.'

And then, with perfect timing, there's a honk on a horn and it's Deano, yelling at me from the van, not that I can hear what he's saying cos he's honking and yelling at the same time. Monica looks at Deano like he's a complete dickhead and I say to her, 'Okay, so I'm still hangin out with Deano, but I'm changing lots of other stuff.'

She just looks at me and she says, 'I want my B section back,' and she closes the door on me and I yell, 'Wait!' and I stick my foot in the door.

'Please, Monz. One last hug,' and I can see she feels a bit sorry for me so she hugs me and I hold her tighter than I've held anyone in my life. I pull the rose heads out of my pocket. They got a little squeezed in the hug and most of them look pretty squashed. I hand them to her and I say to her, 'Whenever you look at those roses, I want you to think of me,' and I leave her, turn my whole body around, and I know I might never see her again.

You know that story in the Bible about the guy who turned into a block of salt when he looked back? Well, that's like me. There's no way I'm going to turn into a block of salt.

I head to the van. Deano looks worried about me and Gav is smiling at me, giving the thumbs up like it's a question or something. I give him the thumbs down, so he knows things have fucked out bigtime.

I get to the van and I say to Deano, 'Hey, did you bring any music with you?' and Deano says, 'Yeah. It's in the car.'

Gav says, 'Don't worry about music, Nige. I got everything from Bob Marley to Hendrix.'

'Oh yeah . . . got any Bananarama?' I ask, staring at Deano.

'Nah,' Gav goes, so I say, 'What about some Bon Jovi? What about the Beatles? What about Bowie? What about Bread?'

Deano looks at me in the eye and says, 'Yeah, I've got all of those – have you got a problem with that, Nige?'

I stare at him and he's got a real serious face on, like he's challenging me in front of Gav. He goes, 'I've also got the B52s, Jeff Buckley, Black Sabbath and the Black Eyed Peas,' and I just look him in the eye and I say, 'Monica wants her CDs back,' and Deano says, 'That's a pity, cos she's not gunna get them.'

I try to get in the Mazda but Deano holds the keys up and says to me, 'Actually, Nige, I reckon you should go in the van with Gav. I've got some business to take care of,' and he winks at me. 'What business?' I say, still angry and that, and Deano says, 'You know, business in Taieri Mouth,' and that makes me think about Jeurgen all over again. I can't get him out of my brain. Deano goes, 'I'll take the Mazda and catch up with you two at Kaka Point. DID YOU HEAR THAT, GAV?' and Gav yells, 'Hoake taua! Let's hit the highway!'

REUNION WITH JEURGEN

DEANO

Taieri Mouth is a small detour on the way to the Catlins. As I'm driving I check the back seat to make sure the axe is still there. It's not like it would have gone anywhere. I loaded it myself just an hour ago, but I guess it's a bit like when you go to the movies and you know you put the tickets in your pocket but you keep checking just to be sure. I'm like that with the axe.

I'm just hopin like fuckin mad that the body is where we left it still, otherwise the moment I show up my goose might be cooked bigtime.

It's not easy leaving Nige in the van with Gav. I know Nige is just pretending to like Gav, but sometimes it feels like he's taking the pretending too far. But it's important that Gav is nowhere near the backpacker. I can't count the number of ways things could be fucked up if he was to know what we were *really* up to.

I drive past Brighton and stare out at the beach. That place has got memories for me and Nige. One Guy Fawkes night when we were about fourteen we snuck out in Nige's mum's car and I hooked up all the fireworks in a bag to, like, this one tennis ball can – you know how they put tennis balls in cans? I cut holes in it and everything was tied up good and proper and me and Nige headed to the beach to light it.

The fucker of the thing was, as soon as I lit it there must have been a gust or something cos it fell over. The can was meant to be pointing up like a rocket, for the good reason that it was loaded with skyrockets, but instead the skyrockets started shootin out of the can along the ground and the can took off too, and I don't remember much apart from yelling out, 'Fuuuuuuuuuuck!' to Nige and both of us runnin away from the thing as it whizzed past our ears.

It was a bit like being in a war zone. You know that movie *Platoon* with Charlie Sheen, and they have that scene where they've just burned a village and shit, and then they have the scene where a whole lot of gooks come out at them in the night and there's like flashes of light everywhere and you can't tell what the fuck is going on – it's just like lots of lights and noises and then you hear a guy screamin and he's been shot and it's real full on and confusing, and survival is a matter of luck and your chances are better if you go a bit psycho, you know, screamin through the woods on a killing rampage and shit?

Well, this was a bit like that. We could hear the noises of the fireworks and I heard Nige scream so I ran in his direction even though I had no idea where he was. He'd fallen in a hole and twisted his ankle. But he wasn't crying or anything – both of us were laughin our arses off. As the last skyrocket spread along the ground I jumped on Nige's body to shield him from any impact, like you'd do if someone had chucked a grenade at you. And then we just laughed more and more. It was one of the fuckin funniest things we'd done.

We walked along the beach afterwards and headed down to the caves and walked barefoot through the water and it was real nice, like . . . I dunno. Memories like those are priceless.

I get to Taieri Mouth and pull down the side road and there's no traffic around so my guess is Jeurgen's body is still there. I make it through the bramble and out to the drainpipe and there's some flies buzzing around the bag. No dogs have found it, which is a good break.

I pull the rubbish bag out of the drainpipe and drag it to some thick bush and I take Jeurgen out from the rubbish bag and he's wearing the backpack and there's a few flies hangin out in his mouth. I go straight to work. I roll Jeurgen over and strip him of his backpack. I take that a distance away to the river and wash off some of the blood from it, cos the backpack is a part of the big plan. Then I take my axe and I slam it into Jeurgen's waist.

It's important that you think of it as a piece of meat, like a butcher dividing up a lamb into several roasts. The only difference is that Jeurgen is a human. But he's still an animal. He's still part of the food chain, and if you just think of him as a sheep heading off to the freezing works then there's no reason to freak out doin what I'm doin.

I do it real professional. There's no point bein grossed out. I have to do what I can to save Nige's bacon, and sometimes friendship involves some unpleasant aspects and that is all this is.

I hack away just below Jeurgen's guts. Getting the last bit to come off is quite hard. After a few goes with the axe, I have to switch over to my pocket knife to cut the last bit of skin, and finally Jeurgen is in two pieces. I realise that to stuff him in the backpack I might need to cut him some more. I draw the line at cutting off his head, though – that would be a bridge too far, even for me.

It's not easy fitting all the bits of Jeurgen into the backpack, especially cos all his stuff is here too, so I have to run to the car and use the cigarette lighter to start a little fire to get rid of some of Jeurgen's T-shirts and undies, which burn pretty easy. The whole time I'm doin it I'm bloody nervous of getting busted, but this seems to be a pretty remote spot, and no one comes within cooee.

I have to work bloody hard on the zip to get all of Jeurgen into the backpack. Like, I've squashed him in as much as I can, but the zip just won't go all the way. I wish Nige was here to help me by holding the other part of the zip together, but in some other ways it's better that I am goin through this alone. I don't think Nige would have very good dreams if he was doin what I'm doin.

The fire has burned most of his clothes to ashes and I take the remaining bits and shove them in the bottom section of the backpack. Then I put on the backpack and walk back to the car.

It feels funny wearing Jeurgen's backpack. Like, I feel like this is what he would have wanted. Knowing it was an accident, it's not like Jeurgen would want an innocent man to go to prison, and I feel like Jeurgen is telling me, 'It's okay doin what you're doin, Deano. You gotta put Nige first in the equation. I'm already a goner so you might as well do with me whatever will help out Nige.'

I take the backpack to the car and I shove it in the boot and head off, down the road towards Kaka Point, to the place where Nige and I spent so much of our childhood together . . .

WELCOME TO KAKA POINT

NIGE

'Bro, I really do love this place. This place is awesome,' Gav goes, heating a couple of knives on the elements of the oven.

'Yeah, me and Deano have got a lot of memories here, Gav. Like, see that tyre swing over there? We used to swing on that swing. Deano loved pushing me. He'd push me higher and higher until I felt like I was flyin like Superman. Do you wanna have a go on the swing, Gav?'

Gav holds the knives together and I suck up some smoke.

'Yeah, okay,' he says.

Next thing the two of us are out there swingin on the swing and goin, 'Yeeeehaaaaaaa!' like cowboys. I've given Gav a push but he's quite big so I can hardly move him. So I hop on the tyre and Gav pushes it with all his might and I'm screamin like one of those primary screams and it feels so good to be out in the fresh air and back on my tyre swing again.

I used to do a lot of thinkin on this tyre swing. Like, about girls and about how sometimes I wanted to kill myself, and about memories too. It was like a spot I could always go to and feel like I knew who I was. Gav is pushin me harder and harder and I'm screamin bigtime. It is such an awesome feeling . . .

Then Deano comes up the path with the toasted sandwich maker in one hand and a pack of cigarettes in the other. Gav gives me an almighty push and my legs almost crash into Deano's face but he swerves just in time.

I say, 'Look, Deano, I'm flying!' and Deano looks at me and he covers his eyes cos for some reason he doesn't like the sight of Gav pushing me on the tyre.

I put my legs down and stop swingin and I say to Deano, 'We got some pretty good memories on this swing, eh, Deano?'

Deano puts a ciggy in his mouth and says, 'We got good memories all over this stretch of land – nothing but good memory after good memory,' and Gav says, 'Ka hoki aku whakaaro ki nga wa o mua. Land of memories . . .'

I quite like that but Deano ignores it and sits down on the grass, lookin out at the view.

'Is that bunk still in our old room?' Deano says.

'Yeah,' I say.

'Good,' he goes. 'You can have the top bunk if you like.'

'I thought I'd sleep in Mum and Dad's old room,' I go, but Deano goes, 'No. We'll sleep in our old room,' and he stares at me, and I can tell from the look on his face that I'd better do as I'm told.

NIGE FREAKS FOR THE NINETEEN-MILLIONTH TIME

DEANO

It must be about two in the morning. 'Niiiiige,' I whisper. I poke my head up and watch him sleeping on the top bunk. 'Nige,' I say.

'Wh . . . whaa . . . wha . . . what is it?' The way Nige wakes up really makes my heart pound. He's like a small child being woken up out of a nightmare. Except when he's awake it's more of a nightmare than when he's asleep.

I once had a dream where I dreamed I was real hungry and there was this banana in the kitchen and I ate it, but when I woke up I was hungry and there was no banana in the kitchen. That's what this was like for Nige. Waking into the nightmare of me waking him up to tell him that the backpacker is in the backpack.

He looks at me and I say, 'Shhhh. I've chopped Jeurgen in half and stuffed him in the backpack.'

'Eh?'

'So we gotta get rid of it. It's in the boot. I figured it was a choice of dropping him over by the lighthouse or maybe down Jacks Blowhole. Whaddya reckon?'

Nige seems to be having trouble with my question. Maybe he thinks he's still in a dream so I slap him in the face to help him get awake, and he goes, 'Owww!' and I'm like, 'Shhhhhh. Don't wake Gav. I'll make you a cup of tea.'

It's funny being back in the crib, especially since it's under new ownership. They've made quite a lot of changes to what used to be Nige's and my place, and I don't like it. For a start, they chucked out my favourite sheepskin rug I used to lie on in front of the fire when I was a kid. They don't use the fire. There's a big bar heater in front of it, so I turn that on. It takes me ages to find the tea-bags, especially in the dark, since the fuckers that live here haven't changed the kitchen lightbulb for like the last four times we've been here. Pisses me off.

Nige comes out in a bomber jacket and some jeans. I hand him a cup of tea just the way he likes it and he doesn't say thank you. Typical.

'You shoulda seen it, Nige. I cut into his waist like about six times with the axe, but I had to cut the last bit with a knife. It was pretty intense but not as bad as I expected.'

'You did what?'

'Sometimes, Nige, you have to think like a soldier. Like, if you and I were in World War One there'd be people dying all around us. In that situation we'd think nothing about this sort of thing. We would have seen much worse and we would be immune to the shock of anything.'

'Eh?'

'You must feel it. Life's different for you now.'

'How do you mean?'

'You've had your first kill, Nige. Your whole mind must

shift after the first kill. You're, like, a different human being. Both of us are.'

'I was thinking Jacks Blowhole,' Nige says, surprising me.

'Good choice, soldier. Do we go up tonight?'

'No. No, I . . .'

Nige is really spacing out, like he's experiencing pain or something. Then I realise I shoulda used kiddie gloves on him cos he starts cryin and runs straight out the front door.

I run after him, down the street, down to the beach. He musta overbalanced trying to run too fast cos I see him go down in front of me and when I catch up with him he has his head in the sand.

I light up a fag. He's still cryin, which makes me uncomfortable, but instead of walkin away I sit nearby, while he tries to wipe his eyes and his nose with a small shell, which doesn't work too well, so I pass him a bit of seaweed and he snots all over that.

He goes, 'I've never thought about, you know, life before. I've never thought about fuckin being alive, till I hit Jeurgen,' and I just smoke my cigarette cos I figure it's best to let him just talk shit if he wants to talk shit.

Then he says to me the weirdest question. He goes, 'Do you reckon there's, like . . . an afterbirth?'

And I'm like, 'What?'

'You know, like, another life after you die?'

I chew away at my ciggy to try and come up with a good answer. I could just make a joke or take the piss but I figure it might be better for him if I kinda make him feel better and that. So I say, 'Um . . . fuck, sure there is. I mean, I'd say you come back and turn into, like, an animal. Like, you and I will come back as, like . . .' I rack my brain for a good animal. 'Like an eagle?' I go. He nods. I can tell I'm makin him feel better so I go on. 'Yeah, an eagle that . . . you know . . . swoops around, collecting stuff and . . . flyin over the mountains and trees and stuff, and catchin rats and mice and shit.'

'What do ya reckon Jeurgen'll be?'

'Fuck, I dunno. What animals do they have in Norway?' Nige is as stumped as me.

'Maybe he'd be, like, a Norwegian rabbit or something,' I say, and Nige says, 'Or like a deer or a polar bear or something,' and I'm like, 'I don't think they have polar bears in Norway, Nige,' and he starts crying again.

Fuck. I mean, I thought I'd made him feel better and then he starts crying, which is just making me feel bad too.

So I punch him. On the arm.

'Come on, man. It's not that bad,' I say.

'I killed someone,' he goes, so I punch him again, a bit harder, and I put on a funny voice.

'Come on, Niiiige, come on, Niiiige,' I say, whacking him again on the arm, and he says, 'Don't fuckin hit me,' but he's got a giveaway smile, so I hit him harder and he starts giggling, and so I jump on him and pin him down, and it's a big WWF wrestle, and I'm yellin, 'I'm gunna give you a dead leg,' and he's goin, 'Nooo OW OW OW!' and we're both laughin and fighting just like we did back in the good old days before Nige became a murderer.

PENGUIN DIVIDE

NIGE

I've just got back to sleep again when I get woken up and it's Gav sayin, 'Nige, it's dawn,' and I'm like, 'Eh?' and Gav says, 'Let's go and see the penguins,' and I say to Gav, 'Nah, not this morning. I need a lie in,' and Gav says, 'C'mon, Nige! I wanna see the penguins!' and he pulls the covers off my bed.

I've been awake all bloody night worryin about shit and now Gav wants me to look at penguins.

'Nah, I'm not coming,' I say.

'Get up, Nige,' a new voice says, and I'm surprised to see Deano all up and ready. I don't get it. I hear a whistle coming from the kitchen and it's the jug.

Gav's makin the cups of tea and I say to Deano, 'I wanna stay in bed,' and Deano says, 'Nige, you know when you get one of those gut feelings that feel like you're gunna have a spew but actually it's your body telling you something? Well, my body just told me to get up and watch the penguins with

Gav. I don't think we should let him out of our sight. That's what my body reckons, anyway.'

'My body reckons I should stay in bed.'

'Well, my body and your body disagree, Nige, but who's smarter? You or me? Answer me honestly.'

'You.'

'So what are we gunna do?'

I'm sitting in the lounge drinking a cup of tea from a tin mug. It's my old tin mug. The new people at the crib haven't thrown that out yet. I used to drink a lot of milk from that mug, and then when me and Deano got older I remember I drunk a lot of tequila out of that mug too.

Outside everything is still pretty dark, which is a bit weird. I'm used to going to sleep when it's light but I'm not used to getting up when it's dark. Doesn't make sense. My body thinks it's all a dumb idea, but Deano's body reckons this is the way to go so I guess that makes it a good idea. Besides, I do like the penguins.

When me and Deano were kids we went down there a few times and tried to scare them. Like, if a penguin is sitting on the egg it won't leave the egg, so you can go right up close to it and it won't move. It's shitting itself but it doesn't go anywhere. Deano used to go right up to the penguins and make, like, penguin noises at them. We were pretty drunk, you know, havin a laugh and that.

One time Deano took a penguin egg and he threw it into the sea, smashing it. He thought that was real funny and I felt a bit weird about it. Deano told me it was just nature. Survival of the fittest and that. He was stronger than the penguin as a human being so he was just lettin the penguin know who was boss, by chucking out its egg to teach it a lesson or something. Deano reckons that animals were put on Earth to give us meat

– nothing more and nothing less, and he has often said to me, 'I wonder what a penguin would taste like.'

I'm driving us to Nugget Point and it's still dark. Gav pulls out his peace pipe and suggests we have a few cones. He lights up in the van. I watch Deano decide whether he'll smoke drugs or not. He says drugs have no effect on him whatsoever but I reckon that's not true. I reckon he goes a bit weird – kinda slower but more dangerous. He thinks when he's stoned that he's actually still as straight as a die, which is weird cos when Deano's stoned he's definitely a bit different.

Anyway, Deano decides to partake. When Gav offers the pipe to him he says, 'What the fuck,' and goes for it bigtime.

'Don't Bogart the joint,' I say after he's been at it for a while.

'Don't what the what?' he says. 'Firstly, Nige, this is not a joint, and secondly, what was that word you said?'

Gav goes, 'He said Bogart, after the famous actor.'

'Well, he can't be very famous cos I haven't heard of him.'

Gav seems pretty keen to talk about Humphrey Bogart.

'You know, Humphrey Bogart? "Here's lookin at you, kid."'

And Deano goes, 'No, Gav. The only actors I know are famous ones, like Tom Cruise. He was excellent in *Top Gun*. You like *Top Gun*, Gav?'

'Kind of.'

'I like how the Ice-Man, who is the bad guy, becomes Tom Cruise's friend in the end and they bond together to fight the real enemy, the Russians.'

'How come the Americans always get to be the good guys and the foreigners are the bad guys?' Gav says, and I say, finally getting a toke, 'Yeah, why is that?'

The view is opening out in front of us and it's like one of

those views that you would take a postcard of if you knew how to. You can see the mountains and the lighthouse flashing in the distance and the sea is roaring and as we drive up the steep dirt road it feels like we're about to drive over a cliff. Me and Deano used to rally drive on this stretch so I pump the accelerator and take us on a joyride just to scare Gav a bit, cos I reckon he might get a kick out of that, and I'm goin, 'This van handles good, Gav.'

We pull up where the penguin bit is.

'Okay, is everyone wasted enough?' Gav asks, and I say, 'Yeah, I'm pretty fucked. What about you, Deano?'

'I don't feel anything,' Deano says.

See what I mean? Deano thinks he's too strong in the head for drugs.

We hop out of the van and the wind is goin nuts, like it's real loud – so loud it, like, whistles in your ears and knocks you around a bit.

'Fuck I love this place,' Deano goes, taking a piss at the first bush we get to. 'Watch out for friendly fire,' he says, shooting a little burst of warning piss our way.

Then another van pulls up in the car park. 'Aaah fuck. Tourists,' Deano says.

'Backpackers,' says Gav, eyeing up their van.

It's one of those rentals that the rental company has drawn lots of patterns on. We listen in and hear them speaking in German or something. I start to feel a bit sick.

Deano spots that and he says to me, 'Nige, it's understandable for you to develop a fear of backpackers, but you need to get over it. Come on,' and Gav says, 'What was that?' and I say, 'Deano just told me a joke,' to cover up, which was pretty smart thinkin of me.

We head down to the path and come to, like, a crossroads.

There's, like, the main path that goes to the hide, which is this big wooden peephole thing where you can watch the penguins from. Then there's a little path that goes down to the beach, where the penguins are.

Deano starts to go down the path to the beach.

'Deano, we're not sposed to get close to them,' I say, and Deano says, 'I forgot, Nige, when was it exactly that you turned into a fuckin square?' and Gav goes, 'I'm heading to the hide,' and heads the opposite way from Deano.

I don't know which path to take.

Do I go with Deano or do I go with Gav?

It's like one of those real hard decisions, especially when Deano hates me hangin out with Gav so much, but he does want me to pretend to be friends with Gav, so I figure maybe I should go with Gav.

'I'm goin to the hide with Gav.'

'You fuckin pussy,' Deano says, and he heads down the hill without me.

DEANO

A lot of things are running through my head. Obviously, there's when do we get rid of the body, and how do we get away from Gav to do that? I figure an opportunity will come our way, but we have to do it today. The longer that backpacker sits in the boot the bigger the stink and the more Nige'll freak out, so today is the day, and I think Jacks Blowhole is the perfect spot.

And I'm also thinkin, what exactly am I doing all this shit for Nige for when he almost ignores me? He treats me like shit. Like, why did he go with Gav and not me? I mean, here I am, his best friend for fifteen years, and he's known Gav for, like, a few months and Nige goes, 'I'll go with Gav.'

'I'll go with Gav.'

Now, those four words might seem like little words, but to me they say a lot more than the words themselves. They say, 'I choose Gav,' to me, and that makes my stomach bubble with anger. I try to tell myself that Nige is just pretending to like Gav, but something deep inside my body is telling me that Nige is pulling away from me, and into the arms of Gav.

It's like a kind of warmth that is missing from him when I talk to him. I had this dream once where I looked at him and I thought to myself, 'Where have you gone, Nige? Where's the real Nige? Where are you?' and it was one of those dreams where he could hear my thoughts, due to ESP.

In the dream Nige said, 'What do you mean?' and I said with my thoughts, 'You never smile to me, or laugh at my jokes any more. You never phone me. It's always me phoning you. How come you don't phone me?' and his brain says, 'I dunno, I'm just tired,' and I say, 'Oh yeah, well, you don't seem to be very tired around Gav. You don't seem to be very tired around Monica. You don't seem to be very tired around my mum, even. How come you're just tired around me?'

That was the end of the dream but I picture it again as I head down the hill towards the penguins.

I stare up at the hide where I know Nige and Gav are and I can feel the bile in my stomach leaking into my bloodstream. About a hundred metres away from me there is some movement in the ocean and the first couple of penguins come to shore. They're all kind of chatty, like they're happy to be in from the cold and back on dry land after a hard night catchin fish and shit. More penguins start to come out and they're all chatterin away like they are real happy birds.

My brain is doing a lot of weird things at the moment, and

the way the penguins are making so much noise and seem real happy makes me feel sad and makes me feel angry at Nige for even letting Gav into our lives.

Nige has no idea what friendship is. Like, Nige thinks friendship is like a relationship – you know, you move on when you get bored – but I think you have to ride out the bad times in order to see the good again.

I haven't changed. I'm still the same old Deano, and I don't know if he gets that. Sometimes I think, 'Fuck him,' ya know? But then I think of living my life without Nige and I think that Nige is more than my mate; he's my family – especially since I don't have any brothers or sisters and I wouldn't want any even if I did have a brother or sister, cos I would have Nige.

I don't know. All I know is that he better start treating me better, otherwise why do I risk everything for him? Why should I take a bullet for someone that doesn't laugh at my jokes any more? Why?

But I would.

I would take a bullet for him.

I would take a bullet in the heart.

More penguins are coming to shore so I light up a cigarette and watch from a distance, but I have a hard time shielding the cigarette from the wind. I can't get the flame up and running so I just sit there tryin to light the cigarette again and again as the penguins come to shore. They're makin a real racket. I don't know if it's my mind playin tricks but I get a mental vision of me and Nige frolicking among the penguins. I pick up a penguin egg and I say, 'Hey Nige,' and I throw it at him and yolk goes all over his face and he laughs and says, 'I'll get you,' and I say, 'No you won't,' and he runs after me in slow motion and tackles me to the ground and we playfight while millions of penguins get in one of those circles around us, watching us and making penguin sounds.

The thought of that makes me smile.

My cigarette still won't light. I see two love-bird penguins in front of me. They do that thing where they stick their heads together like they are kissing and it's real lovey-dovey chunder material but I know my mum would get off on it. I wish she could see through my eyes sometimes, and then she could see the penguins up close and personal. I'm glad she can't see through my eyes all the time though, like, when I'm vomiting or having a wank.

Eventually I head back to Gav's van and wait for the other two, thinkin they would have got bored by now, but they're takin ages. And cos I'm alone, I start crying. I guess I'm going through a lot and I don't know how I can deal with it all. My tears are not tears of joy; they are tears of doom and tears of sickness – that sick feeling where you can feel your best mate of fifteen years pulling away from you like the Picton ferry setting off for the North Island.

I head back to the van to get out of the cold and one of the side doors is unlocked so I get in and and I wipe my nose on Gav's mattress. And then in front of me I see . . . a suitcase.

Gav's suitcase.

And I think to myself . . . why not look?

I've always been a bit of a snooper. I used to look through Mum's undies drawers. Not that I wanted to have sex with my mum or anything. Nothing like that. It's just that I knew she kept a stash of chocolate there quite often, so I would scoff a bit. I think Mum knew I was looking in her drawers but she never asked me about it, so I kept on scoffing a little bit of chocolate. Like, if there was a chocolate bar there I would break off only one bit at a time so she wouldn't notice – that sort of thing.

Same thing with Nige. I would always snoop through his drawers but that was different, cos I started telling him I was doing it and that I didn't mind if he had a look through my drawers. I'd leave some porn under my side of the bed sometimes and I know he watched it cos he never bothered rewinding it to exactly the same spot. That was one of those little things that brought us closer together.

So I'm staring at Gav's suitcase and I'm thinkin . . . should I or shouldn't I?

And then I think to myself, 'Fuck it. Why not?'

I find out a few things, like the fact that Gav's BO is riddled throughout his clothes and is the sort of BO that no scientist could ever wash out, no matter how many chemicals they tried . . .

And I find out that Gav has, like, a set of those aromatherapy candles, which is a bit gay, so, you know, more ammo I guess . . .

But the best thing I find . . .

Is a little black notebook. And what's inside that notebook?

I have a feeling Nige might be lookin at Gav in a whole new light in a few hours' time . . .

THE LONG WALK TO JACKS BLOWHOLE

NIGE

I'm in the car with Deano in the passenger seat, and Gav is convoying behind us in the van. It's almost noon and we've all agreed to meet at Cannibal Bay so I get a shock when Deano says to me, 'Lose him.'

'What?'

'Lose him, Nige. Rally drive and lose the fucker. We got business to attend to.'

'Okay,' I go, and we hit a dirt road and I start amping up the accelerator.

My foot's planted hard and we're makin quite a lot of dust behind us and Gav is in his van behind us, losing ground. It's a real bumpy ride, over big fuckin hills and bits of road that are full of holes that make the car go like it's being shaken around by an earthquake or something. All the time Deano is yelling inside of the car, goin, 'Yeeeehaaaaaaa! Faster Nige! Faaasterrrrrrrr!' and I'm getting amped too, when we come to this farmer taking sheep across the road.

'Just drive through,' Deano says, and he honks my horn for me. I push on through the sheep, giving the odd one a bump in the arse with the front of the car, and they're scarpering in all directions and the farmer looks fucked off as. We get through again and we're off and I clock the speed dial up to one-twenty, which is pretty fast on a dirt road.

Meanwhile, behind us, Gav is stuck behind the sheep. We've pretty much lost him so we take a turn towards Jacks Bay.

As we head down the road my heart starts beating real loud again. You know when you eat something crunchy, like cornflakes, and you hold your hand over your ears while you're eating and it's real loud, but only you can hear it? Well, my heart is like that now, but I don't have my hands on my ears – for some reason my ears are listening to the inside of my body.

It must be my guilty conscious, I guess.

Deano's gone quiet too.

We head past all the old houses at Jacks Bay. Deano and I used to go swimming here a bit back in the day. It's Maori land here, and it hasn't changed much in all the time we've visited. I park us up and Deano looks at me and I say nothing.

'Flick open the boot,' Deano says.

'Hold on,' I go. 'I could do with a cigarette.'

Deano flicks me a ciggy and I light up in the car.

'Roll down a window,' he goes and I get the window down halfway and just sit there lookin out at the sea.

It's a nice day today. One of those days where you get sunburnt if you stay in it too long. Can't see any seals but there's a fisherdude at one o'clock, chucking in his line and hopin for the best.

I say, 'I dunno if I can handle this.'

I keep smoking the cigarette but it starts to run out on me, and when it's finally burned down to the butt I know we've got a job to do.

'Flick open the boot,' Deano goes.

I pop the boot open and for the first time in a while I see Jeurgen's backpack. There are funny lumps sticking out in strange places.

'It's funny, thinking he's in there,' I say.

Deano says to me, 'Most of him is in there.'

I don't know what he means by that. I look at him funny and he says, 'Don't ask.'

He pulls out the backpack and says, 'Open your arms wide,' and he uses all his might to shift the heavy backpack onto my back. The weight almost makes me keel over.

'I wanna be sick,' I say.

Deano straightens the front and pulls a few buckles down and does 'em up tight. 'It's good to spread the weight even,' he says, clipping a buckle around my chest.

'You right?' he goes and I nod, and we head up the hill.

Jeurgen is bloody heavy but I know this is one of the things I have to do to be a man. Deano cut up the body and now I have to carry it. We head past an honesty box. The people who own the land like it if you chuck in a dollar or two. But we've been comin here since we were kids, so we put nothing in. We walk past the old abandoned house at the entranceway to the farm.

Deano helps me climb over the stile and catches me when I start to tip over.

You know how they make people die in their own houses these days? That's what happened to my grandad in Oamaru. He could have died in a hospital but the doctors reckoned it would be better for him to cark in his own bedroom and I'm not sure how Grandma musta felt about that, but the idea was to make him feel comfortable. Like, there's no way this can be a nice thing to go through, but you do your best.

Well, Deano is like that with me. He doesn't walk in front of me or anything. He stays right by my side. He says to me, 'Watch the cow poo,' to make sure I don't step on a big fresh cow poo. He guides me every step of the way.

I know the track, though. Me and Deano both lost our virginity here. We were under-agers at the Owaka pub and Deano met this local mother that lived in the area and she told us to come round the next afternoon for a Devonshire tea and when we got there she gave us scones. Then Deano musta whispered somethng in her ear cos the next thing you know we were climbing this grassy hill and then they lay on the ground goin for gold while I waited further up the hill, looking at the view over the cliffs, where the ocean stretches out to Antarctica.

Then Deano came over and told me to head down for sloppy seconds, and I did what he told me, and that's how I got my first fuck. She went on top and I pretty much just lay there and looked up at the clouds and then I turned my head to the side where I saw Deano in the distance, staring back at us.

That lady died the next year, we heard, of piles complications or something. That made me feel pretty weird too.

Now here we are, walkin up the fuckin steep hill, to another date with destiny.

'I need a breather,' I say to Deano, and I sit down on the grass and we look out at the sea. Neither of us say anything for, like, more than five minutes. There's so many things running around my head it's like someone's doing a big circus in there and my brain can't think any more. All I can hear is a lot of noise and voices of my past and it's all a bit too much.

'Do you wanna hear a joke?' Deano says to me.

I say, 'Nah,' and he goes, 'Are you sure? Sometimes I reckon it's good when you brain is freakin out to think of a joke.'

And I say, 'I don't think I could laugh right now even if you told me the funniest joke in the world.'

Deano says, 'Last night I lay in bed and I wondered what it must be like to be you. And I thought, if I was you, I might be getting mental flashes of the backpacker –'

'Every time I close my eyes I see Jeurgen.'

'It's weird, cos, like, you'd never met him, but now he's, like . . .' and Deano goes quiet.

I finish the sentence for him, 'Permanently stuck in my brain,' and Deano goes, 'That's why all those soldiers who come back from the war go quiet. That's what they're going through, Nige. It's hard to go back to a normal life. I wish it had been me that had killed Jeurgen. I'm stronger than you. I can deal with the bad dreams. But you – you're like a bowl of jelly caught in a bad wind. You'll just wobble and wobble and the wind will destroy you.'

I say nothing to that. I just look over at the view of the south, the big choppy waves, and the trees that have been blown sideways by the southerly, which is always here.

Deano pulls me up and we head further up the hill.

We make our way through quite a lot of sheep. The sheep look like judges with those funny wigs, and they all stare at me like they think I'm guilty. Deano grabs my arm and pulls me up behind him cos everything is getting real steep. My hammies are starting to cramp but I tell myself to keep going. I feel like that guy who tried to get to the South Pole but died on the way.

Finally we hit the top and Jacks Blowhole is in sight.

DEANO

Jacks Blowhole is, like, a big hole in the ground at the top of the cliffs. The hole goes all the way down to the sea. The way it works is the sea comes roaring in, right. The sea here is intense, and it gets stuck in, like, a big cave at the bottom, and it fuckin hits the rocks hard and splashes up, way, way up, and comes out this fuckin big hole at the top of the cliffs where all the farm land is.

It's a weird sight. It's one of those places where you think about committing suicide. In fact, I've thought about committing suicide here a few times, but I figured they wouldn't find my body, and to be honest if I was to top myself I'd rather leave a big mess, like a statement for: 'Look what you did to me, world!'

Nige has definitely been what's kept me alive over the years. He's one of those guys that you know when you meet you'll know until you're an old man. I knew that even when we were at school. I used to say to Nige, 'Nige, when we both turn into old men we should, like, hit the piss harder than ever. I mean, what's the point in turning into one of those bloody has-beens that just drink cups of tea and shit their pants all the time? I reckon we go hard out till the end.'

Nige would just look at me and go, 'Okay,' like he wasn't takin it in.

He's always been a 'go with the flow' guy, which is why he went with me, cos I had the strongest flow of anyone he knew.

Anyway, the moment I knew there had to be a place to drop off Jeurgen where he would never be found, I thought of Jacks Blowhole straight away.

Nige and me are standing at the lookout, and there's no one else in sight. I help Nige take off his backpack. He looks over the edge at the sea, which is going nuts – must be high tide. I'm tryin to think of the best way to send Jeurgen off. I figure we already said what needed to be said to Jeurgen at Taieri Mouth. I figure sometimes words are less important than thoughts, so I say to Nige, 'I reckon you should drop it over the edge, and then have a minute's silence in Jeurgen's memory.'

Nige agrees to it.

I say, 'Don't say a word for a whole minute. Not one word. You should just think about Jeurgen and Norway and stuff like that. I'll do the counting to sixty so you can just think about things and make peace with yourself. Is that a plan?'

'Can you hear my heart?' Nige says, and I say, 'Not really. Can you do this?'

'I hope so,' Nige says, and he places the backpack in front of him.

He kneels down and hugs the backpack as some kind of act of goodwill, and I respect that. Then he picks it up with what is left of his strength. It's a blue backpack, which I think is a good choice, given that Jeurgen is about to be buried at sea. Nige lifts it over the little wire fence. And he lets it drop.

As the backpack drops down the gap in the cliffs, time slows down. It's like the backpack is flying, like an eagle or a big blue pigeon or something. As it drops we see the blue get smaller and smaller and then we see it hit the water below. It's so far below that you don't even hear a splash, since there's white foam everywhere and the roar of the sea is real loud.

I look at Nige as he does the minute's silence. He has worry all over his face. He looks like one of those marathon runners who look fucked but they've still got to do a lot of running, otherwise they'll collapse in a heap. He looks like an old man almost, which is the first time I've seen that. My heart goes out to him and I almost have a little cry, which is weird cos he's the one that should be feeling it more than me. I guess it's like sympathy crying, cos I have so much sympathy for Nige right now. I feel an urge to give him a big hug that lasts for eternity. I don't give him a hug, cos I know he would take the wrong message out of it. Instead, I pat his back a little to make him feel a bit better. First a couple of light thumps, but then some little circles to make the muscles in his back feel better. I stop there cos anything more would be homosexual, and that's one line I know I will never cross.

DEANO AND THE SEA LION

NIGE

We come across Gav's van out at Cannibal Bay. No one's in it, so you don't have to be like an amazing detective to figure out that he must be on the beach somewhere. The weather is real nice down here on the beach, and Deano and I head down to the surf to look for Gav.

I keep thinking about the backpack and I keep seeing it fall away from me, never to be seen again. Deano tells me to take off my shoes and socks so I will feel the sand running between my toes. I say that I don't want to but I do it anyway cos I figure it must be part of his plan or something.

Then he does this weird thing. He gets right in front of me and says, 'Nige, we need to talk.'

And I'm like, 'Eh?'

I can see Gav up in front but Deano gets in the way. He says, 'I got a present for you,' and he reaches into his pocket. And out of his pocket comes a piece of string, and then I see that it's no ordinary piece of string . . . It's the necklace with Jason Farquhar's tooth on it.

I don't get it. I thought I'd chucked it in the rubbish, like, years ago.

'I want you to wear this,' he says.

And I'm like, '. . . Naaa.'

And Deano says, 'You're wearing it, Nige.'

And I'm like, 'Naaaa . . .' like I'm having a real *reaction* or something. I kinda shake my head but Deano tries to put the tooth necklace over my neck. I take it straight back off again. So he grabs it and tries to put it on me again and I'm like, 'I DON'T WANNA WEAR IT!'

Deano says, 'Where are you, Nige?'

And I'm like, 'Eh?'

And he's like, 'Where's the old Nige? I wanna talk to the old Nige.'

'Eh? You're talking weird.'

'Where are you?'

Now he's really freakin me out so I say, 'I'm gunna go and see Gav,' and I head off. He tries to block me but I use a bit of shoulder and barge on through.

'That's right. Go and see Gav!' he says. 'Go and see Gav! Go and see fuckin Gav!'

Gav is crouched down, lookin at a sea lion, like he's studyin it. As I get closer I see a baby sea lion next to it, and the baby is flicking sand up on its mum's back. I wonder if the baby is doing it for attention – you know, to fuck the mum off, like Deano would do to me – but I've heard it's more like a weird camouflage thing so that it'll look more like a rock.

Gav's looking at the sea lions through a camera when suddenly Deano comes running in, yelling 'AAAAAAAAAH!' at the sea lions, and the sea lions run into the sea.

And Gav's like, 'I was gunna take a picture of that,' and Deano just gets up in his face and goes, 'AAAAAAAAAAH!' and I'm like, 'Deano!' and Deano points to me and yells, 'JUUUUDAAASSS! JUUUUDASSSSS!' and runs off again.

I can see Gav is a bit thrown so I say, 'Don't worry about him, Gav. Just ignore him,' and Gav's like, 'Where the fuck did you get to?'

Gav seems a bit fucked off. I try and think of something but I'm not very good at thinkin of white lies and that.

'Eh?' I say.

'You just took off in front of me and vanished. I thought we were a convoy.'

'We were a convoy.'

'Well, the leader should always stop and wait for the next car. It's like a code. What if I'd run out of petrol or something? Where did you get to, anyway?'

I can't think of what to say. I really want to say the truth but if I did I might as well just go and knock on the front door of the police station myself. 'We took a wrong turn and got a flat tyre, and . . . it took us a while to figure out how to get the jack working and the tyre on.'

Gav looks at me funny.

'Nige, do you respect me?'

'Eh? Of course I do.'

'Yeah, well if you respect me, you don't bullshit me.'

I don't know what to say. I feel like I just did a good lie and I must've said it all wrong cos he doesn't believe me. 'Deano told me to take off.'

'So you did?'

'Yeah.'

'If Deano told you to jump off a cliff, would you do it?' he says to me, and I say nothing cos I get a mental picture of

Deano on top of Jacks Blowhole goin, 'Jump, Nige. Jump,' and me goin, 'I don't want to,' and Deano goin, 'Do it, you dick.'

Next thing Deano comes back over and says, 'Can I have a word, Nige?' and I let him have it. 'NO! FUCK OFF, DEANO! JUST FUCK OFF!'

And Deano's like, '*You* fuck off!'

And I'm like, '*You* fuck off!'

And Deano's like, 'Get fucked!'

And I'm like, '*You* get fucked!'

And Deano's goin, '*You* get fucked!'

And I say, 'I DON'T WANNA BE YOUR FRIEND ANY MORE, OKAY? FUCK OFF!' and I just head outta there, away from everyone.

Gav chases after me, saying, 'What's going on?' but I just keep walking.

As I walk away Deano yells, 'Thanks very much, Deano, for everything you've done! Thanks for everything, Deano! Thanks for fuckin everything!' I hold my finger up behind me and I make a beeline for the van.

DEANO

Fuckin ungrateful cunt. After all I've done for him, and this is how he treats me. It's all a bit much. I stare out at the sea and it's like it's daring me. It's saying, 'The faster you run, the sooner you'll drown . . .'

So I finish my ciggy. I put it down beside my shoes, which I just leave there. And I dare myself to run in. I dare myself.

The sea is a big fuckin place and I'm ready to get lost in it.

'The faster you run, the sooner you'll drown,' it's saying.

And I fuckin run.

I run straight for it, and when I get wet up to my waist I

keep running, running until I tip over and I'm swimming as hard as I can, and I get to a point where my feet don't touch the ground any more, and still I swim. I keep swimming, using all my strength to get me out as far as I can. A big wave hits me and drags me back ten metres, so I swim again, straight into the next wave, which takes me back again. I just let go of struggling. I throw my arms and my legs back and I let myself float. Another wave comes and hits me and takes me down and I let out as much air as I can and I go to the bottom and I think of Nige and I picture Nige at my funeral and he's cryin so much he goes to the bathroom to slit his wrists, and a whole lot of water goes up my nose and I'm choking, and suddenly I'm breathing cos the fuckin tides don't want me to drown today. They've dragged me back to the shore and I don't know why God won't just let me die right here. Why should I go on?

I stare up at the blue sky and it's the bluest sky I've ever seen, and above me is a cloud and the cloud looks like a whole lot of hair, like when you've been to the barber's and your hair is lying all over the floor. And I think of that time I got Nige to shave all my hair off and it was everywhere, all over the floor, and we were pissed as and we were laughing cos I'd just said something real funny, and I remember I cut his hair and I kept some locks in a plastic bag, and I think to myself, 'Nige, when did you stop liking me? I haven't changed. I haven't changed, you fucker. I haven't changed, you fuckin fucker . . .'

Some more surf comes over my face and I look over to the left and I see this sea lion, just sitting three metres away from me, just staring at me like I'm a fuckwit.

I stare back at the sea lion and the two of us stay like that for ages, just checking each other out. Man and animal. Not understanding each other. Not knowing why the fuck we're even alive. Just running on instinct and trying to squeeze as much fun into a shit life as we can.

The sea lion flicks some sand over with its flipper and the sand lands on my face, and then the sea lion fucks off, and I think to God, 'Was that a sign?'

God doesn't answer, so I say it out loud.

'Was that a sign, God?' and God says, 'Sure,' and I say, 'What does it mean?' God just looks down at me through the blue sky and says nothing, the big invisible prick.

ME AND GAV AND THE WATERFALL

NIGE

When Gav and me get back to his van this other van pulls up next to us and the moment I see it I go, 'Wooooooohhhhh . . .'

A whole lot of teenagers get out and I nudge Gav in the guts with my elbow and I whisper to him, 'That's my school. That's my fuckin school . . .'

We watch the kids pile out and they've all got clipboards and shit. There's some early developers there, too, among the girls – not that I'd do a schoolgirl. I gave up on that a couple of years ago cos it didn't seem right any more, even though Deano tells me I haven't learned much since school so what difference does it make?

And then I see my old teacher get out, and I think, 'Fuuuuck.' I hide underneath the window of the van.

I say to Gav, 'It's Mr Abercrombie, my old teacher,' and Gav says, 'Why don't you say hello?' and I'm like, 'Nah, I wanna be . . . what's that word where you pretend you're like in disguise?'

'Incognito.'

'That's it. Incognito.'

I look at Mr Abercrombie yelling at one of the kids and I go, 'Fuuuck . . .'

We went to a school camp not far away, out at Tautuku. It was a good time, that camp. I felt Elizabeth Nairn's breasts when me and Deano snuck off to the girls' sleeping quarters. We had a big game of Dare Truth or Promise and I got to pash quite a lot of girls and one of them was dared to feel my dick with my pants still on, and she did it and I was like, 'Woooohhh, I love this game.'

Stephanie Walker had to feel Deano's underarms in the dark and she said she could only feel like three hairs and Deano said, 'Bullshit. You should feel my nuts. I've got hair all over them,' and we all had a laugh. People thought Deano was lying but I knew he wasn't, cos he used to show me his nuts at swimming and they were like big hairy coconuts, pretty gross to look at. It's weird how he has lots of hair on his nuts but he can't grow any under his arms. I guess bodies are pretty weird. You know what they say: no two people are the same.

Gav wants to check out more of the Catlins. I'm keen and Gav says, 'Should we wait for Deano?' and I'm like, 'Nah, fuck him.'

I say to Gav, 'What would you like to see?' and Gav says, 'Well, I got a little map and there's waterfalls'

'Okay, shall we go and see some waterfalls?'

Gav goes, 'Yeah, but first . . .'

That's when he pulls out like a huge doobie. Real large, like a cigar. I look at it and go, 'Woooohhh,' and he says, 'I rolled it myself. Biggest one yet.'

Half an hour later we're parked outside the walkway to the waterfalls smoking this huge doobie and the whole van stinks, like, of the smell of pot, and it's like . . . woooohhhh . . .

If the cops pulled us over now, I reckon me and Gav would be done just like that, and I reckon the cops would get stoned tryin to book us, just from passive smoking and that.

I dunno if getting this munted is a good idea, given the trauma I'm experiencing, but I feel safe in the company of Gav, even if keeping secrets does my head in a bit. Like . . . I do wanna say what happened. I'd love to tell him all about Jeurgen, you know, cos it's on my mind a lot and Deano is the only person I can talk to about it and I'm not feeling too good about Deano at the moment.

I say to Gav, 'Gav, you're a fuckin great guy,' and Gav goes, 'Yeah, I am Nige, but ehara au i te tangata tika rawa – I'm not perfect.'

I say, 'You might as well be, compared to Deano and me,' and he says, 'I'm not perfect, Nige. No one is perfect. In fact, finding the ideal mate is like trying to find someone that has the same kind of imperfections as you.'

'Eh?'

'Like . . . if you're not perfect, then why go and look for perfect people? People are perfect for each other, but they're not perfect.'

'Woooooohhhh . . .' I say, cos I'm just running that thought through my brain. Like, I can feel the message getting carried along the veins in my brain to the bit that learns stuff, and that bit goes straight to my mouth, which just says, 'Wooohh,' cos it's deep what Gav just said.

'Come on. Let's go for a wander,' Gav goes.

So we're walking in the trees and I'm thinking, like . . . how did it all happen, you know, like, life is everywhere, like . . . um . . . my body can feel life all around me, like . . . everything I'm looking at is alive, and . . . and like, all the plants are fighting each other to climb to a place where they can get a bit of sun, and even though we studied photosynthetics at school I never really took in how cool it was until I got stoned with Gav, cos Gav's into this stuff, and I'm walkin through the forest thinkin, 'Anything that Gav's into, so am I from now on.' I don't say that out loud, cos I don't want Gav to know that I think he's the coolest guy on the planet, cos if he knew that he might stop wanting to be my friend.

Gav stops me and says, 'Shhh,' and we both listen to the sounds of nature, like . . . its birds and . . . and water flowing and . . . more birds and . . . my breathing and Gav's coughing and . . . it's like one of those symphonies. There's so many sounds and it's all nature, like . . .

Fuck, I never thought I'd get into nature, but Gav's making me look at a whole lot of things in a new light. It makes me almost forget about the backpacker.

In fact, for now, Jeurgen's death couldn't be further from my brain. Well, it could be further but . . . in fact now I find I can't stop thinking about it, even though I'm looking at a little mushroom growing out of a tree. I bet Jeurgen would have loved this landscape. I can see why overseas people are right into New Zealand, cos it's . . . I dunno, it's like . . . scenery is really cool and . . .

I say, 'I bet Jeurgen woulda loved this place,' and Gav's like, 'Eh?' and I'm like, 'Ohh . . . nothing.'

Then Gav yells out, 'Now will you take a look at that!' and the two of us are staring at a waterfall, and I can feel my cheekbones cracking under the weight of my smile. I can feel wrinkles growing around my lips cos my smile is so big and I can't control it, but the waterfall is, like, soooo . . .

'I love the way the water splits when it hits the rocks and makes patterns,' Gav says, and I look at the patterns and I think, 'You couldn't pay someone to make patterns like that.'

I say to Gav, 'I've never really been into waterfalls before, but this one's fuckin *amaaaazing*.'

Gav says, 'Mother Nature is a beautiful woman, Nige.'

And I'm like, 'Thanks, Mother Nature,' and Gav's smiling a smile that's as big as mine, and I feel like we're sharin a moment I'll never forget, depending on how strong the drugs are and if they cause a bit of memory loss. But even if I don't remember, there'll be this part of my brain that won't forget, and just before I die I'll remember this moment with Gav and the waterfall . . .

And then I start to think of Monica, naked in the waterfall, cos in our first month together we used to do a lot of outside sex; even though it was pretty cold we had a lotta laughs, like, getting dirt on each others bodies and just going for it like wild animals and . . .

I wish I could bring her here and we could do it by the waterfall and . . .

Well, that makes me feel a bit sad too, so I try not to think about it. In fact, all of this stuff is making me feel a bit sad, like . . . I've really fucked up my life, and I've done it by being a real fuckwit, and that makes me feel real bad, and I musta lost my smile and Gav says, 'Are you okay?' and I say, 'I don't know.'

Gav says, 'I recognise your pain. All humans experience pain, Nige, and I want you to know that feeling pain is a part of feeling alive. There's good and there's bad and you can't have one without the other. It's one of the drawbacks of nature. You and me are products of nature, and what you are feeling is one hundred per cent natural.'

I say, 'You don't know what I've done,' and he looks back at me and says, 'You don't know what I've done,' and I look back at the waterfall and right next to us is like the mossiest moss you've ever seen – like, it looks like really wet carpet except more beautiful, like . . .

I touch the moss and stroke it back and forth. It feels nice. Even though you'd think it would feel sticky it's not sticky. It's just like . . . nice . . . It reminds me of when I was a kid, and whenever I'd have a real big freakout, like about death or something like that, I'd cool my face in a cold facecloth and it would make me feel better.

I just stand there strokin the moss and it makes me forget about everything. It makes me forget about killing Jeurgen and it makes me forget about goin to prison for the rest of my life and it makes me forget about how it feels like Deano is strangling my life with his weird shit and it makes me forget about Monica not wanting to have anything to do with me and that I don't know if I can cope with that and it makes me forget about Gav, even though he's right here with me, sharing the moment, showing me the light and . . .

It makes me forget about everything; it's just me and the moss and . . .

And I wish there could be a way I didn't have to go back to the world, cos the world is a mean place. And I think I'd be better off away from it all, somewhere far away from here, just me and myself . . . and maybe Gav can come over for the occasional spot, and Monica for some sex, but other than that . . . I just wanna be alone.

HOW I GOT SAND ALL OVER THE CAT

DEANO

I'm walking along Cannibal Bay back to the car and my clothes are drenched. I walk past a whole lot of kids from our old school, Kaikorai Valley High, and that makes me think back to the good old days. Shit, maybe they were the best days of my life, even though I couldn't wait to get out of school at the time.

I get back to the Mazda and I'm not surprised when there's no sign of Nige or Gav there, but I'm pretty fucked off cos Nige has taken off with the keys, so fuck knows how I'll get into the car, let alone start it.

I check that no one is watching and I rip the aerial off the Kaikorai Valley van, and I try to fit it in a little gap in the Mazda's window. I jam the aerial in and try to bend it around to catch the lock but I can't get it near. I try to twist the aerial and it snaps in two and that makes me really lose it.

I start hacking at the windows with the broken bits of aerial.

Then I scratch paint off the car. I go and get some rocks and I start hiffing them at the car – one rock after another, at the roof and the bonnet. I grab one almighty huge fuckin rock – it's almost too heavy for me to carry, and I smash it into the front driver's door as hard as I can, again and again until it's all out of shape. Then I pick up the rock and smash it into the windscreen. I jump on the hood and just start kicking it and I fuckin get glass in my toe and I sit on the hood and take off my shoe and blood is pissing everywhere, so I reach into the car and find a T-shirt and I tourniquet it around my foot and I yell, 'FUUUUUUCK!' as loud as I can, and that's when I see it.

In the back seat of the Mazda, next to the BMX bike, wrapped in newspaper . . .

Mum's cat.

Poor Patty. I completely forgot to bury her and she's been stinking in the back seat of the car for a good twenty-four hours. So I reach in and take the dead cat in my arms and I wanna make space between me and the Mazda as soon as possible, cos I know the state of it is gunna draw the attention of all of those schoolkids so I'd better make myself scarce.

I grab the BMX from the back seat and try ridin on it, but it's too small and one of the wheels has no tyre and it jams, and while I'm tryin to get it goin the cat drops to the ground from inside the newspaper. I still can't get the wheel to turn so I yell, 'Fuckin stupid bike!' at the bike and throw it to the ground. I pick up Patty, who is coated in sand now. I wrap her back in the newspaper and set off on the walk back along the dusty road, with the dead cat in my arms.

I head off down the road and a car goes past so I walk into the trees and it looks like the car is slowing down, so I pretend I'm taking a piss.

I can see the people in the car staring at me, so I look up at them mid-piss and they look away and take off.

My pretend piss turns into an actual piss, and once I'm done I think, why not bury the cat here? There's a nice view and the ground is soft with a kind of sandy soil and I'm surrounded by a lot of felled orange pine trees. So I lift a tree and I kick a hole in the ground just like Don Clarke used to kick a hole in the ground before he took an important kick for the All Blacks. I dig it out a bit more with my hands and I hiff the cat in the hole and kick some dirt back over and shove a dead pine tree over the top of it. 'RIP Patty,' I say.

Then I set off for the long, long walk to Kaka Point.

I'VE DISCOVERED THAT GETTING WASTED IS A GOOD WAY OF COPING WITH THE TRAUMA

NIGE

I've discovered that getting wasted is a good way of coping with the trauma. So I'm basically wasted all the time, as of half an hour ago. It's like one of those things you get when you realise something that you hadn't realised just before. You know, like when you're a kid and the first time you get a hard-on, but no one's told you, 'By the way, your diddle is gunna get bigger and smaller sometimes,' and the first time you look at it as a kid you're watching it like a magic trick, holding it, shaking it, noticing how if you do certain things with it you can make it go big again, that sort of thing. What's the word I'm looking for? Gav was using it just half an hour ago.

Revelation, that's it.

So I've just had a revelation. When I'm out of it, thinkin about things like Jeurgen, and Monica being heavily pregnant, and Deano's hatred of Gav, and how I'm probably goin to prison – you know, all those things I spend my time thinkin about at the moment – well, getting fucked off my face makes all those things seem kinda weird and strange, like life's just a game and I'm just a player, you know?

I'm not used to my brain thinkin like this but as soon as we got back to the crib Gav gave me the most wicked spot on some special weed he'd been keeping in one of those film canisters – buds from Northland. He said he'd received them in the mail from his whanau. That's like Maori for family – not just family but, like, your family's family, and their family too. I got a bit confused when he explained it to me. Gav uses a little bit of Maori in his everyday life, like when he's chopping onions he'll speak a little bit of Maori, you know, just to keep the language alive. I reckon it's cool. So when he said he'd got it from his whanau, I said to him, 'Maybe I'll start using some of your Maori words,' and he was like, 'Would you really like to learn some reo? Would you really?'

I was like, 'Sure thing, bro! Bring it on!' and he got real excited and went to the van and got me this book.

So in the last hour I've learned to say, 'Kua pa mai taku mate wahine,' which means, 'I've got my period,' and I know that's not very useful. I chose that one out of the book cos I thought maybe Monica might be impressed if I took more of an interest in women's stuff like menstruation and fear of having to give birth to a baby and that.

Gav taught me this word today – it was *empathise*. So empathise means like sympathise but you do it out of like a . . . how does it go again? Empathise is like, 'I understand what you're goin through, cos I too have gone through it.' So, like Gav and Deano can't *empathise* with me being a murderer, cos they haven't killed anyone.

Anyway, so I thought Monica might like it if I *empathised* with her as a woman. These are all ideas Gav taught me – he's quite into treating women like they're human beings, and the more I think about it, the more I think, yeah, he's right. Like, if I see a pretty girl all I'm thinkin about is what her breasts might look like, and, you know, rooting potential – I'm not thinking about her *feelings* and that.

And I'm thinkin maybe it's time to grow up and start thinking about Monica's feelings. Like, start each day with a nice thought, like, 'I wonder if Monica has had enough sleep,' – stuff like that, and just become an all-round nicer person.

Like, what's wrong with being nice? Deano thinks there's something wrong with being nice – like it's a weakness or something. But Deano, as the Maoris would say, 'To hamuti,' which means, 'You're full of shit.'

And Deano, I learned another one too. 'Waiho ahau,' which means, 'Leave me alone.'

Deano has never left me alone, you know?

And I don't just mean alone by myself. I mean alone with other people. Like, I can't go out with someone unless he's around. I can't have my *own* relationship with someone. He has to be involved.

I don't think people have to be as close as that. I mean, it's like I'm in a marriage, but I never agreed to be in a marriage.

So when I happened to chance-score Monica and I went around to her place a few times and didn't turn up at the flat for a couple of days, Deano couldn't handle it. I swear, the second night I slept at Monica's, when I left her flat the next morning Deano was outside, waiting for me in his bus driver's uniform.

I was like, 'What the fuck are you doing here?' Especially cos I couldn't think of how he woulda got Monica's address. He pretty much said to me straight away, 'Don't get too attached to her. She's too brainy for you.' I knew that was true but I kinda got attached anyway. I started getting matey with her university student mates, where everyone gets stoned and says these crazy ideas. I tried telling Deano some of this stuff, like, 'What if we were all brains in a vat and what we see wasn't real?' and Deano was like, 'Yeah, and what if your head was like a video camera and people on another planet were watching it?'

And I was all like, 'Yeah!'

Then Deano stopped being excited and said, 'I was just pulling your tit. Fuck that hippy shit.'

Gav's right about Deano. He's closed-minded. Like, Deano wouldn't even know what close-minded meant, but the stupid thing is he coulda been a real brainy fuck. He was brainier than me at school but he seemed to want to squash it. He always felt like an outsider. And he just thought, 'Fuck it. I'm not gunna be one of those brainy fucks,' and he just stopped trying to learn. Which was dumb, cos Deano not trying to learn was still smarter than me when I was tryin pretty hard to learn.

I've got no problems with it, cos it's the truth. Deano's brainier than me. Most people are brainer than me. If you were to take a hundred people, then ninety-four of them would be brainier than me. I know that cos Deano's really drummed that into me.

Anyway, unlike Deano, I have an open mind. Gav understands that. In fact, he's nurturing my brain at the moment. He's encouraging me to try and say big words, even if I don't know what they mean. To not be ashamed to say, 'I don't know what you're talking about,' if someone says something I don't understand. I'm really lucky to have met Gav.

Deano really split me and Monica up. He did it by being real embarrassing. He'd come into the library when I was helping Monica with her study and he'd try to drag us out for a night on the piss and I'd say, 'No. I'm helping Monica.' He vomited in the library and I got kicked out as well. Monica was *reeeal* fucked off, and I let him have it for once. I said, 'Just leave me alone, all right?' I musta shocked him cos he bought me a fucking electric guitar and amp for an apology present. I said, 'I don't know how to play that,' and he said, 'We could start a band,' and I said, 'I'm not musical,' and he said, 'Neither was U2 when they started.'

Then Deano followed it up by trying to score Monica.

After we had a big fight about it at the golf course we headed to her house and I made Deano apologise to Monica, but he told me to choose between him and Monica in front of Monica and when I didn't say a name straight away he stormed back to the car, and Monica slammed the door on me.

And what did I do?

I went to the fuckin car, didn't I!

I shoulda knocked on Monica's door but I was more worried about fucking it up with Deano, so I went and made one of the biggest mistakes of my life and I got back in the car with Deano.

And now he's tryin to break me and Gav up. Like, can't I have another friend? What's wrong with having more than one friend? You'd think I'd just killed someone, the way he carries on. Oh fuck. Sometimes I forget and then I remember again and it makes me feel real stink.

Anyway, Gav and me have had a lot of spots in, like, one of those head-to-head shootouts they had in those cowboy movies. You know, where they take ten paces and turn around and shoot each other. I have to call a bit of a time out after spot number twelve and Gav slaps his face a few times and says to me, 'Would you like a toasted sandwich, bro? A *real* toasted sandwich. The best toasted sandwich you've ever tasted in your life?'

And I'm like, 'Fuck yeah!'

THE TOASTED SANDWICH THAT GAV MADE

NIGE

Gav just showed me how to make an *amaaaaaazing* toasted sandwich. He had some chicken, which he'd thawed during the day. Like, he got up in the morning and took the chicken out of the freezer – he'd planned ahead that much. He did some onions, which he made into caramel onions by pouring caramel on them or something – I was taking a leak when he made them into caramel so I don't know how he did it yet. He had this chutney he'd found in the pantry that he sniffed and said was still good. And he had some garlic, which I've never had much of. When I was growing up Mum and Dad didn't use a lot of garlic. They didn't really see the point.

Gav explained that the garlic is a good thing for colds, and he said you can use garlic against a vampire, and then as Gav was cooking he pretended to be a vampire and that was a real crackup.

Anyway, I was just amazed watching Gav make a toasted

sandwich. He was so into it. Like, he was actually having *fun*. I've never had fun in the kitchen, but here was Gav, showing me that cooking could be fun. And interesting. Fun and interesting. Anyway, that's when Deano got back and that really put a bit of a damper on things.

DEANO

Most times when me and Nige have had a bit of a scrap we make up pretty easily. Most times it's him that's done something wrong and once I've used a few choice words to remind him of his behaviour he says sorry and I let him off just like that.

He kinda tugs at me that way. He needs me, basically, and when Nige has done something wrong I often see him as a child who has made a mistake and I forgive him. But as for Gav . . .

I mean, the problems really started when Gav came on the scene – let's be brutal about it. Like, how can you know someone for three months, and then act like you've known them for fifteen years? The numbers don't stack up.

Cos let's face it, three months is nothing. Three months in an elephant's life is tiny, cos they live longer than humans. And three months to a turtle must really fly by, cos turtles can live up to 170.

Fifteen years.

Our anniversary is coming up. Not that Nige will remember. He's not a 'details' person. But you would think that fifteen years obviously doesn't mean much by the way he's been carrying on.

Like, I arrive after a fuckin marathon trudge up a hilly dirt road with a fuckin sore bleeding foot that is causing me to walk with a bit of a limp, and you'd think Nige might've been worried about me, but oh no . . . I come in the door and Nige is in the middle of a laughing fit, and as soon as he clocks me the laughter stops.

I feel tears welling up from the inside of my body, but I hold them back for all I'm worth. I say, 'Don't stop laughing on account of me,' and I head to the bedroom.

But before I can get there I have to walk through the kitchen and I can't help but notice that Gav is cooking a toasted sandwich in the toasted sandwich maker I got Nige for his twenty-fifth. And that is a sight that does not fill me with joy. I feel cheated. Like Gav has had sex with one of *my* condoms.

I make it to the bedroom and I look at our bunks and think to myself, maybe it's time to get a bit more independent of Nige. But then I think of life without Nige and that makes me think about all of the good times: like me and Nige as kids running around and around in circles for no reason. And me and Nige having a playfight that time at the pub. Me watching Nige kiss his first girlfriend. Me sitting outside the bedroom door in our flat listening to him fuck some chick. Me and Nige going hang-gliding but changing our minds when we saw how dangerous it was. Me and Nige taking the bus for a drag on the motorway at three o'clock in the morning – fuck, that was funny. Me and Nige urinating on the old-age pensioner's letterbox . . .

Me and Nige both doing 'hump the wall' dancing at Club 118 to 'Strokin' by Clarence Carter, and the lights are UV, and me and Nige are grinning to each other and our teeth come up all bright and purple from the UV lights.

And then I think of me and Nige, here at the Catlins, just sitting out at Surat Bay on a hot day, watching the waves come in . . .

We've had a lot of good times, me and Nige.

I lie down in bed and I can hear the two of them laughing in the next room and I feel like my insides are screaming out loud to me, and I want to scream out loud too. I want to scream out loud like a baby that's just fallen on its head for the first time. Every time I hear them laugh, my guts do a big rumble . . .

NIGE

Wooooohhhhhh . . . That's the closest time in my life that eating has ever felt to doing an orgasm. Gav's toasted sandwich is *that* good. The caramel onions blend into the chicken. Inside the chicken you can taste the garlic, and every now and then I bite into this bit of chutney that makes, like, a real taste explosion inside my brain.

Fuck, I'm singin as I'm eating it. I'm singin, 'Hallelujah! Hallelujah, Gav!' and Gav is smiling and eating, sayin 'It is pretty damned good, if I say so myself,' and I'm like, 'Amen! Amen!' It's funny sayin things like Hallelujah and Amen. I'd never say words like that around Deano, but I've found I'm sayin them around Gav all the time.

Then I say, 'Kia ora, Gav,' and he says to me, 'Kei te pai. Te reka o te kai,' and even though I don't understand what he's sayin I know it was something nice, so I just say, 'Kia ora, Gav, kei te pai, that toasted sandwich was as good as having sex.'

'Wow, you really liked it?'

'You bet. That toasted sandwich should be in the Guinness Book of Records for Best Toasted Sandwich.'

And Gav's like, 'I do make an amazing toasted sandwich.'

'Gav, if you can make toasted sandwiches like this, who knows how many other things you can make. I mean, you're a cook from hell. Hallelujah!'

Gav says, 'I think you're getting heaven and hell mixed up, but we're all made of a little bit of heaven and a little bit of hell, but Hallelujah anyway, bro. I do make a fine toasted sandwich,' and then I kinda forget that I'm mad at Deano cos Gav's put me in such a good mood, so I'm like, 'You should make Deano one,' so I go in to see if Deano wants a toasted sandwich, and he's crying in bed.

That's kind of weird. I mean, why is he crying? It's me that killed a backpacker. So how come it's me that's having a good time while he's crying?

It doesn't make sense.

I really think he's startin to lose the thread.

GAV'S BIG SECRET

NIGE

It's eleven o'clock at night and Deano really catches me by surprise when he comes out of the bedroom and says to Gav, 'So, have you got any of that pot left, please?'

I know he's in a weird mood cos he used the word please. Deano only says please around his mum. I've hardly ever heard him say please.

And also Deano's never been into pot. 'Kills your brain cells,' he says. 'One by one they switch off, like glow-worms in a cave if you yell or shine a torch at them.'

I guess it's good he came out of his room. But I don't know what to say to him about what happened down at Cannibal Bay. I mean, for once in my life I actually said something I *meant*, so I'm not gunna say sorry. No way. But . . . you know, I kinda . . . feel a bit sorry for him and also don't wanna get too offside with him with everything that's happening . . .

I don't know what to say to him, so I don't say anything. I

just let him and Gav do the talking.

As Deano holds the Fanta bottle with the cut-off bottom to his lips and takes in spot number five, I figure he must be completely blotto. Like, I've never seen Deano smoke that much pot. He must be real munted, but he pretends he's not. Deano sucks in quite a lot of smoke and says as he breathes out, 'Marijuana just makes you into a stupid person, I reckon.'

Gav says, 'How do you mean?'

Deano says, 'It makes people stare at their hands and go "Wow," you know? Why would you stare at your hand and say "Wow"?'

Gav says as he puts the knives together, 'Cos you're amazed by the wonder of life?'

'Pardon? Sorry, was that hippy-speak? You'll need to translate. You see I speak *English*; I don't speak hippy.'

Gav just laughs and that really pisses Deano off. Gav heads out of the room and the smile disappears from Deano's face, leaving that face that Billy Idol does on all his music videos. I know I've gotta say something to him, so I just kinda pretend like this afternoon didn't happen.

'Deano,' I say, 'I was wondering if you're smoking pot cos life might not stay the same?'

'Yeah, maybe,' he says. 'Life's short. I think it's important that we do as much getting wasted, shagging and handbrake skids as possible. Live life to the full.'

'Better to burn away than to fade out,' I say.

He looks at me and says, 'Highlander,' and I say, 'With the Queen soundtrack.'

Deano says, 'You and I watched that on your fifteenth birthday. We got pissed in the back seat, and when Queen sang, "Who Wants to Live Forever?" you cried –'

'I did not.'

'You did fuckin so. I was looking at your eyes and they were all wet and salty.'

Next thing Gav's back, and Deano's headed outside. He reckoned he had to reorganise his luggage. Said he's got his clean clothes all mixed up with his dirty clothes and he wants to separate them. Which is a bit of a weird thing to do, but with everything that's goin on with Jeurgen, I'm getting pretty used to people doing weird things, including myself.

DEANO

I'd told Nige I was reorganising my luggage but it was a lie so that I could go back to the van and have a better fossick through Gav's shit for secrets. I look all through the van. And sure enough, I find a notebook behind the sunvisor. I find a notebook in the glovebox. And under the driver's seat I find, like, more than twenty notebooks, and all of them have writing in them. My stomach does a big half hurl, and I get fully caught up in a wave of bubbling anger. I find myself headin straight to Nige and Gav.

'I found this by accident in the van,' I say, and Gav looks at the notebook and his whole face changes, and that's when I know I've cooked his goose bigtime.

'What is it, Gav?' I say.

'That's my journal, bro.'

'Journal? Journal? Who has a journal?'

Gav looks at me and looks at Nige, tryin to sum up the situation. 'Okay,' he says. 'There's something I have to tell you guys . . .'

I stand behind where Nige is sitting and I put my hand on his shoulder to comfort him a little, but then I think it might look a bit gay so I take it away again.

'I don't know whether to tell you guys. It's about whakapono.'

'Fuck a pony?' I say, and Gav goes, 'Whakapono. Trust. I need to trust you.'

'You trust me, don't you Gav? I'd die in a trench for you, mate,' Nige says, and I'm a bit taken aback.

'Would you die in a trench for me, Nige?' I ask.

'Um, I spose,' he says.

'Good. I'd die in a trench for you too, Nige. I'd take a bullet for you.'

'Would you take a bullet for me?' Gav asks me.

I really have to take a hold of myself so I can think of the most cunning response. And I look him square in the eye and I say, 'Of course I would, Gav. Of course I would.'

I musta done a good job, cos I think Gav is quite affected by that. 'Okay,' he says, standin up and rubbin his hands together. 'Well, I don't know how to say this –'

'Blurt it out,' I say. 'Just . . . say it like a big projectile chunder. It's like . . . when you go for a swim in the sea. If you run in you're sweet, but if you go in slowly . . .'

'When the water gets up to your belly-button you start shriekin like a girl!' Nige says, and I point at him and say, 'You got it. And which is better? Dive in, Gav. Just say it.'

I'm quite blown away by what I've said, like . . . I've never been into marijuana but here I am, sayin the best shit I've said for a long time, like I am a wizard of words or something. Nige is blown away too, cos he starts staring at me vacantly like only he can do.

'Okay,' Gav says, getting both of our attentions back. He walks up and down, just like someone going for a swim with cold water up to their belly-button.

'I'm a writer,' he says.

And no one says anything for quite a while.

Until Nige finally goes, 'Woooohhhhh . . .'

'A writer?' I ask.

'Yeah.'

'You sly dog,' says Nige. 'You never said anything. You never said *anything*.'

'Are you in print?' I ask.

'No,' Gav says.

'Have you written anything?'

'Of course,' Gav says, takin the journal out of my hands and thumbing through it.

'Actually, I've got something I just wrote in the kitchen. Do you really want to hear some?'

Nige looks at me and I look at him. I have a hunch there could be something in this, even though I don't know how the cards will play out.

I say, 'Yeah, Gav. I'd really . . . like to hear your writing.'

'Okay,' he goes, and heads out of the room.

'How about that?' Nige says to me, rolling himself a joint. 'Turn-up for the books.'

I don't think Nige has seen the full picture yet. 'Nige,' I say, 'how do we know he's not writing us down now?'

'He'd need a pen.'

'No. In his mind. Recording it to use against us later. In a court of law?'

'What? You think Gav's a cop?'

'No, I don't . . . he's not a fuckin cop. He's a fuckin writer. Stay on the same planet as me, Nige.'

Nige just stares at me, doin that face he does when he's tryin to think but it actually looks more like he's constipated and he's tryin to force out a shit that just won't come. Nige does that look all the time.

'Well, what's your point?' he says.

'My point,' I say, standing so I can make the fluid in my brain flow better, 'is that's quite a whopping thing to *suddenly* tell someone . . . like . . . after you've known them for three months.'

'I spose.'

'You spose? For fuck's sake, Nige, he's a *writer*. Don't you get it? He's *using* you.'

'Using me?'

'Yeah. He's pretending to be your friend, listenin to all the dumb things you say, and quietly . . .' I sit down beside him and whisper in his ear cos I suddenly get worried Gav's gunna come in . . . 'quietly he's *laughing* on the inside, and he's writing it all down in Maori so you'll never understand it. You'll turn up in a bestseller but by that time do you think he'll want to know you?'

'Sure he will.'

'No he won't. He'll have used you up and spat you out –'

Suddenly Gav comes in and I return to my seat so as not to cause suspicion.

'Here we go,' Gav says, with a bit of paper in his hand, 'I did this one yesterday. It's called "The Wall".'

'Isn't there a movie called *The Wall*?' I ask.

'Yeah, with Pink Floyd,' Gav goes. 'I, um, this is completely different –'

'You should change your title,' I go.

'Okay, yeah. What to?'

'I haven't heard it yet so it's hard to say.'

'Oh yeah.' Gav smiles. He starts pacing nervously. And when he talks his voice is all shaky, and nervous too. I've never seen him like this. He's like a naked man havin to give a speech to a whole room full of old women. He looks real shit scared.

He says, 'I wrote this with a hangover. Actually, I'd just been to this party and I was in the hallway and it was real cramped and I was thinkin, why is everyone in the hallway? There's, like, *no one* in the lounge, and that made me reflect on it.'

'Make sure you read it out in a big loud, clear voice,' I say. Boy, I'm enjoying this bigtime.

'I feel a bit shy,' Gav goes, and Nige says, in a masterstroke, 'Gav, it's *us*, like, it's me and Deano,' and Gav nods and starts.

As Gav reads I kinda zone out on him and stare at Nige watching Gav read. Nige is looking up at him with the same puppy-dog eyes he used to use with me when he used to hero-worship me. Gav's first sentence is: 'Frank leaned against the wall of the hallway.'

'Frank, eh? Was it inspired by Frank Spencer? You know, the guy that used to bash into lots of things by accident and make them fall over?'

'Not really.'

'I love a comedy. Is it a comedy, Gav?'

'Yeah, but the humour is quite *subtle*,' Gav says, and I just roll my eyes. I'm about to say something else when Nige says, 'Shhh. Let him read.'

Gav drones on: 'He ran his hand along the wallpaper and felt the bumps on its surface . . .'

As I listen to the rest of Gav's story I feel a huge sense of joy. He is terrible. He is so terrible I stop even listening. I start going over different words myself, like rhyming words in my mind, just so I won't start laughing at how bad Gav's writing is. And I'm thinkin to myself, 'Thank you, God.' The bastard's *bad* at something. Even better than that – he's bad at the thing he wants to be good at. He's a failure. A complete failure.

There's this gap in the talking, before finally Gav says, 'Um . . . it's finished.'

I look over at Nige and Nige just looks a bit of a blank.

'. . . Are you sure?' Nige asks.

'Yeah, it's an ambiguous ending.'

'Ambig . . . uous,' Nige says, tryin to say the word proply. Gav explains it for him, as if Nige was still at kindy.

'Yeah, like, double meaning, like . . . should you feel happy or sad . . . or should you feel happy *and* sad?'

'I've heard enough bullshit,' I say. 'There's no such thing as happy *and* sad, Gav. You're one or the other.'

And Gav goes, 'No, no . . .'

NIGE

I'm with Deano on this one. How can you be happy *and* sad? Like . . . that's impossible, but Gav won't back down.

He goes, 'No . . .' and he takes a while to make the next word, which must mean he's a bit confused. And then he goes, 'Have you ever had those moments where . . . you know, it's like you know you're having one of the happiest moments in your life? Like . . . you're about to score the most beautiful woman and she's naked in front of you and you're about to give her the pleasure she desires and . . . and you're *so* happy, you know? Your dreams are coming true and you're in control and you just feel like a bloody legend, you know, but . . . at the same time, you think . . . one day I'm gunna die.'

'Ain't that the truth,' says Deano.

Gav says, 'So you feel happy, right? But you feel sad at exactly the same time.'

The whole room goes quiet while we think about what Gav just said. And it hits me. He's right, you know?

And I'm like, 'Wooohhhh . . . that is so . . . deep, like . . . wooohhh, you shoulda written *that* down.'

Gav gets excited. He says, 'Did you *like* that?' and I'm like, 'Hell yeah, like . . . it spoke to me. It was better than your story. You should write like that and then you'll definitely make it as a writer.'

'You think so?'

'Yeah, man!'

Gav says 'Sometimes I don't feel very confident.'

I just speak from the heart. I say, 'You're good, Gav. I mean, better than good. You speak to me. You know what I mean? Like . . . I can't find the words, but . . . you can . . . and . . . you just *speak* to me Gav. I mean it. You *speak* to me.'

Gav's real blown away.

'Wow,' he goes. 'I feel embarrassed saying it, like . . . out loud, that I'm a writer. Cos it's such a pretentious thing to say –'

Deano interrupts with this big siren sound coming out of his mouth, real loud. Gav and I both stare at him like he's a fuckwit, even though I know he's not.

'It's the big-word police,' Deano says, and he does another siren and I just crack up laughing.

I say, 'Hahahahahaha that's funny. Gav, you should write *that* down,' and me and Deano are laughing.

Deano says, 'Perhaps I should be a writer, Nige,' and I say, 'Naaa, you couldn't write – you can't even read.'

Oops.

Straight away I know I've just said one of those things I'm not sposed to say. Like, I do that from time to time. It happens when I've had a few and my mind runs off for, like, a toilet break and my mouth just carries on with the first words that come out and . . . and it's a bummer I can't go backwards in time so I *didn't* say it, but I guess if I could go backwards in time I'd be a millionaire, cos I could make a lot of money on the horses by putting big bets on trifectas and that cos I'd already know the outcome cos of my abilty to go back in time.

Also if I'd been able to go back in time Jeurgen would still be alive.

Anyway, I know I've dropped a clanger cos Deano gets a tear in his eye, but he hides it from us by pretending to do up his shoelace, even though it's already done up, so he has to undo it and do it up again, just to hide his crying.

He's always been a bit funny about not being able to read.

I'd known him for two years before I found out. We were about twelve. We were having Kahlua, milk and gingernuts at my house, and I was helping him with his homework. He had to read a book: *The Mouse and the Motorcycle*. 'What did you think of it?' I said to him, and he said, 'It was all right. I like the bit where the mouse rides the motorbike.'

'The mouse rides it all the time,' I said.

'Yeah, I know,' he said, and went quiet.

I knew he hadn't read it. I had his copy due to a mix-up.

I said, 'What reading level are you?'

'Green.'

'You're lying,' I said, and he tried to change the subject.

'Read this out loud,' I said to him, and wrote down on a piece of paper: *The quick brown fox jumped over the lazy dog.* He looked at it, and struggled. He could do 'The', but then he started to go, 'qui . . . qui . . . this is dumb.'

'Read it!' I said, and he started crying. It was like I set off a bomb accidentally, except he just did one of those hissy cries.

I felt guilty, so I said to him, 'You can have my gingernut if you want,' but he wouldn't take it.

'I haven't got a hanky,' I said, 'but I don't mind if you use my sheets,' and he blew his a nose on my sheet.

Outside we were playing cricket and he hit the ball into the trees, so we were in there looking for it.

'How come you can't read?' I asked him, and he said, 'I can't see the words proply,' and I said, 'So why doesn't your mum get you glasses?'

'I'm not a four-eyes,' he said.

The next day at school I brought my magnifying glass and slipped it in his desk before school. He found it and would use it to look at words in class. He'd always hide it, though. And he still couldn't read.

At my place we got the Scrabble letters out. I would make sentences and teach him how to say them by sounding them out. He'd get the hang of it a little, and then get bored again.

One real rainy night, about one in the morning, I was lying in bed and I heard this loud knock on the window. I went to the window and no one was there, but on the windowsill was an ice-cream container. I opened the lid and inside was five snails.

There was a note saying *Thanks for teeching a slow lerner, deano*. I turned my bedside lamp on and watched the snails moving up the side of the ice-cream container, and I pictured him outside the house, wet with rain, smiling to himself.

He never did learn to read proply. He freaks out with books – like, he's got one of those mental blocks. So I know I've just made a bit of a meal of a touchy subject, cos it's sposed to be a secret.

Deano is pretending he hasn't been crying. He says as he ties his shoelaces, 'Well . . . we're all sharin a few secrets today.'

Gav goes, 'Ain't that the truth,' and Deano goes, 'What about you, Nige? You've got a big secret you haven't told Gav about.'

I just gulp.

Gav's lookin at me, all expecting and that. And Deano is lookin at me too. I think he's enjoying watching me suffer like a sheep in one of those trucks that's off to the freezing works. I say the first thing I can think of.

'I'm an athsmatic,' I say.

'Is that right?' Gav goes, and I say, 'Yeah.'

Except I'm not. It was a lie.

Deano says, 'Where's your inhaler, Nige?' and I give Deano the finger. 'And what should Gav do if you have an athsma attack, Nige?' Deano goes, and I say to Gav, 'You know . . . call an ambulance,' and then Gav freaks me out by clapping his hands real loudly.

'Well, how about that!' he yells. 'We're all sharing secrets tonight! I think that deserves a whisky!'

'You got whisky?' Deano goes, and Gav says, 'You bet, bro. I saved it for a celebration and tonight is a celebration. You know what it's a celebration of?' Gav pulls a bottle of whisky from his backpack.

'What?' Deano says.

'The truth,' Gav yells, and he glugs whisky straight from the bottle. 'We are here to tell the truth, the whole truth and nothing but the truth.'

'Fuckin Amen to that,' Deano says, takin the bottle and havin a guzzle. 'Drink to the truth, Nige,' Deano says, handing me the bottle with a smartarse look on his face.

So I say, 'The truth,' and I bloody chug back quite a lot of whisky.

Gav has a big smile on his face and Deano is lookin at me with one of those smiles that, you know, has a lot of different meanings, like that painting of the Mona Lisa, except Deano's smile is a bit more psycho.

INCIDENT IN THE MIDDLE OF THE NIGHT

DEANO

I was furious. Bloody furious ... Words can't describe the emotions I felt when Gav told me off for flushing the toilet.

It was in the middle of the night. I hadn't been asleep all night. Nige was in the bunk above me and I said to him, 'Don't you wanna be my friend, Nige?' and he said nothing. Nothing, even though I could tell he was awake.

So I headed off to the toilet, just for a piss cos my bladder had got a bit full from all the worry, and when I go back to the bedroom Nige whispers to me, 'Gav's not gunna like that.'

And I'm like, 'What? . . . What, Nige?'

'Gav doesn't believe in flushing the toilet,' he says.

'You're kidding me.'

'Gav believes that we flush too much. Cos of all the water.'

'What water?'

'The whole planet depends on it.'

'Eh? Nige?'

'If the planet had no water on it, we'd all be dead, wouldn't we?'

'According to who, Nige?' I say, and I have to tell you, words will never describe the emotions I'm feeling as Nige is talking to me like one of those guys from the Bible that followed Jesus around and then just said all of Jesus' stories for him after Jesus snuffed it.

I go to the hallway and stand outside Gav's room.

'Gav,' I say.

'Don't wake him up,' Nige goes, but I say quite loud, 'Gav! Gav! Wake up, ya cunt!'

I hear a voice groan and say, 'Come in,' and I turn on the light and the fat prick puts his hands over his eyes cos they weren't ready for me to suddenly turn on the light. It's actually quite fuckin hilarious watching him be such a pussy.

'Hey Gav,' I say. 'Nige has been telling me you've got a problem with the way I flush the toilet.'

'Eh?' Gav goes.

He's probly just woken out of some gay dream where he was bumming a wild pig so I refresh his brain back to reality. I say, 'Something to do with water, Gav. The way I'm flushing the toilet is going to cause everyone in the world to die. Something like that. Nige didn't explain too well.'

Gav sits up. 'Well . . . ya know, yeah. I just think there is clearly a water problem –'

'What water problem? We're in New Zealand, Gav. We're surrounded by water. There's fuckin lakes and rivers and glaciers and –'

'It's a world problem, Deano.'

'Oh, I see, so when I flush the loo it affects some poor starving kid in Ethiopia. Is that what you're trying to say, Gav?'

'You're being simplistic.'

I do the siren sound.

'Woo-oo-woo-oo-woo-oo, it's the big-word police!' I yell, and Nige laughs.

'What's the big-word police?' Gav says.

NIGE

I can't believe Gav has never heard of the big-word police. I try and explain it to him.

'It's like, if you use a word with more than three syllables, your mate can do a big siren sound, and you get a fine, or you have to have a scull. It started out as a drinking game but we've adapted it into life.'

Deano looks real pissed off at Gav, standing over him with a crazy look in his eye, you know, like that look King Kong does when he's got that woman in his hand.

Gav says, 'Okay, fair enough. I wanna go back to sleep,' and Deano goes, 'Did you hear that, Nige? Flush the loo as much as you like.'

I know Gav didn't mean it – he just wants to get back to his dreams and that, so he'll say anything. But Deano is really rubbing it in.

Deano's goin, 'Fuck, well, you probably want to go back to sleep, Gav. Would you like me to turn out the light?'

And Gav says, 'Sure, thanks.'

And Deano goes, 'Well, you'll have to say I was right and you were wrong.'

'I was right and you were wrong,' Gav goes.

And Deano says, 'If you're gunna take that attitude the light stays on,' and he storms out of the room.

I go, 'Jesus, Deano,' and I turn off the light and say, 'Sorry,

Gav,' and Gav goes, 'Hei aha. No probs,' cos he's so easy-going. Nothing ruffles his feathers. He's like one of those surfers, except I guess Gav's a bit too fat to surf. But it's an attitude thing.

Anyway, the lights are off and you'd think that would be the end of it, but no. The toilet flushes. And it's obvious it didn't flush by itself. So by a process of insemination I know Deano flushed it.

I go to the toilet and say, 'What are you doing?'

Deano says, 'Nothing, Nige. You go back to bed.'

So I go to bed and there's this flushing noise again. And then one minute later another flush. And one minute later another flush. I look at the digital alarm clock and he's flushing about once a minute. I just know he's tryin to get Gav's attention; I just know he's tryin to turn it into a fight. I just know he's tryin to wind Gav up. I lie there and put the pillow over my head and watch the clock.

Twenty minutes later he's still doin it.

Fuck, Gav must be sleepin like a fuckin dead person cos the cistern on that toilet makes a real high-pitched squeak and that just makes the whole thing worse, especially when you've heard it for the thirtieth time.

I get up and walk to the bathroom.

I say, 'Deano,' and Deano doesn't look pissed off any more. He's hunched on the floor staring into the toilet. His nose must be gettin wet each time he flushes. I hear an echo from the toilet bowl say, 'I'm tired, Nige.'

I say to him, 'Come back to bed, dude. You need to chill out,' and he lifts his head out of the toilet and stares at me.

The top of his hair is wet from water from the toilet. I hope there's no piss in it. He looks at me and shakes his head slowly.

I say, 'Come on, Deano,' and he follows me back to the bedroom, and before he crashes out he says, 'Betrayal isn't an easy thing to take, Nige,' and I don't say anything cos I just want to get to sleep. Deano says, 'I love you like a brother, man,' and then I don't hear boo from him until the morning.

DEANO MAKES UP WITH GAV

DEANO

When I wake up in the morning my brain tells me that today is going to be the last day of Gav's life. Don't ask me why, but the thought really calms me down. Like, overnight, I've stopped hating his guts. There's no need to hate someone's guts when they're gunna cark it in twenty-four hours.

Besides, hate is such a heavy thing to carry around you. It's like trying to carry a suitcase full of bricks. The suitcase is real heavy and after a while you forget why you were carrying all the bricks around. So you leave the suitcase behind.

That's what I've done with my anger for Gav. I mean, I'm even starting to feel sorry for him. It's pretty tragic, walking around on the last day of your life, and having no idea that in twenty-four hours you will be no more.

I almost wish I could tell Gav he's going to die. For his own benefit. Like, if Nige knew I was going to die, I'd want him to tell me. Even though it would freak me out, I would still feel better knowing. Then I could do all the things I'd do if I had twenty-four hours to live, like: write a will, have sex with five prostitutes in one hit, hang out with Nige and do something a bit nuts – like maybe lighting another tree on fire, call Mum and tell her I love her, have a wank and imagine I'm doing it with Princess Di – imagining that my hand is actually her hand, and more general hanging out and getting pissed with Nige.

Poor Gav must have his list of things to do on his last day. So it's a pity he doesn't know, but I'm not gunna tell him.

I push open Gav's door.

'Gav,' I say. 'Gav?'

'Mm,' he says. In bed he looks like one of those sea lions we were hangin out with yesterday. I say, 'I wanna apologise for my actions last night.'

'No sweat,' he says. I think he's trying to brush me off.

'No, I really mean it, Gav. I know you're a good guy. That's why Nige likes you. And it's just been my jealousy getting in the way.'

Gav looks at me. He does a big yawn and says, 'This is pretty heavy for eight o'clock in the morning, Deano.'

'I wanna do something nice to show you I've got no hard feelings. Would you like breakfast in bed or something? I make a real good soft-boiled egg.'

'Yeah, okay, but I'll get up,' Gav says to me, and smiles.

NIGE

I wake up to the radio alarm clock. I keep on tryin to hit the sleep button but I can't work it, and the news comes on and they mention Jeurgen, and how he's missing, last seen in Dunedin. And then they say that he's, like, a soccer player.

And not just any soccer player. Like, Jeurgen once came on for Norway as a substitute.

That doesn't really make me feel good. I mean, I think it makes it worse that I ran over a good soccer player. The upside is that at least he fulfilled his dream of playing for Norway, but the downside is that thanks to me he'll never get to play at a World Cup – not that Norway is that good at soccer. I haven't seen them play; you'd think if they were any good I would've seen them play Brazil or something. But still, I'm a bit blown away that I've just murdered a national representative soccer player. That makes me have a little freakout, so I get up to tell Deano about it . . .

And I get a real shock when I see Gav and Deano sitting outside the house, both of them eating a soft-boiled egg and some Marmite on toast, cut into soldiers. I don't know why, but the sight of it makes my heart feel warm.

Deano and Gav really seem to be getting on. Like, I thought last night that those two would never get on, but maybe what people need sometimes is a blow-out. You know, like, when you bottle something up, like fizzy wine, and you let it pop and it makes a big explosion and the fizzy wine spills everywhere, but once that's done, everything kinda settles down again.

I'm hopin the two of them eating a soft-boiled egg is like some kind of sign to me that everything is gunna somehow work out. To be honest, it brings back my faith in Deano.

Like, he's been real good to me over the years. He looked after me that time when my dog died. He bought me a framed photograph of the dog, and he put it up on the mantelpiece. And Deano's always cooked for me. When he knows I like a meal he'll cook it over and over again until I'm sick of it. He's cooked me so much Wiener schnitzel that if I had a dollar for each time he'd cooked me wiener schnitzel I'd be real rich, and I'd probably be able to buy my way out of the mess I'm in right now.

So I'm listening to Gav and Deano talking to each other – they don't know I'm there – and Deano is saying, 'I agree with you, Gav. Antarctica would have to be the most important continent on the planet.'

And Gav goes, 'I tell you, buddy, if that ice melts, the ocean's gunna rise so much we'll have to live in the mountains.'

Deano says, 'I think fridge-freezers are to blame. Like, we should all stop freezing things. Like ice-cream, for example. It's a luxury, Gav. Maybe if we all ate less ice-cream and stopped being so selfish.'

'There's a hundred things we could do,' says Gav, 'and every little thing makes a small difference. The reason people don't change their ways is cos of consumerism.'

DEANO

When Gav was takin a piss, Nige filled me in about Jeurgen playing soccer for Norway, and I had to say to him, 'It doesn't make any difference. A human life is a human life. If he'd been a dole bludger what you did would be no better, no worse. If Jeurgen had been a spastic with a banana-shaped penis that gave him pain every time he got an erection then the same applies – a life is a life. So he's played soccer for Norway. Good on him, but it's no big deal. A life is a life.'

I was trying to calm Nige down but going by the look on his face I'd made him feel a bit worse.

Anyway, right this moment I'm less concerned about Nige and more concerned about Gav. I mean, today is the last day of Gav's life. Nige has many, many days to go in his, so I should really focus on Gav's needs for the time being.

It really makes me feel sorry that Gav is gunna die. Like, truth be known, Nige would be a much smaller loss to the world than Gav.

And also, I have to say, Gav actually makes quite a lot of sense when you listen to him talking about stuff. Like, we had a good long talk about the world and that, and, I mean, I was really listening to what he had to say, you know? Not just pretending, but actually taking it in all the way to my brain, and he's making so much sense.

Gav is right. The world is in a lot of trouble. Global warming and the population upheaval and all of the plastic bags that are being made and then allowed to float into the wilderness and getting stuck in trees, and then you think about all the animals going extinct – like, did you know that pandas are almost extinct? I mean, don't get me wrong – I think any animal that looks like a toy should be turned into a roast, but all the same, if the panda dies out, then who goes next? The koala? The poodle? The elephant? The crocodile? The donkey?

One by one they are all going extinct, and unless we do something about it, like, you know, next time you want an ice-cream you say to yourself, 'No' – that sort of thing – then there will be no more animals, which means there will be no more zoos, which means all the children of the western world will be unhappy.

And I mean that's just one example of what's goin wrong. So much is goin wrong that we really need to change our ways. It's time to act.

Poor Gav. Billy Joel sang that song 'Only the Good Die Young', and now I know what he means. Just think of Jeurgen and his budding soccer career. And even though I didn't like Gav's writing, at least he put pen to paper, and that's more than Nige and I will ever do. Yet me and Nige are the ones who will grow old. It's not fair, when you think about it.

After brekky I make a plan for the day. At some point we have to pick up the car, which I demoed. Gav is keen to see some of the sights, and hell, it's his last day, so I reckon let's make it a biggie.

A round trip sounds the way to go. Like, let's go down to the Cathedral Caves, then all the way down to Curio Bay and see if we can see any dolphins. Gav'll love those dolphins. Maybe have a surf, even. Over to the petrified forest, which I don't really give a shit about but I reckon Gav'll shoot a load when he sees it – he's that kind of guy. And besides, there's penguins down there too, and I'm sure another penguin fix would do Gav a world of good.

Obviously Slope Point is a goer. The very bottom of the South Island. Further south than Bluff. Not a lot of people know that. I reckon we'll have a sunset at Slope Point, and that'll be a real nice way for Gav to sign off.

And then I reckon we'll come back up to Kaka Point, and me and Nige can say goodbye to Gav there. As far as the last day of your life goes, it would be hard to wish for a better one than that.

GETTING IN TOUCH WITH MEMORIES AT THE CONFIDENCE COURSE

NIGE

We hit the road, and Gav and Deano sit in the front of the van, with me in the back.

I know it sounds like a weird thing to say, but I kinda feel relieved right now. Like, we've done the hardest bit. Getting rid of Jeurgen was a pretty scary thing to think about, and I feel like I really dealt with it like a man would.

In the front Gav is driving at about 30 k an hour cos Gav reckons we should try and look at everything a bit more slowly. Deano reckons we should go 150 k and see what the landscape looks like blurry, but Gav really likes lookin out the window when he's driving and checkin out what all the leaves look like and stuff.

So here Deano and me are, watchin leaves out of the window, but this time it feels even better cos Gav's here, and I'm thinkin if Deano really gets to know Gav – really opens his mind, like he did this morning by talkin about Antarctica

– then Deano is really gunna get to like Gav. I'm sure of it.

And then, like, the three of us can all be best mates.

I'd really like that.

Anyway, Deano offers to be the driver for the day so that Gav and me can get as out of it as we like. That's real considerate of him.

See? He's changing before my eyes. It's like Deano has released all the bad parts of him, like anger and jealousy and hatred for Gav, and he's only left the good parts, and there's a lot of good parts to Deano. If I was good at doin lists I'd list all of Deano's good parts, but I tend to get a bit bored when I'm doin a list, so I won't.

So now Gav and me are smokin up in the back of the van as Deano drives. Deano says, 'What do you wanna listen to, Gav? We've got Black Sabbath, we've got the Beatles, Bananarama, the Bangles, we've got a David Bowie one where on the cover he's naked but the lower half of his body is a dog's body so that he's half man half dog – I imagine you'd like that kind of thing. There's Bread, who I thought would be shit but are actually probly the greatest band that has ever been, I've decided. When they sing a love song you know they mean it. And there's Boney M if you want to have a dance in the back of the van, and there's Kate Bush, who I don't really have any time for –'

'KATE BUSH!' Gav goes, stoned off his nut. 'I fuckin love Kate Bush!'

Now, I know for a fact that Deano can't stand Kate Bush. He doesn't really like women singing, you know? And Kate Bush gets on his tits bigtime. He was gunna chuck out that CD, he told me. It was on his 'To Do' list. I guess he never got around to it. So I'm bloody amazed when Deano flicks on the Kate Bush CD.

She's got a real high voice, Kate Bush. I used to hate her but I guess getting real out of it and hangin out with Gav in the back of the van listening to Kate Bush and lookin at the leaves has really changed my mind.

Gav says Kate Bush changed the way he thought about women. Like, there was a period in feminism where women tried to be men but Kate Bush changed all of that and she was, like, powerful while being a real woman's woman, if that makes sense.

We listened to this song called 'Wuthering Heights', which is about some guy called Heathcliff from some book. I think that's a real interesting thing to do, to make a song after you read a book. Like, if I was a songwriter I'd write a song about the Stephen King book *It*. But I'm not a songwriter so I can't, but next time I see my Uncle Pete, who is a bit of a songwriter, I'll tell him he should write a song about a scary clown.

Kate Bush can sing in three different octaves, which means she can sing higher than the human ear can hear. So some of her most amazing music has never been heard by humans, but only by dogs, Gav reckons. I think he might have been having me on, cos after he said it, he started cracking up, so I had a laugh too.

In the front, Deano looks like he's in a bit of pain. Like, I know women's voices get on his nerves when he's having a hangover, so I reckon Kate Bush must be killing him on the inside.

So you can imagine my surprise when Deano says, 'Yeah, this is quite good, Gav. What an unusual idea for a chorus – *Babooshka, babooshka*. What the fuck's that?'

'Fucked if I know,' Gav says.

'Me neither, but I like it,' Deano goes, and he sings along even – '*Aaayaaa babooshka babooshka babooshka ay yaaa.*'

We go past some trees and a part of road that Deano and I know real well, and Deano yells out, 'Fuck! Tautuku! Tautuku!' and I yell out, 'Yeeeeeeaaah, Tautuku!' as we drive past it, and Gav's like, 'What's that?' and I'm like, 'Our old school camp. Fuck, that place has a lot of memories,' and Deano's like, 'You can't buy those sort of memories.'

Gav yells, 'Stop the van! Stop the van! Take me to your memories!' Deano does a Uey at high speed, scaring the shit out of me and Gav as we go rolling across the van, but suddenly we're headin back and Deano's yellin, 'Let's go to Tautuku, then,' and I'm like, 'The confidence course! The confidence course! Let's do the fuckin confidence course!'

DEANO

Nige loves this confidence course. He's acting like a little kid all over again. We're walking down the little path but Nige gets so excited he starts running, and so me and Gav start running too. Nige runs straight to his favourite bit as a kid, which is a swing rope that lands in a big rope spider's web. It's hard to describe, but you have to jump out of the rope and get caught in the web, you know, like those velcro walls they had in that pub craze a few years back. Me and Nige have always wanted to have a velcro wall in our flat. We talked about it a lot. Imagine your own velcro wall. You'd have such wicked parties . . .

Anyway, Nige is swinging like Tarzan, and screaming in a high-pitched voice that really reminds me of him as a schoolboy. He is so excited.

Gav jumps on the rope and I think he might be a bit big for it, but it swings like a motherfucker and he screams, 'Yeeehaaaaa!' as he catches himself in the big rope net. So

I have a go. I show off by swinging upside down, and when I crash into the web my legs bend over my back and I fall in a weird way, which bloody hurts, spraining my back or something, so I have to sit out for a bit while Nige and Gav take turns jumping on the big web thing.

When they're done, the three of us all sit together. It's weird cos Nige sits on one side of me, and then Gav, of his own choice, sits on the other side of me. Like, he chose to sit beside me instead of Nige. And I'm in the middle of them, like creamed corn in a toasted sandwich.

'It's smaller than I remember it,' Nige says, lookin at all the things on the confidence course.

'That's cos you're bigger,' I say.

Gav goes, 'This place is wicked.'

I say, 'This place has got a lot of memories for me and Nige. Remember Shelley McMurtrie, Nige?'

Does he what. Shelley was my third girlfriend. She was also Nige's second fuck. I dumped her cos back then Nige wasn't very confident, and I wanted them to get together, so I told Nige he should slip on in, cos I knew Shelley was trying to piss off her parents by tryin to root as many boys as possible. I fingered her at the confidence course and then I let Nige smell my fingers afterwards.

Then later on we snuck out in the school van and went back to the confidence course and drunk a lot of beers, and did we go crazy after that. The moon was out so we started howling like wolves, for a laugh. It was an awesome time.

You can't buy memories like that.

And look at us now.

Nige looks all happy.

Gav is definitely happy . . .

Fuck, even I'm feelin a bit happy.

GAV RIDES A DOLPHIN

NIGE

We fucked off outta the confidence course when a whole lot of schoolkids arrived. They kinda ruined our fun. We were pretty much spotted by Mr Abercrombie again, and now we're having to explain ourselves. He's got a whole group of schoolkids with him, and they're all watching while Mr Abercrombie tells us off.

He says to us, 'This is private land,' and Deano's like, 'Sorry, Mr Abercrombie. We're old students, you might remember us. Dean and Nigel? You taught us Maths with Statistics. I wasn't very good at it,' and Mr Abercrombie has a bit of a blank face.

'Anyway, sorry,' Deano says. 'We were just having some fun,' and Mr Abercrombie says, 'Old pupils of Kaikorai Valley High School, eh? So what do you do now?' and Deano says, 'I'm a part-time bus driver and Nige works at the bank,' and Mr Abercrombie just looks at Deano and says, 'A part-time bus driver?' and then he laughs.

Back in the van Gav sits in the front with Deano driving. I'm listening in and Deano says to Gav, 'What a cunt. He knew who we were,' and Gav goes, 'Yeah, bro, and what did he mean laughing at your job like that? Like, I work in security and if someone says to me, "Gav, what are you up to now?" and I say "security" they turn their nose up, like I haven't got a brain. But I have got a brain, see? I know I'm a big guy and it's easy as piss for a big Maori to get a job as a security guard. Then I can save all the money I like and I don't have to use my brain in my work and it really fuels me as a writer, cos I see a side of life other writers don't see. You can't judge someone by what they do. You judge them by who they are.'

'That's exactly right, Gav,' Deano goes. 'I might be a bus driver, but I'm different from any other bus driver I've met. I have my own hopes and dreams –'

'What are they?'

'They're private, Gav, but there's a lot more to me than driving a bus.'

'Exactly, bro. What was that teacher's name again?'

'Mr Abercrombie.'

'I hate Mr Abercrombie,' Gav goes, and I yell from the back, 'Amen to that.' There I go speaking like a Christian again. It's weird, what's happening to me.

When we get to Cathedral Caves it's closed cos of the tides. Gav says, 'I'll see it another day, boys, don't worry,' and Deano says, 'I doubt you'll get another chance to see it. It's a real pity,' which is quite a weird thing to say.

Anyway, Deano is keen to do a lot of stuff today, so he reckons the quicker we get to Curio Bay the better.

The rest of the way to the bottom of the South Island I just shut up and enjoy listening to Gav and Deano talking. Like, they really do click on a lot of things. And when they disagree on something they have a bit of an argument, but it's a kind of jokey argument, like a couple of mates who've known each other for ages and they don't mind giving each other shit. It's really nice to listen to – they're really funny together.

When we get to Curio Bay Deano says to Gav, 'You seen a dolphin yet?' and Gav goes, 'Nah, actually,' and Deano's like, 'In the Catlins we have the smallest dolphins in the world. I can't wait to see your face when you see one of these really little dolphins.'

DEANO

I could never have predicted that Gav would be so amazing with dolphins. You know in *Crocodile Dundee* how that guy can make a crocodile calm down by whispering to it? Well, Gav has a kind of ability with dolphins. There's no other way to describe it.

I mean, I'm in a bit of a state of shock . . .

Like, he swims in there and the dolphins seem to come to him, like they sense something. It's like the dolphins know what I have planned, and they've come to warn Gav. Nige and me are swimming in another part of the bay and the dolphins have shown no interest in us – they've gone straight for Gav.

Gav is screaming like one of those three tenors having an orgasm. But it doesn't frighten the dolphins away. In fact they love it. They're making dolphin noises and Gav starts imitating them, and it's like everyone's talking to each other in dolphin language. Nige tells me he's never seen Gav so happy, and Gav is a pretty happy guy.

And that's when it happens. Nige and I are a good twenty metres away but we both see it with our own eyes . . .

Gav *mounts* a dolphin.

You know that movie where that little girl rides the whale? Well, this is far more amazing, cos Gav is a really, really fat guy, and he's riding a really little dolphin. You'd think the dolphin would sink, but it must be something to do with the strength of the water underneath them or something, cos for about twelve seconds – and I did count – Gav *rides* a fuckin dolphin.

I look at Nige and his jaw has dropped, and I can feel that my jaw has dropped too. Like . . . I mean, I remember one time I thought I'd seen a UFO. It turned out it was a plane caught in a trick of the light, but I was convinced I'd seen a UFO.

That was one of those jaw-dropping moments.

So was seeing the backpacker in the road works for the first time.

Well, here's another one.

Eventually Gav falls in and we wait for him to come up for air. He's down there so long me and Nige are worried something has happened. Like, he's down just long enough for you to think, 'What if he's drowning?' Then he comes back up and yells, 'THAT WAS THE MOST AMAZING FUCKIN THING THAT'S HAPPENED TO ME IN MY LIFE! DID YOU GUYS SEE THAT?'

Nige is like, 'Yeah, I fuckin saw it.'

I say, 'That's not scientifically possible is it? For a man your size to ride such a little dolphin?'

Gav goes, 'I was swimming next to it and something told me to just . . . climb aboard, you know – and suddenly I'm away. Ohhhh mann . . . I'm gunna take a while to come down from this one . . .'

He's not the only one.

I feel grateful to have witnessed it.

And I'm thinkin, good for you, Gav.

You just couldn't *ask* to have a better final day of your life.

A PERFECT DAY

NIGE

Wow. I feel like I'm having, like, one of those days you'll remember for the rest of your life, for all the *right* reasons. Maybe it's all the drugs I'm on. But hangin out with Deano and Gav I feel kind of . . .

I dunno the word . . .

At one. I feel 'at one'. That's something the Daily Lama talked about. The Daily Lama is this guy Gav talks a lot about. He lives in China, and he wears a blanket and travels around the world telling people about how hard it is to live in China. He's become real popular – the Daily Lama is into peace and peacefulness. And he is 'at one' wherever he goes, except for when he's in China. So as I sit on a bit of land, I am 'at one' with the land.

Gav explained that to me and Deano as we watched the sunset go down over Slope Point, the lowest part of the South Island. Like, everyone thinks that Bluff is the lowest, but that's cos the South Island is on a bit of a lean, you know? Like, fuck, it's hard to describe without a map, but the South Island looks like a big steak, except the steak is, like, standing like a person, but it doesn't stand straight – it's actually on a bit of a lean, kinda like the steak is reaching over to pick up something off the ground. With a map I could explain it much better.

Anyway, I'm just practically pooing myself with joy and feeling really 'at one' as me and Deano and Gav watch the sunset at the lowest point of the South Island.

What an *amaaaaazing* sunset.

The orange just fills up my eyeballs, warming them up like a nice electric blanket of orange. It's one of the orangest sunsets I've ever seen, but that might just be the drugs sayin that cos they have been pretty good drugs and I'm so munted I'm not really worried about the backpacker and goin to prison and stuff.

I mean, I know I should be worried, but I'm so out of it, it all just feels like I'm like one of those pieces in a board game like Monopoly, goin round and round the board for no reason, and at some point some of the pieces are gunna become winners, and my piece is gunna become a loser, and I just know that I'll lose the game, but what does it matter? I'm just a piece on the board of a board game called Monopoly.

That's a pretty deep thought to have when you're lookin at a sunset.

The sort of thought Gav would have.

I can really feel Gav and Deano's energies right now, either side of me, lookin at the sunset. We're like the All Black front row. Woodcock, Oliver and Hayman. Two of them are from Otago, so that makes me feel proud. So here we are, the front row: Deano, Nige and Gav. We're at the front row of a show that's free, a sunset at Slope Point, and it's such an amazing sunset you just couldn't ask for better value for money.

Deano says, 'Hey Gav, I was thinking about your writing,' and Gav's like, 'Yeah?'

'Well . . . I reckon you should go for it. Like . . . you shouldn't be shy about it.'

Gav goes, 'Yeah, but how do I know if I'm good? I might be real crap at it.'

'I'm crap at my job at the bank but that doesn't stop me working there,' I say, and Deano goes, 'What you don't want to happen, Gav, is to hit a ripe old age and suddenly go, ohh shit, I wish I'd had a go at that.'

'You've got talent, Gav,' I say. 'Like, you know wise things and stuff.'

'C'mon, guys,' Gav goes.

And Gav goes quiet. Then he says, 'I don't think my family is too keen on the idea,' and Deano's like, 'Fuck your family, Gav. It's your life. Do they own your life?'

And Gav's like, 'Nah, you're right, Deano. This is *my* life,' and Deano's like, 'Exactly.'

I look at Deano cos I'm real impressed by what he just said, and he shoots me a weird little wink.

I am so stoked that Deano likes Gav now.

He definitely likes him. He's not pretending. He's been so supportive of Gav since Gav rode that dolphin. The old Deano would have made lots of jokes and that, like that Gav ridin the dolphin was like he was humping a wild pig – that's the sort of thing the 'old Deano' would have said, but the new Deano is just like, 'Mate, you're a legend; you should be very proud of that.'

See all that positive energy Deano is comin out with?

The three of us sit and stare at the sunset, and Gav says, 'What an amazing fuckin sunset,' and Deano says, 'You could make a postcard out of that,' and I say, 'Amen to that.' Fuck, I keep saying Amen for some reason.

I ask Gav and Deano. I say, 'Hey, do you guys think I'm turnin into a Christian?'

Deano looks at me and says, 'Fuck, I don't know. Are you?' and Gav looks at me and says, 'Don't turn into a Christian, bro,' and I look up at the sunset and stare at the orange that probably contains God, and I think, fuck, I am startin to go a bit Christian, but I better not tell them that out loud or I'll never hear the end of it.

I mean, I went to Sunday School and that. It's not like I never was a Christian, but then I guess I was never really into it, but starin at the sun . . .

I mean . . .

Deano says he talks to God in the shower, with the water vapour and that, and I don't know if he's joking or if he actually believes in God. It's impossible to tell cos he always comes out of the shower shaking his head, saying, 'God keeps telling me to wash my balls better. He's really starting to fuck me off,' and it's kinda convincing, like he is actually talking to God, but his God must be a bit different to my God, cos as I look at the sunset and feel like I am in the presence of God . . .

Well . . .

My God isn't the sort of God who would tell you to wash your balls better.

DEANO

I'm starting to feel excited. Really excited. Like, how a soldier must feel before they land on the beach at Vietnam . . .

That kind of feeling of . . . what's gunna happen?

I've heard that for people who've killed in wars the hardest thing is when you think of the person you're killing as a person – you know, with feelings and that.

Like, what you should do is start thinking of them as not human at all. Like a robot. Think of them and just pretend they're a robot.

But I've really got to know Gav today, and it's a bit hard to pretend he's a robot. He's a good guy. I mean, maybe I could think of him as a robot, but . . .

I'm starting instead to think of him as a sacrificial goat.

Like, you know, they did a bit of that in the Bible. God yells down to the people on the ground, 'I want a goat. Get me a goat,' and they get a goat so that God won't get all angry and make a giant flood like he did that time with Noah.

So I'm lookin at Gav and tryin to imagine him as a goat. Gav is singin 'How Great Thou Art' all in Maori. It's a beautiful thing. He was moved to sing by the peacefulness of the moment, and out come the words . . .

'*Whakaaria mai, to ripeka ki a au . . .*'

I haven't listened to much Maori, but it's a beautiful language . . .

'*Tiaho mai, ra roto i te po . . .*'

You know, it's quite breathtaking. As Gav sings it really tugs at the bottom of my stomach. It's that powerful.

And as I'm watching him sing I'm thinkin, shall I kill Gav by drowning him in the bath? Or shall I kill him in the van by getting him in the back at the edge of a cliff and pretending to reach over for a cassette and 'accidentally' bumping the handbrake? I think that would be a nice way for Gav to go. You know, as he plunged to death in his van he'd get a really nice view of the moonlit ocean, and he'd be staring out at his spiritual home, which is Antarctica, and he'd be in his van, which is like a womb to him. Like, you couldn't ask for a nicer way to die.

But what puts me off that idea is how hard it would be to

set it all up and to make Nige go and take a piss at exactly the right time. And then also what if I can't get out of the van in time after I've let the handbrake off? I mean, then suddenly I'd go down with Gav, and Nige would have lost his two best friends in the world, which would be a real double tragedy for him.

So I run back over the idea of killing Gav in the bath. I could make him have spot after spot, and I could play him some nice music he likes, like Kate Bush, and he could lie in the bath and then I'd encourage him to really relax and enjoy the bath and surrender to the moment of beauty that he must be feeling in such a nice warm bath, which must feel like being back in the womb. Especially with Kate Bush playing, cos her music is the sort of stuff I could imagine you might like to hear in a womb. Anyway, once Gav was relaxed I could just push him down with my hand, like I was holding a cat underwater, you know, just hold his face down cos we have quite a deep bath at the crib and Gav is pretty fat so it's not like it would be easy for him to get out of the bath.

It's an exciting way to do it. Like, seeing his face in the bath as he realises that he has no more fight in him, and watching him surrender to death and accept that it is not his destiny to hang out with me and Nige – I mean, I think if I drown him in the bath I will carry the final look on his face with me forever, and to be honest, I think my life would be richer from such an experience.

Gav's singing is amazing. He really sings beautifully. He's shifted off to a Maori version of 'Morning Has Broken', and Gav's version is just as good as Cat Stevens'. It's breathtaking. I totally get what Nige sees in him now.

Anyway, I decide against the bath option cos I think Nige would freak out and I don't want him to freak out at his crib, which is a place that should only contain nice memories. My fear is that if I kill Gav in the bath then all of Nige's good memories about growing up and summer holidays at Kaka Point would be wiped out by the memory of me killing Gav in the bath. I don't want that to happen to Nige. He already has enough to live with.

No, it's better for Nige if I do it the other way, which was always my Plan A, but the van-off-a-cliff option and the bath option broke my chain of thought.

So I've gotta figure out a way to get us to the lighthouse.

Fuck, Gav's an amazing singer. When he finishes his Maori version of 'Morning Has Broken' I just break into applause, just like that, like my brain had nothing to do with it – my hands just told each other to clap loudly as soon as he's finished. He is *that* good . . .

ANOTHER FREAKOUT AT THE SUPERMARKET

NIGE

We've driven through the night to make it back to the crib. On the way Deano stops the van by the Mazda out at Cannibal Bay. When I see it, it really ruins my good mood.

'Jesus Christ, Deano,' I say. Fuck, there I go again with all the Christian talking – I just can't kick it.

Deano gets out and says, 'Let me explain. I just got a bit upset yesterday. I was angry at you for leavin me in Cannibal Bay without car keys. Like, you made me walk home, Nige, and that's a long fuckin walk.'

I can't believe he's tryin to make me feel guilty when he's just kicked my car in. He goes, 'I mean, we all have our moments, Nige. But I'm over feelin angry. I've accepted Gav into our friendship. I really am a new Deano today. The person that kicked your car in is yesterday's Deano. And all I can do is stand in front of you now and say, "I'm sorry for the actions of the old Deano." I understand why you don't wanna hang out with him. He was mean and he was angry and . . . I mean Gav's really helped me understand this, but dropping my anger has been like dropping a suitcase of bricks.'

I don't know what he means, and then he says, 'Actually, flag the bricks. I'm sorry about the car. I'll get it all fixed up. We've got third-party insurance'

'How's that gunna help?'

'I haven't figured that out yet but with insurance there's always a way. I'm sorry, Nige. I really mean it.'

He looks me in the eye and he doesn't blink or nothing. He just stares back at me and I know in my heart of hearts that he is sorry. So I can't be mad at him. How could I be mad at him? He's been my best friend for fifteen years.

Deano says, 'Why don't we all head to the lighthouse?' and I'm like, 'I'm tired, Deano.'

Deano says, 'What about you, Gav? Are you tired?' and Gav's like, 'Not really,' and Deano says, 'Right. Why don't me and Gav take a look at the lighthouse, and you could go home and get an early night?'

'I've got a craving for scrambled eggs,' I say, and Deano says, 'Well, we're out of eggs – you'll have to pop in to Owaka.'

I say, 'Can I borrow ten bucks?' and Deano says, 'What do you need ten bucks for? How much do you think half a dozen eggs costs, Nige?' and I'm like, 'I just thought maybe I could get a bar of chocolate as well, as pudding, you know.'

Deano says, 'Go and treat yourself,' and hands me a twenty.

'Are you sure it's okay if I don't go to the lighthouse? I mean, we've spent the whole day together. It seems weird leaving you two at a time like this.' But Gav says, 'Nige, your stomach is calling you. Your body is telling you to go and eat. It's important to listen to your body.'

Deano says, 'My body is keen to head to the lighthouse. Is that what your body wants to do, Gav?'

'Totally,' Gav says.

Deano says, 'Well, it's settled then.'

They head off in the van. I start the Mazda and it's bloody hard to drive. I mean, Deano did a real good job of kicking the car in. Only one of the headlights is workin and three of the doors won't open. I have to get in through the back door and climb into the driver's seat. And the windscreen is half there, half not. I'm not sure whether to kick it in or not. It might be dangerous driving with glass ready to smash into my face, but gettin into the car was quite a mission so I reckon I'll just drive to Owaka – I mean, it's not far. Once I'm there I can kick in the rest of the glass.

It's a nice drive on a country road. The Catlins is a special area. It has its own smell. It's kind of a musty smell, like a sack that's been in the rain too long, and inside the sack is an old fish that's gone rotten. It's a nice smell to me.

There's a lot of potholes in the road, and every time I drive over one I get a mental picture of me running over Jeurgen. Poor Jeurgen. It's not easy when you've ended someone's life. Even when you're having a really good day, you end up thinking about them, and it really brings you down.

When I get to Owaka, the little supermarket shop looks like it's just closed. The doors are locked but the lights are all on and I can see the people inside doing their final balances and that. I know what it's like for them cos I work in a bank and I hate finding out whether I've balanced or not, cos I'm not very good at balancing. At work I'm usually a little bit out most days and I don't want anyone to notice that I'm not doin any good, so if my balance is short by twenty bucks I'll put twenty of my own money in.

And the same the other way round. One day I over-balanced by about seventy bucks so I took an extra seventy bucks home with me. I didn't do it for the money. I just didn't want my boss to know that I'm bad at my job.

Anyway, I knock on the window of the shop and the people inside can see I'm hungry, so they let me in but they say they're turning off the till and I've only got, like, one minute. So I say, 'I'll just get a couple of things.' I race in and grab a chocolate bar and I can't find the eggs cos I'm lookin too fast so I'm walkin round and round the aisles – like, I do a full circle and still haven't found anything.

So the lady says, 'What are you looking for?' and I say, 'Eggs,' and she points me where to go.

As I'm paying for the eggs and the chocolate I'm thinkin what else should I spend my twenty bucks on, and that's when I catch it out of the corner of my eye . . .

A stack of newspapers and on the front is a picture of . . .

Jeurgen.

Playing soccer for Norway.

And a big heading in capital letters: SOCCER STAR HIT AND RUN.

I get such a shock when I see it, my bum does a spontaneous fart.

They look at me and I say, 'C-c-can I h-have a copy of th-the newsp-pap-p-per, please?'

And then when I get out of the shop there's a police car outside. A policeman is walking to the shop . . .

I try to act normal and I think it works. The policeman walks right past me and knocks on the door of the shop, but the lady won't let him in cos it's after hours. But the policeman can see that they just served me . . .

That gets the policeman real pissed off, so he comes over

my way. Like it's my fault. I'm not responsible for that shopkeeper's actions.

So I get panicky but I really try to concentrate on acting normal, cos there's no reason he'd want to talk to me. All the same he keeps lookin at me so I have a new sense of, like, urgency, but rushing makes me try to get in the front door of the car, and the front door doesn't work any more so I have to get into the back seat, and I'm in the process of tryin to climb through to the front when the policeman pops his head in the window and says, 'Is this your car, mate?'

And I'm like, 'Yeah . . . bloody vandals. They kicked in my car out at Cannibal Bay.'

'You can't drive that thing, mate.'

So I'm like, 'I know, but . . . I have to drive it to a garage,' and he says, 'It's a bit late for that, isn't it?' and now I'm really freakin out.

So I say to him, 'I'm sorry, officer. I probably shouldn't have driven it. But I've just gone and got it from Cannibal Bay, and I'm gunna park it up at our crib at Kaka Point. It's a long walk out there so I thought I'd drive it there and bring it straight back in the morning to the petrol station garage here in Owaka.'

And he's like, 'I'll tell you what, I won't book you, even though I know you've been driving it. This is what I'll do. You can drive it to the petrol station now and leave it there overnight.'

And I'm like, 'I can't walk that far. It'll take me all night,' and he goes, 'I'll give you a lift if you like,' and then I'm freakin out and saying, 'Okay, I'll take the car to the petrol station, but I've got an aunt here in Owaka, so I don't need a lift. I'll just knock on her door and crash on her couch.'

'Okay,' he goes.

Shit, that was good thinkin.

So now I'm driving and this police car is following me to the Owaka petrol station.

I park it and I get out of the car and walk down the road. Fuck knows where I'm going, but there's no way I'm sittin in the front seat of a cop car when I've just recently murdered a backpacker and the police haven't found out who did it yet.

No way.

As I walk away the police car drives past me and he winds his window down slowly. When he looks at me he just starts laughing, like he's just played a mean practical joke or something.

It really fucks me off. Like, that sort of behaviour really gives the police a bad name. And of course once he's out of sight I give him the finger and head back to the car.

I can really feel myself comin down, back to the real world, and I don't know if I can handle it. As I walk to the car I hear the sound of Jeurgen scoring a goal for Norway. I don't know if Jeurgen scored any goals for Norway, but I bet if he'd played a few more times for them he woulda become a regular in the side, and I bet he woulda scored a few goals.

Before I get to the car I walk past a phone booth and . . . the phone booth is kinda calling out to me so I walk in there and I use some of Deano's change and put it in the phone and I dial Monica's number. I know her number off by heart.

It takes her an age to answer, and when she does she sounds sleepy.

'Hello,' she says. And I don't know what to say, so I say nothing. So she says, 'Hello,' and I don't want her to think it's a crank call, so I say, 'It's me,' and she says, 'Who?' and I say, 'Nige . . .' and I hear her do this big sigh, like I woke her up in the middle of a dream and she's mad at me.

I say to her, 'Monz, I think I'm in a lot of trouble.'

She says, 'Huh?' and I say, 'I can't tell you anything, but . . . I'm having a bit of a freakout and I thought you might be able to calm me down with . . . I dunno,' and Monica goes, 'Nige, I . . . I've got an exam tomorrow,' and I say, 'Can I help you with some of it then? You know, I could ask you some questions. What one is it?'

'Anthropology.'

'What's that?'

'Anthropology.'

'I'm so dumb. I don't know what that is.'

'You're not dumb, Nige. You're just . . .'

And I say, 'Stupid. I'm so stupid.'

She says nothing. And I'm like, 'I'm sorry, Monica. I'm sorry you even met me. I . . . I wanna have your baby with you,' and Monica says, 'Nige, I don't think it's yours,' and I'm like, 'I don't care who helped you make the baby, I wanna . . . I feel like it might help straighten me out,' and Monica is like, 'Please, Nige. You need to let it go.'

And then she says to me the weirdest thing. She says, 'The source of your pain can't be the source of your happiness,' and I think about that and I know it's real deep but I don't know what she means.

I say to her, 'Monica, are you stoned or something?'

'NO –'

'Don't get angry. Please don't get angry with me,' I say, and then there's this bit where none of us talk and we just listen to each other breathing on the phone.

I say to her, 'You might never see me again.'

Monica says, 'Don't do anything stupid, Nige,' and I say, 'I don't know what to do,' and she says, 'Take a deep breath and count to ten,' and I do that, but in the middle of my counting there's a loud beep on the phone, which means I'm running out of money, so I hunt through my pockets for some change but I can only find an extra ten cents. So I put that in and then I count to ten all over again but a bit faster and then I say, 'Now what?' and she says, 'Just look after yourself, Nige,' and I say, 'I want to look after you,' and she says, 'Just look after yourself. Get some sleep or something,' and I say, 'I've smoked quite a lot today,' and she says, 'Well, you're not in a good space. You've gotta clean yourself up,' and I say, 'Okay . . .' and then we say nothing again.

'Goodnight, Nige,' she says, and I say, 'Don't hang up yet. I just want to hear your voice some more,' and she says, 'I'm tired, Nige.'

'Please, Monza, I just want to listen to you breathe for a bit,' and she says nothing but I hear her breathing for a bit and it's real nice to listen to . . .

And then I hear another loud beep on the phone and it cuts out cos I've finally run out of money. I hold on to the phone and listen to the beep-beep-beep sound and I feel like shit all over. But then again, it was nice to hear her voice. And she was nice to me. I don't know what to make of it, but I'm glad I called her.

I get in the car and try to turn on the inside light except it's all munted and it only works when I hold the door open, so I open the door and the light comes on and I look at the newspaper . . .

Fuck, Jeurgen's a good soccer player . . .

He was about to sign to Blackburn Rovers, and soccer at that level is pretty competitive so that's a top effort. Wow . . .

And then it looks like they've spoken to the joker that gave him a lift to Dunedin . . .

And they've ruled him out as a suspect . . .

And below that . . .

Below that is a picture of the road works on Dowling Street . . .

And right then I think, I'd better go and tell Deano about this. He'll wanna know right away.

NO SMALL THING

DEANO

As I drive Gav to the lighthouse I can still picture the sunset at Slope Point in my mind. In a way the sun is setting on Gav's life, and it's so nice to see him really at peace with himself.

I reckon Gav's mum would be really proud of him if she could see the way he lives his life. Maybe his mum wouldn't like the whole drug-taking thing, but apart from that she'd look at her son and think, 'My boy Gav is an excellent security guard, a great thinker, an excellent cook, a good singer, an interesting writer, a good friend, and a really good guy.' Gav's mum must feel real proud.

It's nice for me to know that Gav's life view is about the journey and not the final goal, cos it means that whenever his life may be cut short it will always happen in a time where he is at peace with himself. He has a better inner peace than either Nige or me, that's for sure. Up to this point in my life I haven't really given a second thought to inner peace. I guess hangin out with Gav and passively smoking all of that marijuana in the van must be one of the reasons I'm thinkin about inner peace all of a sudden. I mean, they smoked so much back there and they didn't open any windows, so smoke just kept floating past my nostrils.

So I'm not exactly as in charge of my brain as I would've hoped for, given what I'm about to do . . .

Which is no small thing.

As I drive with Gav to the lighthouse, that's what is going round and round my mind. I'm about to end someone's life. I don't know how I'm going to do it just yet. I just know we'll be up high . . . with a lot of places to fall . . . I'll just wait until the mood takes me and it shouldn't be too hard.

I mean, whenever I've visited this lighthouse in the past myself, I've always felt the fear of falling off the edge. When Nige and I were kids there were no safety barriers, so we gave ourselves big scares by daring each other to stand closer to the edge. At the moment I'm wondering if that's how I'm gunna do it with Gav. Dare him to go to the edge and see how close he can get so that my job of giving him the final push is as easy as possible.

That's what I'm thinkin about as we arrive at the lighthouse and begin the long walk through the safety barriers.

In fact those safety barriers are annoying me as we begin this walk, cos my planning didn't take into account safety barriers, cos I always think of this place like I did when I was a kid, you know, before they put the safety barriers up. I remember when they did it I thought, 'You're ruining the Catlins' best tourist attraction,' cos feelin the fear was always part of the experience for us as kids.

I've been feelin a bit too much fear lately. Like, lookin after Nige after he ran over the backpacker . . . You know, it really has put a bit more on my plate than I would usually handle. Which means I'm at the edge of my abilities at the moment.

But what I lack in ability I have spadefuls of in another department.

And that department is determination.

Determination.

I have great determination to kill Gav.

Gav's a nice guy but that's not really my concern.

I have Nige's future to think about.

So I'm really determined to kill Gav . . .

And I'm a bit fucked off about these safety barriers.

SUCH A FUCKIN IDIOT

NIGE

I drive to the coast, and behind me – like, in my rear-view – there's this other car, right. And the car behind me is drivin a bit aggressive, you know, like they wouldn't mind rear-ending me. So I figure, well, I'm not gunna let this dickhead overtake me, no fuckin way, so I speed it up a bit, and I know this bit of road pretty well, but this fucker stays up with me, still threatening to rear-end me, real aggressive driving, so I suddenly go on the brakes, to give him a real fright, and he almost does rear-end me.

Fuck, now I'm fired up so I speed it up again. I take it up another gear and this bastard's doin the same. And that's when he flicks on his siren, and I see, for the first time, that it's a police car.

I pull over and I think, 'Ohhh fuck, it's the guy at the shop. I'm such a fuckin idiot in so many ways,' and I look in the mirror and sure enough, that's him comin over to the car, tapping on the window.

And he says to me, 'What do you think you're doing, mate?' and I'm like, 'I'm sorry, officer. I don't think that straight sometimes,' and he just stares at me.

And that's when I realise: fuck, he knows.

The police have come to the Catlins to look for me and Deano, and now I'm really crapping myself . . .

But then I try and remind myself that there's a chance he's just chased after me cos he's still pissed off that I got into the Owaka supermarket shop and he didn't, and he just wants to be mean to me again.

Or I guess he might not be wanting me to drive the car. I mean, I completely lied to him about leavin the car at the petrol station, so I could see why he might be pissed off . . .

Fuck, and the car is in a real state. The car looks like it's already been to the car wrecker's but the owner came and got it and escaped with it *just in time*. The car is *that* munted. So I can totally see where he's comin from.

I'm such a fuckin idiot. Such a fuckin . . . there has to be more words for idiot . . . like a moron. I'm a moron. I like that word. Moron. Gav's really encouraging me to increase my vocab.

The policeman just stares at me, like he can't quite believe my stupidity. Then he starts writing on a bit of paper.

He says, 'Fuck, mate, I was trying not to give you a ticket, but I've got no choice now.'

And I'm like, 'I'm sorry, officer. I don't know what to say,' and he shakes his head and writes out a ticket, takes down my name and my address in Kaka Point, and I give him a false address but I'm not very good at lying so I actually say the street we're on but a different number – number 16 instead of number 6 – which is the blue house at the end of the street.

It's not much of a lie and I don't really know if it's helped or not but I've already said it so there's no going back, I guess.

Then he takes a big sniff inside my car.

He says, 'Been smoking pot, mate?' and I'm like, 'Aaah . . .' and he says, 'Don't worry. I don't give a shit. I smoke. You got any in there?' and I'm like, 'Naaah.'

He says to me, 'There's not a lot to do if you're a policeman in Owaka. It gets to be a bit of a drone, you know? So I use it to pass the time.'

'Oh yeah,' I say. 'Well, I haven't . . . you know, got any.'

He says, 'Okay. How far is home from here?'

'Pretty close.'

'Okay, well . . . you'll take the car in first thing in the morning, okay?'

'Yeah. I promise.'

'We never had that . . . pot conversation. Okay?'

And I say, 'Okay,' and he screws up the ticket and winks at me.

'Off you go then. Drive safely.'

I just stare at the policeman.

Like, I stare into his eyes.

I feel like tellin him everything. I just feel this urge for the truth to come out. For me to meet my fate, as Gav would say. Like, it would be kinda a nice load off for Deano if I just came clean now. And, I mean, it's hard livin with a lie. Real hard.

But then I think about goin to prison and I get lots of mental pictures of bein bummed and I don't know if that actually happens in prisons – I mean, it might all be like a big . . . um . . . a cliché. That's what it is. Gav uses that word quite a bit. Cliché. Yeah, so maybe bumming in prison is a cliché.

But then I think, there's bound to be a bit of bumming in prison. I mean, Gav told me that when Captain Cook came out to New Zealand on the *Endeavour*, there was a lot of cabin boys, and their job was basically to get bummed by the officers. So, I mean, if Captain Cook did it, then I guess people in prison are gunna be into it as well. If there's no women you might as well have a substitute and I can just picture them all lookin at me and thinkin, 'He's thin and tall and young. I'd like to *bum* him.'

Fuck, I should stop thinkin about getting bummed. I mean, even if I do go to prison I probably won't get bummed, and if they do bum me . . . as long as I relax my body I might be able to deal with it. And there's worse things that could happen to me in prison, anyway. Like getting beaten up and that . . . And having people yelling at you and that. I hate people yelling at me.

The policeman can see I've gone into a mental spin and he says, 'Is there something else?' and I shake my head.

He takes off, and I take off too. He's headed back to Owaka and I come to the T-junction that separates Kaka Point from Nugget Point. I head to Nugget Point.

AT NUGGET POINT WITHOUT AN OXYGEN PACK

DEANO

It's a real good view up here. The moonlight hitting the South Pacific ocean casts a glow underneath our eyeballs as we stare down the steep, sheer cliff faces far, far below and the enormous gap between us up here and the ocean far below . . .

It really is mind-numbing.

Gav's with me on this one. Like, I don't have to describe to him how beautiful this is. He's staring out at it all in amazement as we catch our breath.

The reason we're catching our breath is that we're up so high it's like walking in altitude, like what they do on Mt Everest. Except those guys that climb Everest have oxygen packs. Me and Gav don't have oxygen packs. And we're a bit exhausted from having the wind blow at us so hard.

Like, the wind usually blows at you from one direction, right? But up here we're getting attacked by wind from all sides. It's like we're at a meeting point for all of the wind. So me and Gav are both pretty shagged by the time we've made it to the lighthouse.

Yet somehow the view gives us energy.

'IT'S AN AMAZING VIEW, EH!' I yell to him, and he yells back to me, 'WHAT WAS THAT YOU SAID?' and I yell back, 'IT'S AN AMAZING VIEW,' and Gav like, gives the thumbs up, cos he's decided it would be more easy up here to communicate with our bodies instead of our mouths.

So I give Gav the thumbs up too, and I allow myself to concentrate and enjoy the view for a couple of minutes before I get down to business.

I love lighthouses. I dunno why. I've always had a soft spot for lighthouses. Maybe it's all the stories – you know, with lightning striking people when they're at a lighthouse. I dunno. It might be I like lighthouses cos they stop ships from crashing into rocks and that . . . I reckon I just like it that it's big and white, like a big white erect cock jutting out of the land with a light on the end of it that goes round and round and round and that white cock with the flashing light is saving the lives of sailors.

It's a nice lighthouse, but you can't get at it like you used to, cos of all the fuckin safety barriers.

Me and Nige's initials are up there, under a couple of layers of paint, but we cut them in so you can still kind of make them out. Fuck, it's a nice lighthouse. I really do like this lighthouse.

Fuck, it's as windy as Mt Everest. It really is.

Still, it's a beautiful clear night in other ways.

In the moonlight I can see the Nuggets really well, even though it must be about eleven o'clock. Yep, they are great Nuggets. No doubt about it. Nugget Point got named after the Nuggets. I'm not sure why they named the Nuggets the

Nuggets. They're like tiny-size islands – I guess they are just kind of like a whole load of giant gold nuggets in the sea. I don't really get why they called them Nuggets. They just look like big rocks to me. They don't look like gold or anything. They don't really remind me of nuggets, truth be told, but they are beautiful all the same.

But I would say that the Nuggets are one of the world's most interesting rock formations. I know I'm biased but, like, I went to the West Coast to that place with the Pancake Rocks, and everyone was goin, 'The Pancake Rocks! They look *so* like pancakes!' and I was thinkin . . . these rocks don't look like any pancake I've seen.

And then I think, what ruined the Pancake Rocks most for me was the safety barriers, which is the same thing as what I'm experiencing here with the Nuggets. The safety barriers are a real pain in the arse.

So I say to Gav, 'WHY DON'T WE CLIMB OVER THE SAFETY BARRIERS?' and Gav goes, 'EH?' which means he can't hear me cos of all of this intense Mt Everest-like wind, so I point to the safety barrier and then I make a sign with my finger to suggest going over.

He just shakes his head, so I climb over myself.

And that is fuckin freaky, cos when I had the idea I was really 'thinkin on my feet', and when I land on the other side I realise there's almost no land to stand on, but I manage to get a footing on some loose rocks, and then I get a foothold on a small triangle of rock on the other side of the safety barrier.

And now, I can tell you, I'm feeling the fear. I am fuckin feeling the fear, staring down at the vast freaky drop below. I stare down at my feet and the rock is hard and uninviting and pretty much vertical. Not quite vertical, like . . . how do I explain it?

It's a bit like a man taking a piss.

Imagine you're standing up nice and straight, taking a piss, right? But it's at the end of the piss where the piss is slowing down to a few little piss-dribbles. So if you look at the spot where your piss-dribbles are landing, then the line between your head and the ground would be at the same angle as the mountain face I am looking down now.

I can sense Gav looking at me with jealousy. And I realise I have just accidentally pulled off a masterstroke. Cos Gav can see that I am feeling the fear. He can see that I am havin twice the experience he is.

And, you see, this is no ordinary day of Gav's life.

This is the day that Gav rode a dolphin. This is a day where Gav cheated probability. This is a day where Gav feels like an absolute legend.

Gav climbs over to join me.

What a bloody legend Gav is. What he's doin takes balls. He's far gutsier than I realised. I find myself helping him when he's trying to climb over the fence. Of course I realise that this moment of 'helping' is a good moment, and I think of havin a good yank there . . .

Like, this *is* the moment I've been waiting for . . .

But I can't do it. Not yet. Something seems ungentlemanly about it.

No, I can be patient.

That was an opportunity, yes, but another will soon come, and it might be nice to say some final words to him.

DEEPLY IN THE SHIT

NIGE

I can't believe that about an hour ago I thought I was having, like, the best day of my life. I reckon that must be the drugs over-relaxing me cos they're wearing off and the closer I get to thinkin like a normal person the closer I get to truly realising that I am DEEPLY IN THE SHIT and it's all closing out a bit faster than I thought it would.

Like, I've been really relying on Deano on the planning front. I just trusted him to come up with a good plan. But Deano's never been a good planner. When he booked us tickets to Surfers Paradise, the accommodation he got was a long way from the beach and it only had one bedroom. Deano isn't amazing at planning. He's just better than me, which isn't sayin much.

And I'm startin to think Deano might not actually be on top of this. I'm wondering to myself, now maybe Deano wouldn't mind if I let Gav in on the secret.

I head through the safety barriers and the view in front of me is so beautiful. I mean, there's the moon, the mountains, the Nuggets, the lighthouse . . .

And just beside the lighthouse there's the shadows of Deano and Gav.

Fuck, I'm really proud of Deano. Like, he has made such an effort to get on with Gav. I didn't know he had it in him. I really thought Deano hated Gav's guts. But no – cos look at them.

They look like a couple of good friends, close together by the lighthouse.

Hold on . . .

H-hold on . . .

I'm getting a weird feeling . . .

BITE THE KNUCKLE

DEANO

I'm havin trouble thinkin of what my final words to Gav should be.

And I'm also tryin to think up a good plan for the next five minutes.

I've got Gav here beside me in the worst position he could possibly be in: right on the edge of a cliff face and on the wrong side of a safety barrier. The only problem is that I am also in a terrible position. If I was to push him at this point, and there was a struggle, I would be goin over too, which is the double-tragedy-for-Nige scenario that I've been most worried about.

This is exactly the sort of situation that my subzero would usually get to the bottom of. And my subzero tells me something very important. My subzero knows that if I climb back over the safety barrier before Gav, then Gav is truly fucked.

Which means it's time for the last words.

Fuck, now, that's quite an awesome responsibility. Coming up with the last words someone is going to hear in their life. I'd like them to be . . . somehow . . . comforting.

I motion Gav to put his ear to my mouth, and I cup my hand over and make a direct sound tunnel from my mouth to his ear. And I say to him 'Gav, you're a great guy,' and Gav waves to me and gets me to put my ear up to his mouth and he makes a good sound tunnel with his hand that means despite the loud wind, I can really hear him quite well. He says to me, 'Hey Deano, I've got a confession to make. I really didn't think I was gunna like you. I really . . . try to see the good in people, and I looked at you, and I tried to see the good . . . and I couldn't see it. But you know what? Now I see the good in you, bro. Now I see the good in you.'

Fuck, what an amazing thing to say. So I get him to put his ear to my mouth, and I say, 'I see the good in you too, Gav. Kia ora,' and Gav smiles. I look him in the eyes and he looks at me in the eyes, and we're looking at each other, like friends . . .

Wow . . .

Like it's quite possible that right now I am better friends with Gav than Nige is. Sure, Gav's known Nige for three months and me for about five weeks, but all the same, as we look at each other I feel a real . . . connection. It's surprising, and it makes me feel good.

I give him the thumbs up and I climb back over the safety barrier and I am standing behind him with only a safety barrier between us and I yell, 'GOODBYE, GAV,' and I mean it quite sincerely. I'm not trying to be a smart alec. I really mean, 'Goodbye, friend.'

Then I push him as hard as I can on the square of the shoulders.

Gav makes a scream and turns around and he realises

what's happening, and he struggles as hard as he can. He's so off balance with havin to turn around that despite his size and strength, it's hard for him to fight back. His hands swing up and grip onto my shoulders, so I whack him in the ribs real hard and he lets go, and now he's hangin on to the safety barrier with just one hand, and everything else is basically over the edge . . .

And I bite into the back of his hand. Like the hardest bite you could imagine. Like a werewolf – I mean, it is a full moon. We are at a lighthouse. I mean, I get carried away by the moment, you know?

I bite hard at his hand and I can taste the blood of his hand in my mouth, but his hand won't budge, so I bite into the knuckle on his finger, right where the bone is, and I must half bite the thing off cos that's what tips the balance, cos he's gone, he's gone in a second. My last sight of him is a face that has just seen a great big 'The End' sign, and he does not look pleased with me. Not one little bit. I only see him for a microsecond but it's enough time to clock the look of a wild bear, ready to get revenge, ready to destroy me, dying to rip my body to bits, but it's too late, Gav, cos you're over the edge and I'm not.

You're plunging down a piss-dribble-angled mountain face and I'm not.

You're meeting whatever destiny awaits you, and me . . .

I'll be gettin my destiny soon, but I'm gunna get my destiny *alive.*

That's the difference between me and you, Gav.

I'm alive and you're not.

Next thing I hear another noise and it's Nige, yelling, 'NO NOOOO NOOOOOOOOO NOOOOOOOOOOOOOO!' and I realise he's just seen the whole fuckin thing . . .

MAN'S INTUITION

NIGE

Have you heard of those twins, they're in different countries, and one of them has a heart attack, and the other one feels like he's having a heart attack, even though they're in a different country?

Well, I feel like something's going badly between Deano and Gav. I feel it in my stomach. Gav told me all about Woman's Intuition – how women can feel things like a sixth sense. Gav says men get it too; it's just that when men get it, it's usually some kind of breakthrough on a minor matter, like where they last put the remote so they can turn the telly on. Gav calls it Man's Intuition.

Anyway, I get a real strong feeling of Man's Intuition. It's such a strong feeling it takes over my brain, and I just run.

I just run, and the further I run the more I know something's goin wrong.

And I have to run through a patch where I can't see Deano

and Gav but then when I can see them again I see it with my own eyes – there's some sort of fight goin on, so I shout, 'NO! NO! NOOOOOOOOO!' and now I can only see Deano and I keep running, running and yelling at the same time, running and yelling, 'NOOOOOOOO NOOOOOOOO NOOOOOOOO NOOOOOOOO NOOOOOOOOOOOOOOOOOOOOO!'

SAFETY BARRIER WRESTLE MANIA

DEANO

Nige runs straight to the edge and looks over, and sees nothing but a big drop.

No Gav. Nothing but the sea and the wind.

And then he looks at me.

And now is not the time to pretend nothing just happened.

Like, even if I could get away with lying I wouldn't want to. Nige has to know the hard, brutal truth. We have to be responsible for our actions. When you go to the supermarket and you get a piece of meat you forget that it came from the slaughter of an innocent cow. I prefer to be able to look my food source in the eye. Nige has to come to terms with the fact that I've killed Gav. I don't expect him to be cool with it straight away. He's gunna be real mad at me for a long, long time but eventually he'll realise that I did it for him. I did it cos Nige couldn't be trusted not to tell Gav one day, and Gav couldn't be trusted with not tellin anyone. I don't care how good a guy he is. Was. You can't have a secret with three people. Even two people knowing is taking a real chance.

Nige looks at me. He goes, 'WHHEEERRRE'S GAAV?' and I try and stay real calm.

I say, 'I chucked him over.'

He's like, 'WHAT?' and I have to yell it louder than the wind: 'I CHUCKED HIM OVER! I'M SORRY.'

Nige looks over the barrier and he calls out, 'GAAAAAAAV! GAAAAAAAAAAAV! GAAAAAAAAAAAV! GAAAAAAAAAAAV! GAAAAAAAAAAAAAAAAV!'

I just watch him calling it out, 'GAAAAAAAAAAAAAV!'

'GAAAAAAAAAAAAAAAAAAAAAAAAAAAAAAAAAAAAAAAAAAAAAAAAAAAAAAAAAAAAAAAAAAAAAAAV!'

It's very moving, Nige's reaction.

He's really lettin it rip. I didn't know he could yell so loud.

'GAAAAAAAAAAAAAAAAAAV! GAAV! GAAAAAAAAAV! GAV! GAAV!'

And finally he stops.

And then there's like this squawk from a bird or something. Nige yells again, 'GAAAAAAAAAAAV!' and the bird squawks again.

'That's him,' he says, and he starts climbing over the safety barrier.

And I'm like, 'Hold it. Where are you goin?' and he's like, 'I heard him. He's alive,' and I have to shake some sense into him.

I say, 'It was a fuckin bird squawking.'

'It was Gav.'

'It was a bird.'

'It was Gav. I could hear him.'

'No, it was a bird. Or if not a bird then a possum or something. It wasn't Gav –'

'I heard Gav –'

'Gav's dead, Nige. And if you go over you're dead too.'

And he yells, 'FUCK OFF!' and he tries getting over, so I wrestle him back. I pull him back off the safety barrier and we both fall hard to the ground.

Nige falls hard on his elbow and he yells, 'AAAAAAAAAH!' and I'm like, 'I didn't mean to hurt you,' and I let go and he gets up and tries to get over the barrier again. So I wrestle him to the ground again, and this time I jump on him. I jump on him and restrain him. I restrain his hands with my hands. I restrain his feet with my feet. But I'm unable to restrain his knee and he smacks it clean into my balls, and I swear I can hear one of them popping open. I scream high-pitched like one of those chipmunks from *Alvin and the Chipmunks.*

Now he's on top of me, showing no sympathy for my crown jewels. He's on top, yellin loud in my ear, just yellin, 'AAAAAAAAAAH! AAAAAAAAAH! AAAAAAAAAAAAH!'

Like, I really think he's gone off his trolley, then he starts strangling me, right in the neck. I can feel everything getting cut off – my air supply, everything. I'm struggling like fuck but he's really got a good grip on, tightening around my neck, but I'm able to get my hands together next to his face and I somehow manage to make sign language – the big T you do with your hands to say 'Time out, time out!' I see his eyes drop to my T and he lets go and stares at me, shakin his head . . .

Then he spits on me – a big drooly dribble between the eyes.

And he smiles.

I don't know why he smiles.

He looks me in the eye, and then . . .

And then . . .

Then he jumps over the safety barrier and I hear him go, 'AAAAAAAAAAAH . . .'

. . .

. . .

. . . and then nothing.

THOUGHTS ON THE WAY DOWN

NIGE

I'm screaming bigtime, just yelling in the wind as I find myself falling and getting faster, and I'm tryin really hard to grab on to any rock but, like, I'm falling too fast to grab anything so I basically kinda know this is the end for me.

As I go down I'm thinkin, this is like a suicide – only I didn't mean to commit suicide. I knew things were shit but I didn't think this would be the end of my life . . .

I fuckin grab at anything I can. I manage to get hold of a bit of rock but it only stops me for half a second, and then I just keep getting whacked by rock after rock, like I'm in one of those boxing matches with Mike Tyson and he keeps hitting me on different parts of my body. Only it's not Mike Tyson; it's the rock. And then I start falling sideways and now I don't know which way's up and which way's down and then a bit of rock hits me square in the stomach and suddenly I come to a stop.

Fuck, I just feel all the air goin out of my stomach as I land.

And I'm like, 'What the fuck just happened?'

And that's when the pain hits.

OHHHHHHHHHHHHHHHH I fuckin felt that. I was in shock, so I didn't feel the pain straight away, and I still haven't looked up to find out where the fuck I am or what's happening. I'm scared to look and my guts . . . it's like a fuckin surgeon's been at me with a knife . . . or like Mike Tyson's been at me with a knife. It's a bit like Mike Tyson had a go first and then he tagged in the surgeon.

I dunno where my kidneys are, right, but I reckon they're down close to your arse, and I certainly feel somethin screamin blue murder down there.

I realise I have done a full faceplant cos all I can see is black. And my face is . . .

AAAAAAAAAAAAAAH MY FUCKIN FACE IS FUCKIN AAAAAAAAAAAAH! Actually it's not as sore as I first thought. Like, it is sore, but my first reaction was to freak out. It's actually not that sore, although my jaw does feel a bit wobbly. I bet I'd find it hard to eat an apple right now.

And then I lift my head up and I see where I am.

. . . Okay.

. . . . Okay.

. . . Okay, well that's not exactly good news, but at least I'm alive . . .

. . . for now.

YOUR BEST FRIEND IN THE NEXT LIFE

DEANO

Ohhhhhh fuck. That was the double tragedy I feared, but worse than that: I'm the only one left up here.

And I mean . . .

I'd do anything for Nige.

And maybe Nige was right.

Maybe that was Gav down there.

Like, maybe there's a way . . .

But I look over the edge and I don't think there's a way.

I just can't see a . . .

I mean, I don't reckon Edmund Hillary would have a go at that.

I reckon if you showed Ed Hillary the cliff face I'm thinkin of havin a go at right now, and you said to him, 'Will you go down there, Mr Hillary?' he'd say, 'Fuck off, are you mad?'

Certain death.

I'm certain of it.

Fairly certain. 'NIIIIIIIIIIIIIIGE!' I yell. 'NIIIIIIIIIIIIIIII-IIIIIIIIIIIIGE!'

'YOU STUPID FUCK!'

'YOU DUMB FU . . .'

Then I realise that now, more than ever, I have to drop my anger. This is like a test. I have to think like a man and be a man. I mean, this what it was like for those jokers at Gallipoli. They didn't have a chance, did they? And still they did it, for God and Queen and Country. Those mad motherfuckers. My grandfather fought in World War Two so I can feel his spirit in me right now. And I also somehow feel like Nige is still alive.

So I yell out, 'NIIIIIIIIIIIIGE!' and I hear this fuckin noise, the same fuckin noise Nige heard.

Only I could swear it's a bird.

'NIIIIIIIIIIIIGE!'

And that sound again, but it doesn't sound like Nige. It really does sound like a bird.

And I know I've just gotta do it. If this is meant to be a triple suicide then that's what it'll have to be.

Actually, double-suicide and one homicide . . .

I climb over the safety barrier. 'Ohhh fuck,' I'm thinkin. 'Ohh, fuckin Nige, fuck Nige, you fuckin stupid . . .' and I just shake my head and I try to put a foot on a rock and I start sliding . . .

As I go I think of Nige. This locks me and Nige together forever. It's like identical twins have the same birthday – well, me and Nige are identical twins of a different kind cos we share the same death-day.

I'm slidin down the mountain so fuckin fast, I've barely got time for final thoughts . . .

Except for I love you, Nige.

I'd take a bullet for you.

Nige's mum used to say to him when I got us in trouble 'And what if Deano jumped over a cliff? Would you jump too?'

Well, Nige, if you jump off a cliff then so do I.

If you jump off a cliff then so do I.

And when I hit the bottom and we both make it to the next life, I'll be your best friend in that one too.

A PICTURE IS WORTH A HUNDRED WORDS

NIGE

Okay, I've come to, and my senses are back in place and my face isn't as sore as I first thought – it was like the shock that I had a sore face made me think I musta had a broken face. I kinda screamed at the thought and I thought I was in a lot of pain but . . . I mean, I think I'm feeling pain right now, but the pain is nothing compared to the sight in front of me.

I'm in the middle of a rock face, right? Halfway up the mountain. And the sea is roaring away and the sound of it echoing on the rocks is just unreal. And there's sea spray everywhere. And wind. And here I am, in the middle of it all, on the ledge of a steep rock face and the rock is all wet and I'm concentrating so hard just to stay where I am, cos if I make one mistake up here, then that's it.

Trouble is, if I stay put I'm fucked too. I may not be an A or a B student but I know that.

Fuck man, like, you know how they say a picture is worth

a hundred words? Well, this picture is worth more than a hundred words. This picture is worth four hundred words . . .

The moon's out and I keep thinkin I might be dead cos I should be dead, so maybe I am dead.

Actually, I bet this is like a weird sort of dream like you might have if you were in a coma . . .

So I think, am I in a coma? You know, in a nice safe hospital bed and all I have to do is wake up? So I try and wake up but nothing happens, so I guess I'm alive and not in a coma, which means that . . .

It's all a bit much to take in. I'm not very good in situations like this. Like, I reckon if I was on that telly programme *Survivor* I'd get voted off in the first week. I reckon Deano would go good on *Survivor*, though. And Gav . . .

Gav! That's the fuckin reason I came down here – I mean . . . I almost forgot about him, I was in such a state of shock, but . . . 'GAAAAAAAAAAAAAAAAV!' I yell. 'GAAAAAAAAAAAAAAAV!'

And then there's this voice. This quiet little voice that says, 'Is that you, Nige?'

And I know that voice straight away. That's the voice of Gav.

And then I hear the voice of Deano, goin, 'AAAAAAAAH!'

And I yell out, 'DEEEEEAAANO!'

And Gav's goin, 'Is that you, Nige?'

And Deano's sayin, 'Is that you, Nige?'

And I look above me but I can't see him, so I yell, 'Are you all right, Deano?'

Deano goes, 'Oh, you know . . . I can't pretend that didn't hurt.'

And Gav goes, 'Is that you, Nige?' again.

And I head to the sound of Gav, like a son moving to the sound of his father . . .

Fuck I wish I'd abseiled at school camp but I pulled a bit of a sicky that day so I wouldn't have to do it, but now here I am *rock climbing*. I put my foot down into a gap and find a good hole down there, and I move down, holdin on to slippery bits of rock that are stickin out and I just think to myself, as long as I don't look down I can do this. Just don't look down. Don't fuckin look down.

I reach down with my foot and this hand grabs my leg to support me and fuck me if it's not Gav. And he's like, 'There's a sheltered spot here. Come on.' And he helps me in and it's amazing – it's like a little cave cut into the side of the rock. Gav hugs me and I hug him so tight like you wouldn't believe.

Gav says, 'We've been blessed, Nige. We're stuck but we're safe.' And he just starts laughing. Like, laughing real hard, like a mental patient. Real intense laughing, and I'm laughing too, cos it's too fuckin weird.

Then we stop laughing and I just go, 'Fuck!' to Gav. Gav talks real fast, sayin, 'We'll need to be rescued. You know, if no one rescues us we're fucked but . . . I mean, I guess if that happens we won't have to eat food and one of us might have to eat the other, like in that movie I saw on telly called *Alive*, about the Argentinian rugby team. Did you see that one? Boy, am I glad to see you!'

He hugs me real tight again. Then he looks at me and he says, 'Did he push you too?'

'Eh?'

'Did Deano push you? Is that why you're here?'

'No man, I heard you.'

'Bullshit.'

'Were you calling out?'

'Of course.'

'I knew you weren't a bird,' I say. Gav shakes his head . . .

Then there's another noise.

'NIIIIIIIIIIIIIGE!' Deano yells.

'NIIIIIGE, GIVE US A FUCKIN HAND, YOU SELFISH CUNT!'

And I see the look on Gav's face change. Like, it goes from bein happy to something completely different in, like, a second. So Gav goes to give Deano a hand. And seconds after he does it, I clock what he's gunna do. It's that Man's Intuition thing all over again.

I see Deano's leg float down, and I see Gav rugby tackle him, pulling at the legs, and Deano's like, 'FUCK! NIGE! WHAT THE FUCK?' and he hasn't even twigged that it's not me, so Gav says, 'Hi, Deano,' and now Gav has Deano upside down by the legs, his head dangling high above the sea, and Deano says, 'Ohh. Hi, Gav,' real quiet, but then he yells out, 'HELLLLP, NIIIGE! HEEELLLP MEEEE!'

I dunno what to do. And I'm like, 'Please, Gav!'

Gav yells, 'Stay out of this, Nige!'

So I yell, 'PULL HIM BACK UP, GAV!' and Gav yells, 'HE FUCKIN TRIED TO KILL ME!' and Deano's goin, 'AAAAAAAAAAAAAH!'

Gav lets go of him and I yell, 'NOOOOOOOOO!'

Deano manages to hold on to Gav's arms so I jump at Gav but he's fuckin strong and I end up slidin over Gav's back, flipping over his head, and catching Deano. That makes Deano let go of Gav's arms, and no one's holding on to either of us, so now Deano and I are headin straight for the fuckin sea – a huge fuckin drop straight into the sea!

EVERYTHING I OWN

DEANO

Nige holds my arms and stares at me as we begin our rapid fall. We look at each other and we're both screamin hard out. And then I feel my scream turn into a smile, cos I know at this moment I have never felt closer to Nige.

Unless I'm mistaken, Nige just tried to save my life.

And yes, he may have cost me my life in the very same moment, but he tried, that's the important part – it's the thought that counts.

And I mean . . . I've done a lot of sacrificing myself lately. I think of that Bread song, 'I Would Give Everything I Own' – the joker who sang that song knows exactly what I'm going through. I would give everything I owned so that Nige could be happy. Everything. I could own nothing, but if Nige was happy, I'd be happy. I'd give away my bed, my old photos, the contents of my savings account, the TV, my grandad's hip-flask, my entire porn collection, my chest expander, my inheritance that I'll get from Mum's house when she carks – not that that'll add up to much, but still: I'd give it all away in a flash. I'd give away the clothes off my back. In fact, I'd give all my clothes away and then I'd be naked, but it wouldn't matter, cos I'd give up everything for Nige. Even parts of my body. My kidneys. My heart. My lungs. My cock. My nipples. My face, even. Just like Bread – I'd give everything I own.

That's poetry, that is. I can hear Bread ringin in my ears as we plummet toward the sea. And I have a strange sense of calm. And even though we are falling fast it feels like we're falling slow. I want to say something to Nige but he won't hear, so I just stare at his eyes . . .

And he stares back at me . . .

And then we hit the water.

MEET THE MAKER

NIGE

I'm deep in water. No shit. I'm deep in the depths of water, and I'm still going down . . .

And down . . .

Like . . . Wooohhhhh . . .

Cos this isn't a drug trip. This is reality. I'm underwater and going down, down, down, and my eyes are wide open and I can see stuff underwater. A school of fish swim past me and I'm still heading down, down to who knows where . . .

I feel like I'm in another world.

Kind of peaceful.

Some seaweed floats past me but then I see this big eye and I realise it's not seaweed. It's a big octopus that is just staring at me, not blinking. The octopus waves its tentacles at me and I feel like it's sayin goodbye to me on behalf of God, like some kind of fishy angel or something. I drop even further, underneath the octopus – I'm on a path to the bottom of the sea.

It's really peaceful down here. I didn't expect it to be so peaceful.

And then I feel myself getting pulled up.

It's like I'm getting pulled up by a higher force. Like, I am finding out first hand that there is a God. I can feel him pulling me by my collar, taking me to the next life. God is pulling me up and up and away from this shithole of a life, and as I get pulled up through the water I think, Mum and Dad, I'll miss you. Monica, I'll miss you and I'm sorry I caused your exam results to suffer. And your baby, our baby, I mean it might not be my baby but I reckon there's a fair chance, so hey there, little unborn dude, I . . . I mean, I haven't met you, but I hope you don't come out too much like me. I hope you take after your mother, cos she hasn't got shit for brains like me – she's got brains for brains. I hope you don't grow up to be as thick as me . . .

And Gav, I'll fuckin miss you. You taught me a lot of stuff that is the kind of stuff you can't even put into words, and I'm not even gunna try to, cos the words I would use would be dumb words that would just cheapen something, really . . . really special . . .

But most of all I think of Deano. Deano, you bastard. I don't know if you've ruined my life or made my life. All I wanted to do was head out on my own for a bit. Like, you think I was gunna just toss away the friendship? I wouldn't do that. How can you be so fuckin . . . I can't think of the right word . . . *unconfident* about yourself? Deano, you've been my best friend ever since you punched Jason Farquhar for me and gave me his tooth as a present. I'll never forget what you did for me. But why can't I just do my own thing? All I wanted to do was hang out with Gav for a bit, and then maybe one day go to Shepherds Bush in London where all the Kiwis are. All

I wanted was to go to Shepherds Bush by myself, and maybe go flatting with someone else for a change, but you couldn't handle it, Deano. There's a song by The Police called 'If You Love Somebody Set Them Free'. It's not a very good song but it makes a very good point.

And as the hand of God takes me to the top of the ocean, I realise that in the last week I have thought about life so much that I musta got ten times brainier than I was before, and I can only thank Jeurgen for that.

I know it's time to meet the maker:

Our Father who art in heaven,

hallowed be thy name,

thy kingdom come,

thy . . .

um, thy . . .

Okay, I don't know the rest but I'm comin with you, God.

And I see a light above me . . .

Everything's getting lighter and lighter . . .

I can see the moon from in the water . . . and still we go up . . .

And I look up at the hand on my collar dragging me up to the surface . . .

And I realise it's not God . . .

It's Deano.

FUCK ME, IT'S A NUGGET

DEANO

That was some fuckin fall. That was freakier than doin a bungee jump off a bridge, that's for sure. I've got Nige back above water, but the water is freezing beyond belief and the weather is as choppy as it would be on planet Jupiter. Nige has almost passed out. He's taken in a whole lotta water and I reckon we'll last about ten minutes, tops.

'SWIIIIIIMM!' I yell to Nige. 'YOU GOTTA SWIIIIM!' I let go of him but he goes straight under again. I think he's half dead or something.

So I haul him out and I fuckin doggy-paddle like I've never doggy-paddled before, with Nige at my side, pulling him behind me.

But we're not goin anywhere cos the fuckin water is swirling round and round, and I'm doin well just to stay afloat. And now a tide's got us, and it's pulling us away from the coast, and ohhh Christ, I couldn't swim to the coast if I tried, even though I can see it's not far off. I'm bein pulled in the opposite direction, and I'm usin all my energy just to keep Nige afloat.

We're bein pulled further and further from the cliff we just jumped off, and fuck knows how we survived that one . . .

I thought when you fell from a certain height the water was sposed to become like concrete, but this water was like water, you know? I really feel like I've been shot like a bullet from a gun – we've gone deep into the water and now we've come up for air for a few last moments of hope and panic before we die proply.

Like, I'm pissed off at God, as usual. There's a lot of sea vapour about, so I yell to God, 'You fuckin cunt!' and God says, 'Why are you mad at me? I'm taking you exactly where you need to go.'

And I'm like, 'Eh, God?' and I look around and I see we are headin straight for a little island . . .

Fuck me, it's a Nugget. We're heading for a Nugget. Nige still feels pretty dead in my arms and I fuckin use my last bit of energy. You know when a rugby player says he's given 100 per cent, and then they started saying they gave 110 per cent, like 110 per cent is better, you know, and then lately in the interviews they've started sayin they're giving it 120, so I'm thinkin, I'm gunna give it 130 per cent, so, I give it a full 130, and I drag Nige behind me. I'm doin breast stroke cos that's the only swimmin stroke I know apart from doggy-paddle, and doggy-paddle won't get me and Nige to the fuckin Nugget.

So I do breast stroke, but it's bloody hard to pull Nige while doin breast stroke so I kinda invent a new swimming style and it might not look too flash but it does the job and we get to the Nugget.

I drag Nige as high up the Nugget as I can, and it's fuckin

not comfy for him, but we can't stay too close to the water. The wind is howling all around us and God has really just made quite a big statement to me, one that I'm gunna take on board.

Who woulda known that I would find God on this journey? Like, that is a turn-up. Like, I suspected he was in the shower with me all that time but I also thought I was talkin to myself, like one of those schizos. But here God is, you know, and he's blowin a fuckin gale all around me and Nige.

God is sayin, 'You've been bad and you deserve to go, but I'm gunna give you another chance, Deano.'

I say to God, 'What about Nige? Can you help me out with Nige?' and God says nothing and I'm like, 'Fuck, I hate it when you go quiet,' and I look down at Nige and I see some water comin out of his mouth . . .

So I remember one of the things we learned at high school. Mr Downes was giving mouth to mouth to a dummy and me and Nige were sniggering, and then it was my turn. And before I gave mouth to mouth to the dummy I said to Nige, 'I'm gunna give the dummy some tongue,' and as I gave mouth to mouth to the dummy I licked inside its mouth with my tongue – real classic tongue-kissing, and Nige was laughing hard.

Then Mr Downes said, 'Your turn, Nigel,' and he was like, 'Ohhh, what? Shouldn't ya clean it first, sir?' and Mr Downes said, 'Your turn, Nigel,' and just smiled. He was a hard case, that Mr Downes. And I remember the look on Nige's face as he gave mouth to mouth to the dummy I just tongue-kissed.

I think of that as I give mouth to mouth to Nige, here in the moonlight, except I don't use my tongue. My bigger worry is Nige's tongue, and that it doesn't go down his throat, so I have to pull it out a little to keep it out of the way. And I breathe

the breath of life into Nige's mouth, and I'm fuckin praying to God and sayin to him, 'Please, I'll fuckin do anything,' and breathing into Nige's mouth again, breathing into his mouth, and as I breathe into his mouth . . .

I can feel him breathing back.

Like, our mouths are locked together and I can feel his breath on my breath. Like, we're breathing *into* each other. And I'm like, 'Thank you, God.' I lie on top of Nige, shielding him from the wind and the rain, holding him tight, keeping him alive, feeling his breath on my face and just thinkin, the feeling of Nigel's breath on my face is the most amazing thing I've ever felt.

And then I think I'll make that a *private* thought. Like, I don't think I should tell Nige that my favourite thing is being *breathed on* by him.

I might keep that to myself.

WOULD YOU TAKE A BULLET FOR ME?

NIGE

I wake up on top of the hardest rock you can imagine. My face has been on its side and there's a whole lot of drool on the rock.

So basically the first things I see are: 1. Blue sky, 2. Rock, and 3. My drool.

And then I hear the sound of the sea.

And I have no idea where I am. So I get up and take a look . . .

And then I sit down again. And I close my eyes. And I'm thinkin, 'Okay, I'm on a little rock in the middle of the sea with no one but Deano. How do I feel about this?'

I mean . . . I'm alive.

Fuck, I mean, that's a bit of a surprise.

I remember last night seeing God and stuff, you know, pulling me out of the water, but I pretty much blank out about there and . . .

Where the fuck are we?

I stand up, and this time I turn around and I see the cliff face. I see the lighthouse, high above me . . .

And slightly blockin my view of the lighthouse is Deano, who is tryin to dry a cigarette on a rock. And he says, without lookin at me, 'There's gotta be a way I can light this thing.'

I look at his cigarette and it's pretty fuckin damp. Deano is squeezing it like a sponge and water is coming out. He tries drying it on a rock again.

'Hey Deano,' I say. 'Am I dead?'

Deano goes, 'No. You're alive,' and I'd half suspected that was the case.

I say to him, 'I hope Gav's okay.'

Like, it's my way of sayin I'm not just gunna blank out the fact that Deano tried to kill Gav. He puts his cigarette in his mouth and fumbles in his pockets for a lighter.

'Yeah, I reckon Gav's okay. I mean, I've been tryin to see him on the cliff, and I did see some movement in a cave, but I think it might have been a gannet.'

'A gannet?'

'Yeah, you know, the bird.'

I don't know if they have gannets down here but I'm not gunna pull him up on it. What's more important is that Gav's okay.

'I sense he's okay,' I say. 'You know, I sense it with my body, like . . . I just got this feeling. It's hard to explain –' and Deano goes, 'Fuck, I must have lost my lighter in the ocean,' and he's really stressing now cos he always has a cigarette first thing in the morning.

He tries drying his cigarette with his finger again, and some of the tobacco comes out all mushy. Deano squeezes the tobacco back into the cigarette, using a lot of skill.

'Deano,' I go, 'I think I might believe in God now.'

And he says, 'Yeah, I know what you mean, Nige. I believe in God too.'

I don't know if he's taking the piss or not.

I say, 'No, I'm really serious, I mean –'

'You don't need to explain it, Nige. I feel his presence totally.'

I still don't think he's getting me. Like, he thinks I'm just telling jokes or something. Cos I know he doesn't believe in God, cos his God doesn't sound realistic. I say that to him. I say, 'I don't think my God is the same as your God.'

He goes, 'Eh?'

And I'm like, 'My God doesn't tell me to wash my balls,' and he says to me, real serious, 'There's only one God, Nige.'

Now Deano is just staring at me like I'm stupid. He's got this stare he's worked out. Like, we both know it well. It's the 'Are you stupid?' stare.

I say, 'Yeah, but God would never tell me to wash my balls. I've been thinkin about that a lot.'

He says, 'Yeah, well, maybe there's more to God than you think. I mean, yes he lives in water vapour, but –'

'My God lives in the sun –'

'Okay, well, he lives in the sun for you and water vapour for me, but he also lives inside us, Nige. So cos he's inside me, he speaks like me, he thinks like me. He reminds me to wash my balls cos he knows that if he didn't remind me, I'd forget. God knows me pretty well, Nige.'

I have a think about that and I kinda half get where he's comin from.

I say, 'Does God know me as well as he knows you?'

'God knows you, Nige, but you don't know God very well. I'm not surprised you're suddenly into God, though, cos he was totally there with us last night. He helped me save your life.'

'Oh yeah.'

DEANO

I don't think Nige is being very grateful right now.

I say, 'Aren't you going to say thank you?'

'For what?'

'For saving your life. The reason you're alive is cos of me.'

'You just said God did it.'

'No, we worked together, Nige, and believe me, God left a lot of the really hard stuff to me. I swam you to this Nugget. I gave you mouth to mouth resuscitation. I kept you warm by sleeping on top of you so you wouldn't die of hypochondria.'

And Nige looks at me and says, 'When I woke up this morning there was a lot of drool. Was that your drool?'

'No, Nige. You really drooled a lot last night. It was horrible.'

And Nige just nods.

Fuck, I've gotta prompt him every step of the way. 'Say thank you,' I say, and he goes, 'Thank you,' and I feel a little bit better now, so I turn my attentions back to the cigarette.

God doesn't seem to want me to have a cigarette. Fuck him. He knows I'm dying for a cigarette, but what does he do about it? Sweet fuck all.

I search my pockets for a lighter again. Nige sees me struggle, so he says, 'You could rub two rocks together.'

Like, that might be the dumbest thing Nige has ever said, and that's really saying something. I just snap.

I say to him, 'Great. You start rubbing two rocks together now, Nige. And while you're at it, why don't you remind yourself that I have been your best friend for fifteen years . . .' and Nige goes, 'Eh?'

And that's when the helicopter flies over. For the second time – Nige slept through the first time.

Nige really works hard to get their attention, wavin his arms up and down and yellin out, 'HEEEEEYY! OVER HEEEEEERE!' and I'm like, 'They can't hear you, Nige,' but he doesn't listen, he just yells, 'OVER HEEEEERE!' again.

It flies close to the cliff, and you can see a rope drop down. And then I see a tiny figure that must be Gav, hooking himself up to the rope . . .

'Well, would you look at that,' I say. 'Good for Gav,' and Nige says, 'What if they don't see us?' and I'm like, 'They've seen us, Nige. That's not what you should be worried about. What you should be worried about . . . is that's a police helicopter Nige. How do you think that's gunna go? I bet they're really lookin forward to your story. As a matter of fact, I'm looking forward to hearin it myself.'

He looks at me, that pathetic look he does. He says, 'Help me, Deano. I don't know what to do.'

'Don't worry about it, Nige. I can help you. You're lucky that I am brighter than my exam results from school would say. You're lucky that I've figured a way out of this. But it'll come at a price. If you want my help you can never talk to Gav again.'

Nige goes, 'Fuck you,' and I shrug my shoulders and look up at the helicopter, and the little figure of Gav at the bottom of a ladder.

Good for Gav.

And then I look at the way Nige looks at Gav, and then I get a mental picture of the way he's been lookin at me, and it really gives me the shits – you know, after everything I've done for him – and I'm not sure if he actually likes me or if he's just pretendin to like me.

It makes me wanna cry. But now is not the time for crying. Now is the time to be a man. So I look at Nige and I say, 'Did you mean that, what you said?'

'What I said about what?'

'What you said about us not being friends?'

'I dunno. I was pissed off.'

I look him in the eye and I say, 'I'd take a bullet for you, Nige. Would you take a bullet for me?'

NIGE

And I'm like, 'Eh?'

I look over at the helicopter and Deano walks in front of my view. He says, 'No, don't look at the helicopter, Nige. Look at me. Answer me truthfully. Would you take a bullet for me?'

And I'm, like, thinkin . . . what am I sposed to say here?

I say to him, 'You're talking all weird,' and Deano says 'I'm talking like the *real me,* Nige. No more bottling up of feelings. From now on you get the real me. Do you know what friendship actually is, Nige?' and I'm like, 'Eh?' and I just go quiet, cos I figure if Deano wants to have a rant, let him have a rant.

'Friendship,' he says, like he's talking on a stage to a thousand people. 'It's just one word, but it's a very big word. And here's another big word for you, Nige. Loyalty.'

And I think I've heard enough. Like, he's seriously freakin me out with all his new-age talk. I don't get why he's suddenly into new age. And then I figure it out. He's all into new age all of a sudden cos of Gav.

Now he's telling me off like a fuckin schoolteacher.

'I've got one more word for you, Nige,' he says. 'One more word I'd like you to think about. Commitment. What do you think about that word, Nige? What do you think about commitment?'

I yell, 'Stop it! You're talking weird!'

And Deano goes, 'It's the real me, Nige, and I'd like to talk to the real you!'

I don't know what to say. I really don't.

Deano goes, 'Okay, your brain's not working yet. I'll get your engine running. Commitment is when two people need each other. Ying and Yan. They balance each other out. Two hearts beat as one. U2 sang a song called "Two Hearts Beat As One". U2 know what friendship is. They've kept that band going for over twenty years. U2 understand commitment. I understand commitment. It's about always bein there. Who do you call in a crisis? In good times or in bad times. Willing to go to any lengths. I'd take a bullet for you, Nige. Would you take a bullet for me?'

And I look at him and it's like . . . I think I'm finally hearin him . . . like . . . the real Deano wants to hear from the real Nige, and I look him in the eyeballs and I think to myself, 'Fuck it, if that's what he wants, I'm gunna answer this one honestly . . .'

And I say, 'Yeah, I would.'

That throws him. 'What was that?'

'Yeah, I would.'

I've really taken him by surprise. I've taken myself by surprise. But I would, you know. Fifteen years doesn't count for nothing. I've known him since we were kids. We're like family. I mean, I might hate his guts sometimes but that's how it is with family.

He nods, and then he smiles. Then he stops smilin.

'I didn't hear it proply,' he says. 'Say it louder.'

'I would.'

'Look me in the eyes and say it.'

And I look him in the eyes and I say, 'I would take a bullet for you, Deano.'

And Deano holds his hand over his chest like he's gunna break into the national anthem. And he says, 'I would take a bullet for you, Nige. If a bullet was heading your way I'd dive in front and catch it in my heart . . .'

It's a real quiet moment, shared between men.

And then Deano reaches into a zip-up pocket in his pants. And he pulls out a necklace . . .

But not just any necklace.

He holds Jason Farquhar's tooth in his hand. It's quite old now, that tooth. All the plaque in it has gone hard and a dark yellow. I look at the tooth, and then I look at Deano. And Deano says, 'Say after me: I believe in Friendship –'

'I believe in Friendship.'

'I believe in Loyalty –'

'I believe in Loyalty.'

'And I believe in Commitment . . .'

I've gotta admit it. I find that one a bit of a hard one to say. Like, that would be easier to say to a girl. It seems weird sayin it to Deano.

Deano says to me, 'Surrender to it, Nige. Life has got you on a leash, and the only way you'll ever enjoy it is to just stop fighting the leash and just go where you're taken.'

And he's right. Like, that's such a deep thing to say. Like, if Gav had said that I would be like, 'Wooohhh,' so I think it's pretty cool that Deano said that, cos the old Deano hated all that kind of way of talking.

So I say to him, loud and proud, 'I believe in commitment.'

Deano holds the tooth necklace up and puts it around my neck like I've just won a gold medal at the Olympics. He looks at me and does a real big smile.

Then another helicopter comes up over Nugget Point. I jump and wave when I see it, and as I'm jumping and waving I say to Deano, 'When you said you had a plan, how do I know it's not another dumb plan?' and Deano jumps and down and waves to the helicopter and says, 'Nige, believe me, I've had so many dumb plans that when I think of a good plan it really sticks out. It sticks out like dogs' balls, so trust me on this one,' and I'm like 'Okay,' and then we both jump up and down and wave to the helicopter.

The helicopter flies straight above and opens its hatch over us, like it was one of those pigeons taking aim to poo on a car.

As it gets into position I stare at the blades goin round and round, like one giant circle, and as I look at that circle I think of a dog runnin round and round in circles, chasing its tail, and then I think, that's exactly what I've been doin my whole life – runnin round and round in circles, goin faster and getting nowhere.

The helicopter drops out a rope and it swings down to us and a voice from above says, 'Hook yourself on and hold on tight!' so I hook myself to a winch thing and Deano does the same, and we shoot up in the air and it's a beautiful clear day and you can make out every mountain and every beach and every lake in the Catlins.

Fuck, it's a beautiful part of the country. Paradise.

As we fly above all of it I look down at Deano and he's lookin up at me with that crazy smile he does. And he yells, 'ISN'T THIS AMAZING?'

Fuck, is it what.

NOTHING COMPARES TO THURSDAY
(ONE YEAR LATER)

DEANO

I'm really excited. I'm always excited on a Thursday. I get up earlier on a Thursday, cos I can't sleep thinking about it.

Like, Monday night's a good night for telly at the moment, and actually Saturday is a great night for telly, and then Friday is pie day and I like a pie, but really . . . nothing compares to Thursday.

That morning I'm up and in front of the mirror. The mirror is more like just a part of the wall that's steel, you know? I'm looking at my eyes. And there's no bags, so that's good. I'm obviously sleeping well. I look at my skin, and that is a bit yellowish, but it could be the crappy light in my room.

I'm losin more hair and I blame that dishwashing detergent I'm forced to use as shampoo. I haven't used conditioner for ages and my hair is payin the price. I'm tryin to decide at this early point whether I should go for the comb-over or not. I say, 'Whaddya reckon, God?' He's been hangin out in the leftover water vapour from me washing my face. God says, 'Grow a moustache,' and I say, 'Fuck off, God.' He loves givin me shit advice and havin a good laugh if I use it.

I look at my head and I chuck a bit of water on it and go for the comb-over. Fuck it. Gotta make the most out of what you've got. Then in my reflection I catch these muscles . . .

They're my biceps. Like, they are definitely getting bigger. A girl would stop and stare at my biceps right now. And I've got pecs and abs and I'm workin on a six-pack. Like, there's a long way to go – I still look like a scrawny runt compared to what I will look like, but I'm really starting to think I've got body-building potential.

You know, I picture myself in all of that brown wax they put on, and the little undies, and I reckon that with a full head of hair, maybe . . . I might look quite hot. Compared to before, anyway.

I do a big grin to the mirror. It's not cos I'm happy, although I am very happy with it being a Thursday. I'm grinning cos I want to make sure my teeth are as white as possible. I haven't been able to use smoker's toothpaste for a while and my teeth are paying the price.

Still, other than that, I'm lookin okay. My room-mate tells me to 'Turn off the fuckin light' and I look at the digital alarm clock and it's only four in the morning, so I'm like, 'Sorry, dude. May the Lord bless you,' cos I've found myself quite a safe passage in the last few months by talking about God a lot. A few of the punters here are quite into that shit, so I'm looked after by the Christians, so, you know, I play up the God thing a bit.

Whenever I'm taking a shower God sniggers at the way I'm suckering up to those Christians. Put it this way – I'm not really a big fan of communal showers. I'll say no more on the subject.

Ah well. You gotta do what you gotta do, eh?

NIGE

I half forgot it was Thursday and when I realised it was I got a real fright, and I forgot to fill the Mazda with petrol again and I had to ride it down with the engine off to get to the petrol station again. Fuck I can be a dick.

And even after I've put petrol in it, the car is running like a real bastard. Like, the clutch sometimes gets stuck to the floor, which is a real pain when you're trying to change gear, you know? You're goin from second to third and suddenly you're just rolling with the clutch all the way in, and to get the clutch back out I've found a way to wiggle my toe under it at a certain point, which means I have to drive barefoot, but I always forget and I have to take off my shoe while I'm driving and then wiggle my toe in the right spot, just to avoid havin a crash and that.

I've got quite good at it though, on the upside.

Gav got published yesterday. I was so excited. Like, I haven't spoken to him since . . . you know . . . but I've followed his progress as a writer.

Well, I guess there hasn't been much progress to follow. Like, this is the first thing he's had published. It's like a book with lots of writers and he's one of the writers and he's got a photo and everything. And it's a story about being happy and sad at the same time, which is what I told him he should write, so I'm pretty stoked.

It's a great story, even though nothing really happens. I mean, I did get a bit bored when I read it, but the important thing is that the quality of his writing is five-star.

I tried phoning Gav a month ago, but he won't answer my phone calls. I guess he's still pissed off that I let Deano into his life. I tried talking to him at the first court hearing but he wouldn't have a bar of it. That made me feel pretty sad. I'm glad he didn't try and make things worse for me, though. He didn't really give anything away on the whole Jeurgen thing. He pretty much just concentrated on Deano trying to kill him, and that's fair enough, I reckon.

He's gone back to the Far North and I can picture him chillin out smokin a joint on a big sand dune somewhere. He's such a good guy.

But I do wish he'd call me or something. I miss him, you know?

I made Deano lunch today. I hate cooking but I've had to learn. When you make a sandwich the hardest bit is choosing what to put in the sandwich. Like, I never have any ideas. But mostly I've been goin for Deano's favourite, which is corned beef and pickle. He also likes cheese and tomato, but he complains a lot when I make him cheese and tomato, cos I can't be bothered grating the cheese. It's like I have to wash all of my own dishes now, and I think using the grater is unnecessary. Only I don't cut the cheese thin enough. He complains that I cut the cheese too fat. Just before he takes a bite he looks at the inside of the sandwich. He'll say, 'Look at this,' and point out a real fat bit of cheese to me.

So today I've made him corned beef and pickle. He'd better like it, cos I got pickle on my uniform, and I've only got one shirt at the moment, and people at the bank will look at me funny cos it's quite a large pickle stain.

It's hard livin by yourself. Like, I thought all the mess and stuff just cleared itself up like magic but now I realise Deano did it.

I mean, I'm appreciating Deano more and more each day.

I head into the roundabout and then up the hill, and finally I get there. When I park up I look at my hair in the rear-vision, and I reckon it looks okay. Deano gives me shit, but I reckon it looks all right. It's a new direction for me, you know?

I head up to Mrs Tuckett. She's always at the front desk. She takes a look inside my tupperware container and points to the book and I sign, and when I sign I look at all the other signatures in the book, and up the page I keep seein my signature, and I think to myself, 'Woooo,' you know?

DEANO

One of the things I like most about Thursday are the clothes I get to wear. I've got these special grey overalls with no pockets in them for when I get a visitor. They do good laundry here. It smells real nice and it feels good next to my skin.

When we head out I find myself almost running, just out of excitement, so I slow it down to a jog, but even that looks funny, so I just do one of those walks with a bit of a skip in it. We have to walk single file. I don't know why. Like, why can't we just walk out as a bunch? Why all the single-file shit? It's like school all over again in some ways. I liked school. I was a good survivor at school. It brought out the outsider in me, but the outsider always found a way to get by. That's why Nige is lucky I took him under my wing. Back then, and now too. He really needs my guidance.

I'm glad I am still deeply involved in his life. I can't wait to see him. I can't wait to see him. I'm *that* excited.

I wonder how he's going with that hair-straightening experiment. Like, Nige has always had a bit of a curly mop, and now he's got his hair straightened, I can't take it seriously. I always laugh when I see him.

I laugh this time, too.

I really piss my pants when I see him cos the new straight-haired Nige looks hilarious.

He says, 'Stop it.'

I say, 'I'm sorry, Nige. It's just so . . . funny seeing you with straight hair. How are the results? Are you pulling? Does Monica like it?'

Nige looks real sad. He says, 'It's not going so good. Monica's taken out a restraining order against me.'

I'm like, 'Ohhhhh Nige, that's such bad luck . . .'

I put my hand on his shoulder, cos this is a real blow for him. Ever since the blood tests revealed it wasn't his kid he's been around there anyway, asking if he can just 'hang out', and . . .

Poor Nige. It's been hard for him.

'Shit, Nige,' I say, 'that's terrible,' and Nige has a tear comin out his eye. He was obviously always into Monica bigtime, and the idea he might be a father was just more an excuse so he could try and get back together again. She won't have a bar of it, and he won't accept it. I mean, they have got it on five or six times in the last year, cos she quite likes having sex with Nige, but she doesn't see a lot of other use for him. You know, Nige is good in the sack, so I can see why she takes him in from time to time, so to speak. I tell you, he's got a real talent for sex. I should know. I've listened to Nige having sex many a time and he always leaves the customer satisfied . . .

Shit, Nige is really taking it hard. He's, like, real sad today.

He says, 'I really miss her, you know?'

'Are you masturbating?' I ask.

'Shhhhhhh.'

NIGE

Like, he's embarrassing me, asking questions like that here. I'm lookin around at people in the room – you know, it's like a big old school hall and there's even lots of kids running around. None of the chairs in the room are the same. It's like they picked up all the reject chairs from the Salvos. The guards always look bored off their nuts, even though all sorts goes on in here. Like, three weeks ago I saw someone getting a sneaky blowjob under the table. Me and Deano found that pretty funny but Deano told me not to laugh out loud, just in case.

Deano can see I feel a bit weird talkin about that in front of all of these people but he says, 'Don't worry about them. How often are you masturbating?' and I say, 'About four times a day,' and he nods, like he reckons that's a good amount.

'It's good you manage to find the time alone,' he says to me, and rolls his eyes.

Deano's having a real masturbating issue in prison. He keeps getting himself off but he's scared his cellmate's gunna catch him and think the wrong thing. He says to me, 'Sometimes it's better than the sex, you know?' and I think of myself when I have a masty, and the feelings of loneliness I get after I'm done.

Deano goes, 'Well, you know what I always thought about Monica.'

'Yeah, I know.' She's too brainy for me. He thinks I need to find someone who is about as brainy as I am. I don't really know how brainy I am, that's the problem. I mean, how do you measure how brainy you are? If it's about life experience then yeah, I reckon I got lots of brains, cos I've done things a lot of other people haven't done cos they were chicken, and I know a lot about the things you do when you're wasted and you're havin a laugh and if that is a way of measuring how brainy I am then I would say I'm pretty brainy. I get out of it quite a lot and I enjoy gettin really wasted and tryin to cope with a normal day at the bank. I've found that quite entertaining. Ever since I found out it was hard to fire people I've really started acting up. I guess in some ways I'm not doin too good out here. Like, to be honest, Deano looks in better shape than me, and he's the one who's locked up.

'I need to find someone less brainy,' I say.

'That's right. But not too stupid, either. Just not hypo-intelligent like Monica. What about God? Have you been goin to church?' says Deano.

'I can't be bothered. Church is so boring.'

'Yeah. Okay, fair enough on that one,' he says.

I look around a room that I've got to know real well. Like, every time you come here there's a lot of emotions. It's like being at an airport. People get upset, people laugh, people are really pleased to see each other – I have really noticed that. I'm one of the regulars, of course, so I know some other regulars, like this old granny that goes and visits her grandson, and she's nice cos she likes baking for her grandson, and she always gives me some of her baking, so that's a real bonus. Today she gave me a lamington. I shoved that in my pocket cos I didn't want to share.

I pass Deano his lunch and he has a look at the insides of the sandwich and nods, like I've done a good job this time. Then we both eat our sammies and that's when I say to him what I've been tryin to build the strength up to say . . .

'I want to go to Shepherds Bush, Deano –'

'Not this again –'

'I just wanna hang out with some Kiwis overseas and that. Why are you so scared of me goin to Shepherds Bush?'

'You'll never come back.'

'I will.'

'You're not going there, Nige. London isn't right for you.

You're going to Surfers Paradise. I've already booked your ticket on the internet. I was gunna wait until your birthday but there – the secret's out.'

And I'm like, thinkin, he always does this. I mean, I get so angry at him. I say, 'Fuck, Deano! When will you get it into your head that I don't want to go to Surfers Paradise? I've already been there!' and Deano raises his voice and says, 'It's hard walking around every day, knowing you told a big lie. Sometimes I think to myself, "Fuck it, I should just tell the truth . . ."' and I, like, put my head in my hands cos he really likes reminding me of the power he has over our friendship.

Like . . . I guess it was pretty good of Deano, saying he killed Jeurgen and that. He reckoned I wouldn't be good in prison. I mean, I agree with him, but he's always quick to remind me how easy it would be for him to just get the truth out of his system.

So, you know . . . it's like . . . what can I do?

Anyway, I took a vow, didn't I? For better or for worse.

You know, Deano's right. Sometimes you've just gotta accept that life's got you on a leash. Like you'll never be in control of it. It's just a fuckin . . . illusion – that's the word. You can fight the tug of the leash or you can just go wherever you're taken and enjoy the walk.

I'm a dog on the leash. And Deano's my owner. Is that a nightmare or what?

Not really. He has just got me a ticket to Surfers Paradise.

I'm like, 'I mean . . . at least the weather's nice in Surfers,' and Deano's like, 'Never mind the weather, think of the strippers . . . all-over tans . . . the nightclubs where you get a nut and all the ladies get a bolt and you have to screw your nut into all the ladies' bolts and when you find the right one you pash her and win a prize, I mean . . . you can't get better than that, Nige. I want photos of everything.'

'Okay, I'll go,' I say, and he goes, 'Happy birthday for next week,' and I'm like, 'Thanks, Deano.'

DEANO

When Nige has finished his sandwich I ask if I can have his crusts and he doesn't mind. And then I say, 'Hey Nige, just think . . . in ten years I'll be out of here, and we can go flatting together again. Won't that be awesome?' and Nige just kinda nods and shrugs his shoulders. Then Nige goes, 'I thought it was fifteen,' and I'm like, 'Fifteen is the *actual* sentence, but people think I'll probably do ten.'

As I tuck into Nige's crusts I get a mental picture of us as old men in an old people's home, sharing a room, eating some meals on wheels and having a laugh. I might have a hole in my neck from my cigarette smoking, and I'll have a funny voice as a result, but I'll still say lots of classic things, and me and Nige will always be ten minutes away from cracking up with laughter at any given time.

I say, 'I love you, Nige. Not in a gay way. You know that.'

And Nige says, 'Yeah I know. I love you and not in a gay way too,' and then instead of hugging him I give him a dead arm. I punch him so hard he almost falls off his seat, and the guards notice. So I hold my arm under the table and he punches me out of view. He's punched me real hard too. Both of us are holding our arms with our hands in pain, cos our arms are throbbing with the pain we've just given each other, but it's kinda funny too.

I'm crackin up, saying, 'Fuck, Nige, you look classic right now,' and Nige looks *sooo* funny, holding on to his arm like I'd hit it with a fuckin brick, doin that face he does when he wants to take a shit but nothing'll come out. He looks at me holdin on to my arm and he says, 'You look fuckin funny too,' and a guard tells us to 'Shh . . .' and we just start giggling into the table, just like we did at school when I was hiding from the teacher on the top floor of the library and I hid under a desk and Mrs Pritchard came lookin for us and I saw up her dress and she wasn't wearin any undies and she was hairy as. We had to laugh so silently then – otherwise we'd both get detentions – and we stuck at it for a while, but I heard Nige crack up and then we were both laughin and we got detentions, and me and Nige are laughin exactly the same way now. The guard goes to another part of the room, and we just start laughin out loud.

I'm goin, 'HAHAHAHAHA!'

And Nige is goin, 'HAHAHAHAHAHA. Classic.'

And I'm like, 'Classic – HAHAHAHAHAHAHAHA!'

And Nige is like, 'FUCKIN CLASSIC, HAHAHAHAHA!'

As Nige laughs, the tooth on his neck bounces up and down on his Adam's apple. Fuck, Nige has a funny laugh. He laughs like a machine-gun. I love the sound of his machine-gun laugh.

'HAHAHAHAHAHAHAHAHAHAHAHA!' he goes.

And now we're both just *cracking up*, goin, 'HAHAHAHA HAHAHAHAHAHAHAHAHAHAHAHAHAHAHAHAHA HAHAHAHAHAHAHAHAHAHAHAHAHAHAHAHAHAHA HAHAHAHAHAHAHAHAHAHAHAHAHAHAHAHAHAHA HAHAHAHAHAHAHAHAHAHAHAHAHAHAHAHA!'

THE END

ACKNOWLEDGEMENTS

Thanks to Geoff Walker, Jeremy Sherlock, all the other people beavering away at Penguin, Rachel Scott, Sara Bellamy, Seven, Rob Sarkies (for egging me on bigtime), Toby Leach, Nigel Collins, Grant Roa, Fenn Gordon, Marianne Hargreaves, Tony Paine, the Christchurch Arts Centre (who helped me keep the novel alive when no one else would fund it), Fiona Farrell, Simon O'Connor, GT, Mel Johnston, Tilly from Unity, Nick White, Aaron Watson, Mick Rose, Craig Sengelow, Lisa Warrington, 'The Modern Library Writer's Workshop' by Stephen Koch, Antonia Wallace (who I had a lot of laughs with and learned so much from), Fergus Barrowman and Victoria University Press, Simon and Anna (my married couple friends from Lyall Bay), Stanley Sarkies (plays a mean ukulele), Georgio Ormondio, Sean O'Brien aka Joe Blossom aka 'Big Sky Country', Andy Brophy, the punters who turned up to the 'I'd Love To Have a Beer with Duncan' shows, Mighty Mighty, Bar Bodega, Bats, that little pub in the Kapiti, Rich Neame, Hone Kouka, Quinton Hita, Nic McGowan, Sebastian Morgan-Lynch, Tao Wells, Jemaine Clement, Miranda Manasiadis, Anna Cameron, Vicky Pope,

Abby Dunlop, Greg Wikstrom, Matt Grace, Radar, Amelia Pascoe, Rochelle Savage, Sam Auger, Sara Gilbert, all of the Gobbledygook Eradication and Evaluation Knowitalls (GEEKs) at Write Group, the guy who I spoke to who'd been up Everest, everyone at Deluxe (I promise I'll pay my tab soon), Rebekkah Pickrill, Margaret Gordon, Eve and Jimmy Wallace, Mum (we drove round Saddle Hill and ate KFC), Dad, Catherine, all the rest of the rellies, Steve Turner (I decided against the dwarf option), Roy Colbert, Annabel Alpers (go Bachelorette!), the German backpacker who I met by the sea lion, and all of my friends who encouraged me.

Special thanks to the people of the Catlins. You look after a beautiful part of the country. I don't know if you want too many visitors so I'll try to keep it secret that the Catlins is so beautiful. Oops.

Love from Duncan.

ABOUT DUNCAN SARKIES

In New Zealand, Duncan Sarkies is best known for writing *Scarfies,* which is New Zealand's tenth highest grossing film. He has also written two episodes of the *Flight of the Conchords.*

He has written many plays, including *Lovepuke,* which has been performed throughout Australia and New Zealand. Another play, *Saving Grace* was the New Zealand Play of the Year in 1995.

He is also a performer. His show *Instructions for Modern Living* (a collaboration with musician Nic McGowan) has played around the world. He regularly performs a pub show, *I'd Love to Have a Beer with Duncan,* as a fundraiser for the blind, with free entry for the blind.

His book of short stories, *Stray Thoughts and Nose Bleeds* won Best First Book at the Montana New Zealand Book Awards in 2000. *Two Little Boys* is his first novel.

A note from Duncan about *Two Little Boys*:

I need to explain something. It has never been an ambition of mine to write a novel. When I wrote the book of short stories Stray Thoughts and Nose Bleeds *people repeatedly said 'When are you going to write a novel?', as if short stories were some kind of step towards 'being a grown-up'.*

I've never seen it that way. Many of my favourite writers are short story writers. The concept that a novel was somehow more grown-up riled me a touch. So, to prove I'm not very grown-up I've written a novel featuring the most juvenile, immature and uncouth characters that I could think of. I'm scraping the bottom of the barrel here. My writing is hitting a new low. I'm proud of that.

The characters Nige and Dean have been haunting me for the last five years. I like their company, even if they leave a mess wherever they go. Nige and Dean started writing their own story, and they chose to write it as a novel. Who was I to disagree?

Two Little Boys *is a crime story. You know all of those 'bizarre crime done by an idiot' stories you read on page 5 of the newspaper? This story is one of those. So I guess you could find it filed under 'White-Trash Darwinist Penthouse-Forum-Influenced Stoner Crime Fiction'.*